Off The Beaten Path

OFF THE BEATEN PATH

GUSTAVO BONDONI

GUARDBRIDGE BOOKS
ST ANDREWS, SCOTLAND

Published by Guardbridge Books,
St Andrews, Fife, United Kingdom.

http://guardbridgebooks.co.uk

Off The Beaten Path

Edited by David Stokes

Cover art © Salvador Sanz

ISBN: 978-1-911486-40-4

To Sofía

CONTENTS

Editor's Introduction

Gustavo Bondoni was a world-traveller from an early age. Although he was born in Argentina, his parents worked for a multi-national company, so at age three he moved first to the United States, then all over Europe. He returned to Argentina for high school and college, but never stopped travelling. He has been all over South America and Central America, and he worked for a company in Syria. He also works for a travel company which can lead him all over the world.

This travel influenced his writing in multiple ways. For one, his early schooling in the United States and Europe means he writes primarily in English, one of the few Argentine authors to do so.

Also, it gives him an interest in far-flung places which he explores in his stories. He has been to many places, and when he writes about somewhere he hasn't been, his exposure to many cultures gives him the sensitivity to try to get the details right. He usually knows someone from the area who can help him convey things correctly.

His background shows through in this collection. His fluency and skill in the English language and his knowledge of its literary tradition shine in his writing. And these stories were chosen to to show a multitude of settings around the world.

Bondoni writes in a multitude of genres. This collection contains his speculative works of science fiction, fantasy and horror. He also writes mystery and mainstream works. In fact, one story here, *A Position of Power*, is a classic detective story, just given a steampunk setting. Really, what he does is go where the story leads him, regardless of genre.

Likewise, his writing embraces several styles, as well. Many of his stories feature a dramatic and often catastrophic twist. Others reach for the heartstrings, drawing readers into feelings of the characters. The best may be when he combines the two, and you experience the the emotions of characters in the face of shocking circumstances.

And many of the situations are shocking. He is not specifically a horror writer, although he has written a monster novel: *Ice Station Death*. But his characters are not often safe. As he said, "I set out to write a happy ending and then end up with dead bodies all over the place and no idea how they got there..."

This collection tries to cover some of many of these styles. A surprising twist alters the direction of *Happy Hour at Lilu's*, as well as several other stories. *Primal* is a post-apocalyptic horror, as nature is pushed too far by humanity and strikes back. On the more emotional end are stories such as *Anchored Down in Anchorage* and *Racial Memory*, each of which combines a strong speculative idea with characters we come to feel for.

This volume collects the Poupée Cycle: currently a trio of stories featuring the same characters. The collection starts with the first of these stories, *Wyrm of the Mangroves*. The sequel, *Poupée's People*, continues the story at about the midpoint of the book. These stories were crying out for a follow on, so new to this collection is *Superior Beings*, the most recent Poupée tale, near the end of the book.

Scratching Through Rock is another new story, appearing for the first time in this collection. It is a heartfelt story delving into a painful chapter in the recent history of Bondoni's Argentine homeland, with a bit of a horror touch. I am proud to be publishing its debut.

This collection also includes introductions to each story written by Bondoni. These give some insight into his writing process and his growth as an author. One example of that is his changing relationship to writing about his home country. We try not to give too many spoilers in the introduction, although if you are worried, you can skip over them and read them once you finish the story.

Since Bondoni has over 200 published stories in at least 7 different languages, this collection can only scratch the surface of his body of work. If you enjoy this book, I encourage you to seek out more of his writing, and keep a look out for more to come.

—David Stokes
Guardbridge Books, 2019.

WYRM OF THE MANGROVES

This story was written in October 2009, at a point in which my writing career was just beginning to feel a bit more serious. I was selling stories regularly in multiple genres and feeling good about life. Looking back at those early days, however, most of my stories had a "Golden Age" feel to them: all of them had a big idea at the core, and the plot was the driver. Characters could be well-realized or less so, but weren't necessarily the center of the story.

"Wyrm of the Mangroves" was one of my first successful efforts to break away from that pattern and create a truly memorable character without sacrificing the big idea at the core... by accident. The central driver was supposed to be the rogue geneticist but, halfway through the story, I realized that Poupée was the truly fascinating member of the cast.

And, as befits a more mature tale, the mag it appeared was also beautiful: *M-Brane*. This was a project that published character-driven SF in what looked like a pulp-era wrapper. A most attractive publication which I still miss. The nice thing is you can still buy ebooks of the issues on Amazon.

We'll meet Poupée again in two other tales (one written specifically for this book), but this was her first closeup and, ten years later, it's still one of my favorite stories.

Under the canopy, in the twilight of noon's mottled illumination where colors seemed twice as intense not because they were bright but because they seemed to fade into the depths of the forest, Philippe watched two yellow eyes disappear under the surface. The water was clear enough that he could follow the creature's progress for a few seconds, but then it was gone for good. He sighed. It would take him another two hours to get it to come that close again the following morning.

All he could do was wait for his visitors to arrive. The

animal's sudden retreat could mean only one thing: people were coming down the path. The only human presence the creature tolerated was his own… maybe it sensed that he was its father.

A young boy and girl approached. Seven or eight years old, they were as clean as could be expected of village children whose playground was a rain forest, but their clothing was new and they looked happy and well fed. Their black skin, nearly blue in the dim sunlight that made it through the canopy seemed to glow with health.

"Hey there M'siu Phillipe," the girl said. "Watcha looking for?"

He essayed a stern look, but the children were unfazed. They knew him too well. "Dragons."

"Really?" They both moved closer to the water's edge. "Where are they?"

"You scared them away."

Amelie, the little girl, cocked her head. "How can we scare away a dragon? Don't dragons eat kids?"

"Not these. They're still too small, but if you come back in a hundred years, they'll eat you, no problem."

"Don't be silly. None of the animals live a hundred years. Not even the chimps." She seemed to take as a given that she, herself, would live forever.

Actually, Philippe wasn't quite sure he was telling her the whole truth. He'd been seeing some unusual scarring on the local manatees: long parallel scratches as though the manatee had been scratched by a cat. But big cats, even the few that lived in the Gabonese rain forest, preferred to hunt on land. They most certainly wouldn't be hunting in water deep enough to hold manatees.

But he said nothing. He really didn't want to alarm the villagers. Africa was still laissez-faire in its attitudes towards most transgressions, but dragons living in a swamp would definitely bring attention from Tchibanga, and then from Libreville. And that would lead to a whole bunch of questions

Philippe really preferred not to have to answer.

All he wanted from life was to be left alone in his shack beside the mangroves, and to be allowed to watch his creatures grow. He needed the children to think about anything except dragons.

"Would you like to look through the microscope?" he asked them.

They squealed. This was a rare treat. Slides were easy enough to prepare because the swamp water was teeming with microscopic life, and they could spend hours watching what they imagined to be wars between tiny alien empires. And, most importantly, they'd spend the next few days talking about it, too.

***

Dishonor, heartbreak, and the end of his former life had come in the night, completely unexpectedly.

Black-clad commandos broke through his windows, violated his privacy and invaded his inner sanctums and jealously guarded secrets while he slept. Or so he imagined—he hadn't witnessed it himself.

Those self-righteous bastards who thought that they could keep science from advancing just because it offended their sense of what was moral and what was natural, who believed that the fact that they represented the whim of the ignorant, but numerous, masses gave them the right to act.

How ironic that their first act was to kill the very creatures against whose 'enslavement' they'd railed, the controversy reaching the highest levels of government. Even more ironic was that one of those very creatures, those 'crimes against the genome of humans and who knows what other species', had been responsible for getting him awake and out of the house just ahead of the strike force that the French government had, in its infinite wisdom, decided to send against its most famous scientist.

They hadn't missed by much.

***

The small ball of fur dropped from a branch, arms akimbo, but balance uncompromised. Her overlarge head bobbed a few times, but she was used to that already.

"Hello, Phlip."

Philippe gave her a fond look. He might be engrossed in a new project, but Poupée and her now-deceased sisters had been his first great triumph. They'd told him that it was impossible to get near-human intelligence in a creature the size of a spider-monkey. They'd told him it was abomination to even try.

He'd proved them all wrong, as usual. While everyone expected him to attempt splicing human DNA with that of a small primate, he'd gone off in a different direction and used hamster genes as the base instead. They were actually easier to modify, and, with a liberal sprinkling of dung beetle and scorpion DNA thrown in—Philippe refused to let his expertise in insect genetics go to waste—a series of small, light-furred beings had slowly emerged from the chaos and miscarriages.

"Hello, Poupée, and my name is Philippe, not Phlip. Try saying Philippe."

"Phlip." She attempted to smile, but looked like an angry rodent.

They'd grown more and more intelligent as he learned from his mistakes until, one glorious day, a being that walked upright after only a few hours was born. The fact that she looked like one of the heads from Easter Island with a stickman body thrown in was not something that concerned him. Back then, he still thought he had all the time in the world to get the balance just right. He would have been able to create miniature humans in a few months more.

"Children go 'way?"

"Yes, and I'm very happy that you didn't come when they were here. Thank you."

She beamed at him, immediately making him wish that he'd

had the time to engineer away those enormous incisors. If given another chance, and access to his earlier research, it would be his first order of business. But he knew he shouldn't complain. Disproportionate teeth and all, Poupée was the only reason he wasn't sitting in some jail in Marseilles waiting for his media-hyped trial.

"Where were you, anyway?"

"Explore jungle," she said. She didn't meet his eye, and that made Philippe suspicious. But then he relaxed and reminded himself that anthropomorphizing what were just very smart animals was the first sign that he was losing his grip on reality.

"Did you find anything interesting?"

"No. Just walk around."

She followed him inside and took her accustomed place beside the hut's single western window, which offered the best illumination in the afternoon. She opened a book in front of her.

Philippe watched from his armchair. He wasn't certain how well his attempts at teaching Poupée to read had taken. On one hand, when he'd tried to teach her the letters, the whole concept seemed alien to her, as if the logical constructs of spelling were just something her brain wasn't hardwired for. On the other hand, she'd long since left the single picture-book in his library aside, and preferred to attack the classics on his shelf. Every once in a while, she would turn a page, even.

As he watched, Philippe wondered whether it had been a mistake to abandon that line of research. Perhaps his decision to create something a little larger and more rugged to suit this larger and more rugged landscape had been premature. Poupée seemed to have little trouble navigating the byways of the Gabonese jungle.

And yet, he couldn't deny that it was fitting. Intelligence should occupy the highest branches on the tree of life, and his new project would do that magnificently—while any descendent of Poupée's line would always be a snack, no matter how well they were armed.

He dozed off as the tiny creature turned a page.

***

The next few days convinced Philippe that he was utterly, completely and irremediably losing it. It not being the first time that this had happened to him, he knew how to handle something like this.

Peace could only come in the arms of some beautiful young ebony skinned angel of mercy. Preferably one who thought he was a tourist and pretended not to charge him—just asked for money to buy herself "some pretties". He packed a couple of shirts and a few shorts.

Intellectually, he knew it was all in his mind, but he just couldn't seem to shake the idea that Poupée was watching him intently all the time. On the few occasions he'd turned to look, however, she seemed to be intent on reading his old, weather-beaten copy of "Pride and Prejudice". Considering that the novel was written in English, and Poupée hadn't really managed to conquer French just yet, he felt she probably wasn't making much progress.

He forced himself to turn away again.

"Where you go?"

Philippe almost jumped out of his skin. He had to force himself to turn back to her. It's just the jungle getting to you again. You've been in here alone for much too long with nothing but the sound of the insects keeping you company—that and a dragon which is getting bigger and bigger and seems to thrive on humidity and dark green. He shook his head to clear it and walked slowly to where the tiny figure sat by the open book.

He knelt. "I need to go to Tchibanga. I'll be gone a few days."

"Can I go with you?"

"You know I can't take you there."

"Is it because I'm different? Because people won't like to see me?"

"They might like to see you, but they wouldn't treat you well. They would hurt you, and I don't want you to be hurt."

"Why would they hurt me?"

He sighed. "It's hard to explain, and I have to go."

"Is it because I'm a monster?"

"What? Where did you get such an idea?"

Poupée gestured towards the book.

He frowned. "There are no monsters in that book."

Poupée waved at the shelf absently (stop anthropomorphizing her, Philippe thought furiously). "Other books have monsters. I don't have brothers, sisters, mother, even friends. And I think you not my father."

"No, I'm not."

"I have no father?"

"No."

"But I'm alive. How can I not have a father?"

"I see that we need to have a long talk about this when I get back. Don't worry about it for now, all right?"

"All right," she replied innocently while her eyes said to him: 'no way'.

He shook his head. He really needed a couple of weeks in the old colonial neighborhoods in Tchibanga where the few remaining wooden houses held the moisture of decades past beneath their peeling yellow paint, and the love of a sweet girl would find little wrong with his wad of Euros, even if they were of the old design.

He set off down the path, nearly at a run.

***

But there was, could be, no peace in Tchibanga. Even scented candles and the musky smell of Angélique that should have filled his world while she filled the room with movement could not drive away the accusing gaze.

He wondered whether he should just leave Gabon. There were other places he could hide, and he'd been out of the public eye long enough that it was doubtful whether anyone would even care anymore.

Just as he thought this, the beautiful ebony enthusiast in the room with him managed to get things just right, and he forgot about everything. But only for a few minutes.

When the darkness stilled, and the only sound in the room was of contented breathing as she slept, two little rat-like eyes stared out from the darkest corners.

****

Daylight, and a week or so under full sunshine, found him laughing at himself. He would go back, explain things to Poupée and continue to live his life of seclusion. There was no need to look for a safe haven somewhere in tropical Asia. He was fine where he was.

When he felt that he'd accepted that in more than an intellectual way, he headed back, driven by both his resolve and the fact that he couldn't leave his other project unsupervised for so long with people living nearby. Not with a clean conscience, anyway.

The hut, however, was deserted when he arrived on another warm wet midmorning. There was no sign of Poupée anywhere, and no piping voice calling him Phlip. For a second, he felt an icy fist rummaging around inside his chest, looking for something to grab, but the moment passed. So what if the little hamster had gotten herself eaten by something nasty? She knew it was dangerous to wander too far from the hut and the tiny folding flap in the door. Besides, he had other projects to worry about—bigger things from both a physical and philosophical perspective.

He dropped his bag unceremoniously on the floor and walked towards the edge of the swamp, his feet sinking slightly into the soft clay.

Now it was just a question of waiting. The creature was most active during the mornings, disappearing after noon to sleep—at least Philippe assumed it disappeared in order to sleep; he had no real way of knowing other than trying to track it through the mangrove swamp, which was not something he was particularly eager to try. There were other things in that swamp besides what he'd placed there. Nothing too deadly, but some would bite and others were contagious.

He sat down at the point where mud gave way to water, buttocks planted on a relatively dry root, and waited. He knew that the eyes would be there sooner rather than later, they trusted him more and more as the days went on.

A ripple in the distance telegraphed the presence of something huge in the water. He thought the creature had grown a quite a bit in his absence, more than he would have expected. Another data point to measure the interaction of the genes it held.

"Aren't dragons supposed to fly?"

Philippe almost jumped out of his perch into the lake. The voice came from just above, from amid the thick leaves of a coula tree. He thought for a moment. "Poupée?"

The tiny creature's arrival was heralded by the rustling of leaves and the fall of a couple of nuts into the swamp. "It looks like the drawings of dragons in your books, and I saw you looking at pictures labeled 'wyrm', which I've found out is just a fancy way of saying dragon when you were working in the lab. He even has wings, so why can't he fly?"

The silence that greeted this question was filled with various things: the return of all of Philippe's misgivings regarding the mental state of his diminutive companion, the sudden cessation of all the wildlife sounds in the swamp as the v-shaped ripple wound its way between the thickest clumps of mangrove roots. The French geneticist sat petrified, the toes of his boots dipping into the warm water.

Poupée, the least threatening figure one could ever imagine, both comically misproportioned and physically weak, walked slowly towards him, and Philippe scooted away. But, short of running into the jungle, there was no escaping the questions.

"And if he was going to have to swim all his life, why didn't you give him gills? Or at least a body better suited to living underwater. What you designed only serves to make him suffer as he drags himself from one end of the swamp to the other."

Philippe finally found his voice. "He?"

That seemed to stop the flood. "What do you mean?"

"You keep saying 'he'. How do you know it's male?"

The head, objectively tiny but huge on the furred body, cocked to one side. "How could you not know? Isn't that part of the way you build us?"

Philippe ignored the word 'us' and focused on Poupée's question. "I never choose the sex. I could, it would be child's play, but I don't. I've always believed that a parent shouldn't be able to choose the sex of their offspring."

Poupée's eyes widened. "A parent?" She stamped a tiny foot, a gesture that would have been ridiculous had it not been for the darkness of the humid swamp and the fact that the ripples had almost reached them. "How can you possibly think of yourself in that manner? Parents are supposed to love and teach. You don't love and teach, you watch and study. You throw away the children you don't like."

"What? How can you say that?"

"If you don't want me to know something, you shouldn't write it down in your notes, and then leave the notes where anyone can get them."

Philippe laughed, forgetting about lurking bodies in the swamp. "I see my projections about the balance between instinct and acquired learning was spot-on. Your brain seems to be functioning at adult level—and you're only what, six years old?"

"Seven. A good parent shouldn't forget his children's ages. So what are we going to do now? Are you planning to create some more freaks that can't function in the real world? Perhaps a bird without feathers that has to use its beak to climb trees? Or maybe a fluorescent insect that can be seen from miles away by anything that feeds on bugs? That would certainly make it miserable, don't you think?"

"Listen to me, Poupée. It isn't like that. I never wanted any of you to suffer."

The misshapen doll snorted.

"Really!" Philippe went on. "Can't you see? You are something beautiful, something that wasn't possible until a few years ago!"

"If I'm so beautiful, then why can't I go to a ball and show myself off? How do you think they'd receive me in the village if I showed myself to them? I know what I look like. They'd call me a goblin—or worse." She pointed towards the lake, where the two yellow eyes could clearly be seen. "And what about him? If he were beautiful, he would be soaring through the skies."

Philippe shrugged. "They'd just shoot it down. It's better this way. Soon, it will be able to walk, and then everything will be all right—if I got the proportions right."

"Oh, you got the proportions just perfect, all right. He's a magnificent creature."

"How do you know? And why do you keep calling it a he?"

"I call it a he because he told me he was male—I wish you'd cared enough to give him a name, though. And as for the proportions, I can say it because I've seen him walking. He looks just like the dragons in your photos. The wings are magnificent."

"How could it tell you anything? It shouldn't know how to talk yet."

"Oh, I've been teaching him. I taught him all about you. How you made us. How we can never go out in the world because everyone will hate us. How you can go to the village when you're feeling lonely. And how we can't. How I saved you from being captured by the police." She seemed to remember he was there. "Oh, yes. Your theories about combining the steep learning curve of animals who need to be prepared to fend for themselves from the day they hatch with the intelligence of human beings seems to be working perfectly. But why would you want a talking dragon, anyway? And how did you get it to be so big—did you combine whale genes with the alligator stuff?"

Philippe, flabbergasted by the barrage of questions, but more surprised by the high level of the dialogue, raised a hand. "Dragons have to talk. They are the smartest of the mythological creatures…"

"Oh, I don't really care about that. You see, mainly, I've been telling him about how I'll never be married. How I'll never have a debutant ball, and how I'll never meet Mr. Darcy. Because I'm a freak, because you wanted me to be a freak. I told him that I was alone, and he asked me what it meant to be alone, and I explained. Then he was sad and disappeared for a few days."

"There's no need for him to be alone. I can produce as many of his species as he wants."

"I told him you'd say that," Poupée replied.

"Of course I say that. It's the truth."

The tiny creature lowered its voice to a whisper. "But I've convinced him that it's a lie. You see, if you make more of him, then he'll forget about me, and I'll really be alone. At least this way, there are two different freaks out here."

"But…"

Poupée emitted a shrill whistle and the water began to part around a long grey snout. She turned back to Philippe, her eyes dead. "He's very angry with you. I really wouldn't stop to try to convince him that I'm lying. The crocodile genes aren't particularly worried about the fact that you're his father."

"What do you want from me? Are you trying to kill me?"

Poupée shrugged. "I'm not really sure. On one hand, I'm grateful that you gave me life. On the other, I'm furious that you forced me to live this way. Maybe it would be best if you just ran into the jungle and we'll see how this plays out."

He took a step towards her, but she danced away, nimble as

any forest creature. He had no illusions that he'd catch her.

The sucking, splashing sound of a heavy body exploding from the swamp interrupted his reply.

"I think you'd better run, now," Poupée said.

Philippe stared at the beast for an instant. The doll was right; it was completely magnificent. Huge and powerful, with a tail that seemed to go on forever and obvious cunning behind those not-quite-reptilian yellow eyes. He knew a rush of pride as is spread its wings and shook them to get the water out of the folds.

Then it turned to look at him and Philippe held its gaze for a moment, trying to understand what lay beneath.

And then he ran.

BRIDGE OVER THE CUNENE

I love to write stories for themed anthologies. The constraints placed upon the writer forces the creative juices to flow along different channels. "Bridge Over the Cunene" was written for *The World is Dead*, an anthology set after the zombie apocalypse has come and gone, and humanity is settling down to deal with the new reality.

Like many other stories in this book, it's set in Africa. I believe Africa, with its huge diversity of terrain, wildlife and social structures is the most fertile ground an author can explore. A nice bonus is that every time I write a story set in Africa, I'm transported to a place I've never been before.

This is often called my saddest story, but I think it shows hope for the human race in a bleak situation—it shows why we're human, and why zombies aren't.

Botoso was singing some innocent rhyme about the horrors of the great change at the top of his lungs. It was a new phase, and Lara was fervently hoping that it would pass as quickly as the rest had.

It seemed only last week that the little five-year-old had contented himself with running around inside the stockade, happy to let his universe be defined by the log walls. But, suddenly, he'd become obsessed with the world outside. First, he'd gone through a period of curiosity about the Pale Ones, never going to bed unless he'd first been told a story about them, and the things that had happened during the change. He'd cover his head and pretend to be terrified, but never had nightmares, and always came back for more.

Then, seemingly simultaneously, every little one in the village had begun to sing the songs that their parents had sung. Songs about the Pale Ones, songs about the change. It was incredible how these songs, that had been buried for years, reemerged all at once. Nonsense songs, but their verses contained references to the horror of the times.

Lara noted that her son was looking at her quizzically. But he was silent at last, which was a relief. She could get back to mending the shirt.

"Mama," his thin voice piped up. "Do you think I could be the headman, some day?"

"Of course, dear," she replied absently.

"Just like Simao Zaboba?"

"Yes, dear."

He wandered off, and she breathed a small sigh of relief. There were clothes to mend, thatching to do. And he could be a demanding child sometimes.

***

He'd done this for all of his adult life. His predecessors had done the same. It was as natural as life on the veldt, and had been part of the cycle of life even before the great change, and would be part of it after the Pale Ones were a faded memory.

Simao Zaboba was at peace with himself, with the bright noon sun and the fresh June breeze whispering through the trees. He knew enough to be thankful for his role in the natural cycle. Twice a month, the offering was made, and twice a month, it was accepted. A pig on the full moon, valued for its brains, a goat on the new moon, desired for its blood; and safety, even a measure of protection, for the village all month long. It had always been thus, although in the times of his grandfather, the offering of a chicken or a cow were made on a less regular basis, to other, less tangible, spirits. But even those sporadic devotions must have had some effect, since the village had survived nearly unscathed, while others... well, others had been absorbed into the nests.

Today, he was leading a well-fed goat on a leash of metallic rope, enjoying the three-hour walk to the neutral zone across the river. Today was a clear day, and he could see forever, but knew that he would never see one of the Pale Ones during the day. Like all spirits that had once been day-walking humans, they were nocturnal creatures.

The bridge was a rickety affair, long poles lashed together with vines. His father had told him that the Cunene had once been bridged by dozens of concrete structures designed to last for generations. But these had been torn down in a desperate, failed attempt to stop the plague from spreading north to Angola. The village had avoided the change only because it was so far off the beaten path. By the time they'd been rediscovered, the Pale Ones had evolved, and had even reached the point where they could be reasoned with. Spirits were like that.

As they approached the neutral zone, the goat began to show signs of nervousness. It seemed to sense, somehow, that hundreds of its brothers and sisters had perished very nearby. Close enough that the smell of death was still present.

Or maybe it sensed something else. Something hungry.

Simao was unconcerned. He dragged the now openly resisting, panicked animal towards the clearing the way he'd done hundreds of times before. The stained ground and scattered bones seemed to give the animal added strength, and it left four furrows in the dust as its feet slid along.

He reached the tree and looped the end of the metallic rope around the trunk. As always, he double-checked the clasp; the consequences of the goat escaping were too ugly to contemplate.

Leaving the grunting goat straining against the unbreakable rope, Simao walked, as he'd done countless times before, back towards the village.

He wasn't expecting to see little Botoso crouching behind one of the bushes, because he'd never been there before. And that was probably why he didn't.

***

Botoso knew he was in trouble. He had no idea how in the world he was ever going to get back to the village. He had no idea where the village was. This was the first time he'd ever been outside the stockade without his mother or one of the other village adults to take care of him, and the sun was setting redly over the horizon.

But he wasn't frightened. He told himself that a future headman would never be frightened just because night was about to fall. He would laugh the night off, and keep walking until he found the river. He knew the river was near his village.

He also knew that he would make a great headman someday. He was smart and compassionate. After Simao Zabobo had left the clearing far behind, Botoso had emerged from hiding and immediately noticed that the headman had forgotten the goat. The boy knew how important goats were to the village—he was old enough to know that the village's very survival depended on the supply of goats.

So he worked at the clasp tying the goat to the tree and began his walk back the way he'd come. At some points, it was difficult to decide which way he had to go, since one patch of low grass or clump of trees looked just like the next, but he wasn't worried. A headman would never get lost.

But he had. And now the sun was all the way down, and it was hard to see where he was going. The goat, sniffing the air, had been getting more and more restless, and, suddenly, it gave a mighty jerk and broke free of Botoso's five-year-old grasp, dragging the leash off into the darkness.

Botoso gave chase, following the tinkling of the metallic cord until an unseen hole in the ground sent him tumbling onto a patch of thorns. He lay there silently, listening to the tinkling which grew fainter and then died out, and to the night, which was suddenly alive with scurrying and wildlife sounds. He knew that some of those sounds weren't alive.

He told himself that he wasn't afraid, but the tears that streamed down his face seemed unaware of it.

***

Lara was frantic. She'd been waiting for Simao Zaboba outside the village ever since she'd realized Botoso was missing. Now, off in the distance, she could make out a dark, tiny speck coming towards the village from the south. She knew, she had to believe, that the speck, as it grew nearer, would resolve itself into two figures, a large, thin one, and a slightly rotund smaller speck less than half the height of the first.

As the speck grew into a smudge, her hope waned, but then she rallied. The headman probably made Botoso walk behind him, as a punishment. That's why she could only make out one figure approaching in the afternoon glow.

But even that hope soon faded. She ran out to Zaboba, stood before him, clutching his arm, getting her breath back and finally panted, "Did you see Botoso?"

The headman looked her over, perfectly still, his impassive gaze showing no emotion. "There was no one on the path. How long has he been gone?"

She hung her head. "I'm not really certain. I looked for him, to eat the midday meal, and he was nowhere to be found. We looked all over the village." Lara was holding back tears now, desperate, her nails digging into his motionless forearm.

Zaboba looked at her knowingly. She felt that he could see through her, that he knew her deepest secrets, that he knew she was holding back. Finally, she could hold back no longer. "I think he followed you," she sobbed, and broke down completely.

"This is grave news," Simao said. "Go gather the elders." He pushed her gently towards the village, and walked slowly after her as she ran, stumbling, to do his bidding.

Other than Simao Zaboba, there were four village elders, and they all looked gravely on as she explained her plight. Finally, Satumbo, a toothless old man, by far the oldest man in the village, broke the silence. "A boy lost in the night is a job for the father," he said.

"My husband is dead."

"The uncle, then."

"He had no brothers."

"Then the boy is lost. The village cannot risk the men we have. No wife will let her man go. There is no way we can defend ourselves from the Pale Ones outside our walls in the night. The night belongs to them, and if we violate that agreement, we forfeit our lives."

Simao Zaboba spoke unexpectedly. "I will go," he said. "I know where the boy is. The mother must come as well—she will have a choice to make."

Lara swallowed. Nothing was more important to her than her son, but what Satumbo said was true: the night belonged to the Pale Ones. She was suddenly imagined herself being torn to shreds, her bones cracked for their marrow, her blood drained from her body, her brain sucked from her skull through a hole in the top of her head. But then the image in her mind changed, and she saw Botoso there in her place.

"I'll go," she said.

"You will go alone," Satumbo replied. "Simao Zaboba is much too valuable to the village."

"No, I am not. I am just a silly old man whose only value to the rest is that he leads a goat to a dangerous place once a fortnight. And besides, I will certainly return tonight. I speak the language of the Pale Ones."

"The Pale Ones will kill you when they see you."

"It may be so, but I don't think so. They have changed since your childhood. And even since mine. I will be all right." He turned to the still-open gates of the village, retracing the steps he'd taken to return to the village that afternoon. He didn't look back to see whether Lara was behind him.

And he didn't seem at all surprised when she appeared beside him. Only Lara knew that she almost hadn't come. Only she noticed that no matter how confident the headman had been of his own return, he'd said nothing about her.

***

It was a typical night. The veldt was cool and the sounds seemed somehow louder than they did from inside the village compound. That was ridiculous, of course; the open-topped wall of logs wouldn't have done much to filter the sounds of the nocturnal animals—the hoot of an owl, or the scurrying of rodents, or the buzz of insects. But it still seemed that the sounds were louder out here without the wall.

They'd been walking, their way illuminated only by the starlight and the knowledge of Simao's feet which had tread this same path for thirty years, for two and a half hours. At first, she constantly called out for Botoso, but, as they neared the bridge, Simao Zaboba told her to be quiet. Sound carried a long way on these grassy plains, and soon, the sound would carry all the way to the nest.

He didn't know where the nest was located, exactly, but he suspected that it was just a little beyond the clearing in the neutral zone—a clearing that was less than half an hour away on foot.

The night sounds seemed to get louder and louder the farther they got from the village, as if the animals, far from the noise and smell of human habitation, grew bolder. But Simao knew it had less to do with the actual noise than the fact that he was listening harder, trying to distinguish the sounds that didn't belong to the night. The sounds that meant that there was a something out there walking noisily on its two hind legs—something that hadn't been designed to prowl in the darkness, despite having originated near there very same plains millions of years before.

Something that, despite not being human, would have the arrogance and fearlessness that had, until the great change, allowed humans to walk the night knowing that no matter how much noise they made, no matter what they stirred up, it could be dealt with.

But now, with the few surviving humans huddling behind

thick walls or in underground bunkers as soon as the sun went down, only the Pale Ones walked the night that way. They could be easily heard by someone who knew what to listen for. And it wasn't long before Simao Zaboba distinguished the telltale sounds. His heart sank when he realized that the noise of multiple Pale Ones milling around was coming from the clearing where he'd left the goat that afternoon. It came from their destination.

He looked over at Lara, but she seemed lost in her own thoughts and not to have heard anything out of the ordinary. Her features were set, and she was grimly putting one foot in front of the other. She thought that he would know where to look.

She was right. He knew exactly where the little boy would be, but he dreaded what they'd find once they got there. He began to hope that they would be intercepted before they arrived, dreading each step. Soon, his fear had grown to the point where he was only reluctantly putting one foot in front of the other. By the time they were a hundred paces from the clearing, Lara was dragging him along.

Even in the dark, he could tell the clearing was crowded. Darker shapes could be made out in the darkness, and Simao Zaboba felt as though someone was running cold hands up his spine.

"Welcome," a voice said out of the darkness in front of him.

Lara jumped, but Simao had known it was coming. The word had been spoken in their harsh guttural language, the language that the villagers feared and reviled. They called it Palespeak. The Pale Ones themselves called it English—it had been the tongue of the southern land before the change. Only the headman and a few others could speak it.

The voice went on, "We suspected you come soon." It was a ragged, sighing voice—as if it had been unused for so long that it had to be dug up from deep within the Pale One's thorax. And yet, the speech was clearer than what he'd heard when, as an apprentice, he'd accompanied the old headman to make the agreement that exchanged an occasional goat and pig for their lives. During that meeting, the Pale Ones had spoken in grunts and single, almost incomprehensible words—and it had been impossible for them to understand any but the most rudimentary concepts.

Simao knew that how he responded could make the difference between life and death, but he also needed to understand the situation a little better. "I make fire to see," he said, glad he'd practiced his Palespeak all these years, despite never having had to use it.

His pronouncement was met with hissing and an unseen step forward from his right. Zaboba tensed, but the original voice replied before any action was taken against him. "Small fire," it said.

"Small fire," he agreed. One of his precious, irreplaceable matches was used to light a torch.

The clearing was bathed in flickering yellow light. The Pale Ones looked much worse for the wear. Nothing with skin as tattered and decomposed as the inhabitants of this clearing had any business being animate. Their once-mahogany skin, already pallid from the change, had become even more gray with the years. They looked like dolls made of stained rags.

Zaboba looked around desperately, searching for a smaller figure. His gaze was attracted by a commotion behind the nearest Pale One.

"Mama!" a high-pitched voice screamed, and suddenly a small brown bullet shot from the shadows and buried itself in Lara's stomach. She cried and bent over to hug him, protecting him with her arms. "Thank you, thank you," she was saying, to no one in particular, without thinking about it, just repeating the mantra—happiness and disbelief mixed.

"Thank you," Zaboba told the Pale One in front of him.

The other acknowledged, inclining his head. "We no eat little ones. Little ones grow, turn big ones. Bring us food. Other nests eat little ones, eat big ones too. Other nests die out. No food."

Zaboba was shocked at this. He couldn't believe what he was hearing, couldn't believe the sophistication of the Pale One's thought processes. But he had no time to dwell on it then. "We leave now," he said, bowing.

"No."

Zaboba realized that the semicircle of Pale Ones in front of them had expanded, and was now a complete circle, ahead and behind. They could not leave unless they were allowed to. There was no way they could break through that line unscathed—and even a scratch meant the end of human life, and the beginning of a twilight existence as a Pale One. He turned calmly back to the spokesman.

"We no have food," the Pale One said.

And suddenly, Zaboba lost his calm. He understood that what had been his worst fear, in the back of his mind, had actually come to pass. He knelt beside little Botoso and, trying to keep the fear and urgency from his voice, said, "Where's the goat?"

And Botoso, sensing the fear, began to cry. "It ran away. I tried to catch it, but I fell." And, finally, accusingly, "You forgot the goat."

Zabobo turned back to the Pale one.

"We no have food," it repeated. "Give food."

Lara turned to him, eyes wide, understanding. She seemed on the verge of panic, so he calmed her down. "Do not worry," he said. "I will stay. I am an old man, almost fifty summers. The village does not lose much."

Gratitude flashed on her face, but was almost immediately replaced by doubt and then fear. "But how will I find my way? It is still a long time until dawn. What happens if we get lost?"

"You must not become lost."

"What happens?"

"If you get lost, you will both die." He cursed the moonless sky. Even the small illumination from the barest crescent might have made the return trip possible. "Once you leave the neutral area, you are fair game unless you are on a clearly defined path towards the village. If you are anywhere else, other members of the nest will take you, since they have no way of knowing you are from our village."

And Lara knew it. She cried softly, silently, as she accepted what she must do. Botoso, who had lifted his head to see what was troubling his mother, suddenly crying again as he found himself transferred to Simao's care.

Simao took a tight grip of Botoso's hand. He knew the boy would have to be kept in check.

"Will you take care of him?" Lara said.

Simao nodded.

"What will become of him, an orphan? His options will be few."

"His options," he replied, "will be one. He has seen the Pale Ones, and it seems he will survive the encounter. He will be headman. I will take him on as an apprentice."

Pride flickered across her face, but lasted only a fleeting instant. She had remembered that she would not be there to see it. "Tell them," Lara said.

"One will remain," he told the leader of the Pale Ones, who nodded in reply.

A rustling sound behind caused Simao to turn. The Pale Ones behind had disappeared.

"Ones who go, go now."

Simao Zaboba took a tight grip on Botoso's hand and began to walk towards the village. At first, Botoso came readily, but then realized what was happening.

"Mama!" he said.

But it was too late by then. The circle had reformed, with them on the outside. The headman dragged the resisting boy towards the village. He was even thankful for the boy's calls for his mother, as they somewhat drowned out the screaming. At first, a single cry of protest, then a series of long, drawn out screams of agony which grew hoarser and hoarser. The final scream was a ragged cry, mercifully cut off in the middle.

The boy seemed to understand; his struggles stopped.

But the sick feeling in Simao Zaboba's stomach wasn't caused by the sounds of a pretty young mother being torn to edible chunks behind them. It was caused by the knowledge that the Pale Ones had, in their way, discovered farming—or at least a way to get small but sufficient quantities of live food without having to hunt for it. At present, they needed the village to supply their meat, but how long would it take them to figure it out for themselves? After that, the village would serve no purpose other than as a breeding ground for their favorite dish—or, worse, the site of one spectacular nighttime binge.

His reverie was broken by a slurping and panting noise from the feeding ground behind. He shuddered and hoped it would fade soon.

But sound carries a long way over the veldt.

EYES IN THE VASTNESS OF FOREVER

This story was originally published in *Innsmouth Free Press*. As you can imagine, anything related to Innsmouth is an eldritch fantasy (I believe this is the first time I've ever written the word "Eldritch" for publication). This particular piece, however is not related to any of Lovecraft's worlds, except for spiritually.

What I liked about it most, however, was that it was the first piece I ever wrote set in Argentina. I'd avoided my home country like the plague, but Tierra del Fuego in the time of Magellan seemed far enough away to be safe.

Every few moments, one of the lights would blink. It was just an instant, and almost unnoticeable because of their sheer number, but Joao De Menes was watching intently, defying the devil-eyes to come closer. If they did, he would show them the power of a Portuguese right arm.

Magalhaes had laughed at him, simply saying, "If you fear the Indians' camp-fires on the coast so much, perhaps you should take all the watches tonight," and had then ordered the anchor dropped.

The captain might be an arrogant fool, but Joao knew the truth: those eyes were watching and weighing, the eyes of hundreds upon hundreds of hungry demons, waiting for the foolish Europeans to sail their ship beyond the edge of the world.

He didn't know what lay beyond the end of the world. Some men told of a magic mist that you wandered around in forever, with no exit and no heaven, while demons feasted on your spirit. Others simply said you dropped off the edge of the planet, straight into the fires of hell. Still others spoke of eternal blackness, impossible torment.

Whichever was true, there were demons, and those demons possessed eyes which were staring down at the ship malevolently from the cliffs that marked the edge of the world.

And every once in a while, one of them would blink.

***

Dawn broke lightless and drizzling, but Magalhaes was adamant: a boat was lowered and a fearful crew selected. It was impossible to fault the captain's courage—he was the first to nominate himself—but easy enough to resent his cruelty. Of the ten men selected, five were the strongest on the Trinidad, while the other five were the most superstitious. Magalhaes was convinced that they could be cured of their foolishness by force and exposure to the fact that what they believed were demons were just natural phenomena.

Predictably, De Menes was among them. He hadn't even bothered to go to sleep following his watch because it was obvious that he would be on the boat. He boarded sullenly, ignoring the wind-driven spray. That wasn't what was bothering him; his concern lay in the fact that he had no inkling as to what devils might await them on the barren patch of rocky land ahead.

The place looked innocuous enough: an empty brown and grey shore with low cliffs broken by periodic inlets. But De Menes knew that daytime often found malignant forces dormant, waiting. They were still there, of course, but they wouldn't show themselves, just feel out the sailors and take them in the night, when their power went unchallenged.

They landed without incident, and Magalhaes led them a small distance inland and halted in front of a fire pit surrounded by the bones of some small animal. He pointed at it, looked straight into De Menes' eyes, and laughed. "Here are your demons Joao. Hungry savages, from the look of it." Turning to the rest of the men, he said, "Be wary, they can't have gone far. This fire was burning an hour before dawn—I marked it especially."

The men shifted uncomfortably. All were well aware that being harpooned by seal-hunters who'd never seen a European before would only destroy the body, as opposed to the eternal ravages that falling into the clutches of a demon supposed, but it made no difference to them. Death was what they feared, and they would worry about their immortal eternities at a later time. They stood straighter, attentive to the approach of any savages.

The natives they'd encountered along the interminable coast they'd sailed down to get that far hadn't been particularly aggressive, but it was never advisable to let down their guard. Everyone who'd ever boarded a ship bound for spice or glory had heard the tales of fearsome ceremonies, strange rituals in pitch-colored jungles and unholy banquets in which Europeans had served as the main course.

They need not have worried, however. An hour after sunrise, a small group of natives approached them from behind an outcropping of rock. They walked slowly, their skin just slightly darker than the pale brown grass which their passage seemingly did nothing to disturb.

As they came nearer, the sailors could discern that the every member of the group, composed of three women and two men, was as bare as the day they'd been born, their skin covered with some kind of thick grease or paste, a bright red color. Presumably, this must have kept out the winds which, this far south, were cruel even in the spring—and would be deadly in winter.

The three women walked boldly to the group of Spanish and Portuguese mariners and spoke in their own language, a tongue that sounded harsh and hollow to De Menes, as desolate as the moaning of the ever-present wind. There was no threat in their gestures. The men were unarmed, and the spokeswomen seemed unsurprised to see them.

Magalhaes turned to Herrero, a Spaniard who could understand any tongue, no matter how uncivilized. Rumors, given strength by his dusky skin and quick temper, told that the interpreter's affinity for the tongues of the savages was due to his being half-savage himself. Others said it was a gift from the devil. However he'd come about it, though, the ability had proven both useful and profitable on the journey so far. "Stay ashore and learn their tongue. I will have the ship send you a boatload of supplies. De Menes and Carrizo will stay with you." Herrero nodded.

De Menes said nothing. He should have felt fury at the captain for belittling his beliefs once again, but there was no anger within his soul. He'd known what was coming, felt as though he was walking a predetermined path, with an already decided ending, albeit one he could not see. All he saw when he thought about it was the grayness of impenetrable fog, an indeterminate future.

He simply walked behind Herrero as the linguist selected a campsite. This was not hard to do, as the whole hillside was dotted with pits, each of which held the remains of some discarded campfire.

The rest of the morning passed peacefully. Herrero had wandered off and was seated in the center of a group of natives, gesturing, laughing, making gifts of beads and other trinkets which seemed to go down very well with the natives. Soon, they were gesturing for Carrizo and De Menes to join them.

The two sailors did as they were told. De Menes sat down gingerly between a graying old man and a woman who could not have been more than twenty, with jet-black hair. He tried to keep his eyes away from the exposed anatomy of the locals, but the circular seating arrangement made that difficult. Carrizo stared openly, but none of the women seemed to mind.

Herrero was already making progress with the language. Interspersed with the gesturing, there was now a word here, another word there, which seemed to please their hosts, who tried to correct his pronunciation and laughed at his efforts.

One woman, however, was paying no attention to Herrero. The girl De Menes had sat beside seemed to have eyes only for him, and stared the entire time. At first, he thought it must simply have been the close up view of his light skin and strange clothes, but he soon realized that the girl had not even glanced at the equally exotic figures of Carrizo and Herrero.

He smiled at her and placed one hand on his chest. "Joao," he whispered. Her dark eyes invited him to speculate about the rest of her, and he tried desperately to keep his own gaze locked on them while she spoke.

"Teuhuech," she replied, placing his hand on her own chest. He pulled it back quickly as she said something else, a rapid-fire string of words in her own language, delivered in a husky monotone. The man on De Menes' opposite side chuckled.

At that moment, a couple of men from the Trinidad arrived, carrying sacks of provisions. "Your tent is down in the boat. If you want to sleep under cover, I'd suggest you get it. We aren't coming back up here."

Grumbling, but relieved to be able to escape from the strange natives for a few moments, Carrizo and De Menes walked down the hill. Herrero, of course, was much too important to be bothered with menial tasks. They joked with the oarsmen as they pulled the poles from the boat. "Magalhaes says we'll be back tomorrow or the next day. He wants to sail beyond that outcropping." The man pointed to a peninsula some leagues away, "To see whether we can replenish our water."

De Menes' heart sank. They would be alone, without even the comforting sight of the flotilla to keep him sane, on a small spit of land at the edge of the world. But he would not give the tyrant the satisfaction of begging to be allowed back on board. He gestured Carrizo to pick up his half of the burden and set off toward the campsite.

The wind, already a desolate howl, had picked up even more as they began to pitch the tent. By De Menes' reckoning, it was about three in the afternoon, and there were still hours and hours of late spring sunlight remaining. And yet the sunlight seemed weak, thin, as if its force was being drained by invisible fog. De Menes shivered.

The girl, Teuhuech, realized he was back almost immediately, and joined them just as Joao attempted to position the final tent pole. He watched her walk in their direction, unable to ignore the fact that there was a young and supple body beneath the red paint.

She playfully took hold of the tent pole, her surprisingly strong grip resisting his efforts to tear it from her grasp and his attempts to twist the pole without making contact with her skin only made the native girl laugh.

Finally, she relented, allowing De Menes and Carrizo to finish erecting their tent, a medium-sized piece of canvas suitable for three men. When it was done, she smiled and crawled inside. De Menes tried to look away, but Carrizo had no such qualms. He stared at the indecently exposed flesh and then turned to his companion and winked lewdly. "I would go in after her, my friend, but I don't think that would make her happy. You, on the other hand, should hurry before she changes her mind."

De Menes gave him a dark look. While he wasn't a saint, by any means, and certainly wasn't averse to the occasional dalliance with one of the native girls, this one's single-minded determination made him nervous. It was impossible to shake the feeling that there was something deep and disturbing lurking just behind those smiles. Maybe it was just his dread at having been abandoned by his ship at the edge of the world with nightfall approaching fast. But he felt that his soul and his immortal existence were at the mercy of forces no mortal could ever hope to control.

He shook his head and returned to the circle where Herrero was still holding court. The Spaniard complemented his limited—yet still impressive, considering how little time he'd taken to create it—vocabulary with wild gestures and vocal sound effects. His audience sat at rapt attention.

"I'm telling them the story of our Atlantic crossing," he explained. "Although they seem to believe that we're sorcerers from the sky, because they saw the sails of our ship, and think it looks like a bird."

De Menes nodded and sat on the cool ground, squeezing between two of the local men who'd arrived in their absence. The red paint did little to cover them, either, but it was still less distracting than having Tehuech beside him. As the story went on, more men arrived, none aggressive, all painted red. The girl, disappointment evident on her face as she saw his new seating arrangements, sat straight ahead of him.

The long afternoon's anemic light soon gave way to an eternal twilight, and the men began to drift to the nearby fire pits. Soon, the demonic eyes once more lit the hills, but this time De Menes sat among them. He wondered what else walked the night, connecting the dots between the warmth and light.

The sailors were left to their own devices as night came down and the last vestiges of the day's warmth and cheer were swept away before the howling wind. De Menes had difficulty believing that the savages could bear the chill without clothes, and found himself wondering whether they insisted in that same lunacy during the winters, which he imagined must have been merciless in those latitudes.

Their own fire was an unimpressive affair, built close to the tent and casting a small ring of light from which De Menes refused to venture even to relieve himself. He could feel the demon lords watching them from the darkness, present in every shadow and trying to find the doorway that led from their own gray and boundless kingdom into the world of the living.

Knowing sleep would be beyond him, he'd offered to stand guard. So he sat with his eyes open long after Carrizo and Herrero had drifted into snoring slumber. He cringed at each sound, ready to defend himself, but, when the demon crawled into his tent and took his hand, he could do nothing but follow it out.

It led him endlessly across the stiff grass to the embers of another of the bonfires. By its light, De Menes saw that no demon held his hand, but that Tehuech had brought him there. He knew exactly why. She was still naked, but she'd also scraped off the paint.

He pulled his hand away, trying to remember the way back to his own fire and the security of the tent, but fear had made him an unthinking being, a sheep led to slaughter. He turned back to the girl, and a movement above her breasts told him that she wasn't completely bare. A necklace of stone and shells and driftwood danced above her breasts.

Seeing where his gaze lay, she smiled. "Joao," she said. She removed the necklace and held it towards him with both hands, saying something incomprehensible, and then "Joao," again.

He shrugged and bowed, allowing her to pass the offering over his head. It caught on one ear, but was soon in place around his neck.

"Thank you," he said, and she smiled back, understanding the meaning, if not the words.

Joao felt more relaxed. Having accepted her gift, he felt that it would be all right to return to his camp. He turned away from the fire, the afterimage of the embers dancing in his eyes. He waited for them to subside, for his night vision to return.

But, instead of disappearing, the moving lights came into sharper focus, resolving themselves into points of light just beyond the ember's illumination. Eyes that stared unblinkingly back at him, seemingly an arm's-length away. De Menes recoiled from those eyes, his steps taking him straight into Tehuech's waiting embrace.

He knew that the fire was all that kept them away, and that the girl was all that kept the fire alive, and that the creatures of the netherworld were not there to interfere, but to bear witness to a consummation.

***

The following day dawned bright and clear, memories of the previous night burned away, but De Menes was still surprised to wake inside the tent. He had no recollection of having returned, and his memory of the rest was blurred, as if veiled in gray fog. But it had not been a dream: the clicking of his new necklace as he crawled out of the tent assured him of it.

"Come on, sleepyhead," Carrizo chided. "The sun's been up for an hour, and Magalhaes is back. He found some more savages a little further west, and they seem a bit more advanced than these. We have to pull up the tent and return to shore."

The manual labor allowed De Menes to temporarily forget about midnight rendezvous and ghostly eyes and, as he approached the sea and its waiting boat, he felt an enormous weight lifting. Each step felt lighter than the last.

A small party awaited, natives mixed with sailors. The savages even helped to load the boat, only asking a few trinkets and some cloth in return for their unnecessary help, which were given gladly—too often the sailors had had to fight natives who took a dim view of outsiders. Tehuech, among the local group, said nothing and kept her eyes on the ground.

Finally, as De Menes was about to step aboard, one of the older women came forward, and said something to Herrero.

Herrero listened, and turned to Joao. "I'm not really sure what she said, but I think it was 'that man wears a wedding circle', and she pointed at you. Do you know what she's talking about?"

De Menes hung his head. "I think I do." He pulled the necklace back over his head and walked to where Tehuech was standing, heart heavy with dread and remorse. He held it out to her, but she made no move to take it, and refused to meet his gaze, eyes resolutely turned away. Finally, he left it at her feet and stepped back. Still she gave no sign of acknowledgement.

Joao walked back to the shore and boarded the boat. None of the savages made any move to stop them.

***

As the Trinidad left the hills with eyes far behind, the crew began to taunt De Menes, asking what had happened, and attempting to get the details of what they imagined must have been one of the more sordid escapades of the journey. But he refused to elaborate and the speculation soon passed into the realm of wild orgies and fantastic pleasures.

De Menes heard none of it. The lewd shouting seemed to him a far-off whisper. As the ship advanced, it grew fainter and fainter.

Even the ship itself seemed to be fading. It had sailed into a fog which became thicker as they sailed through it. The Trinidad's prow became a ghost of itself, and soon, even the mainmast, scant meters away, seemed a specter.

A small tremor of panic coursed through him as he realized that the deck beneath him was no longer solid, but made of ethereal mist, but he simply shrugged it off. Understanding had replaced fear, and a broken trust was suitably punished. Perhaps the endless, featureless grey at the end of the world would not be as bad as the visions of fire and torment that the hell of his own land promised.

And perhaps, just perhaps, he would be called upon to bear witness in some distant future, thereby remembering what it was like to tread upon the grass at the end of the world, and share the love of one of its guardians.

OFFLINE

The first scene of "Offline" came to me complete: a desperate young woman in a darkened room right out of a noir detective story, but instead of Los Angeles in the 1940s, she was living in an equally bleak future.

Then came the challenge of building the society around her and making it believable. Once that was done and the geography established, this story almost tells itself.

It was originally published in the Irish magazine *Albedo One*, my first ever publication on the Emerald Isle.

Three blue lines.

Damn. To think that that was all it had taken to change my life beyond recognition, beyond recovery. To think that those three insignificant blue marks had been the bridge from what I was before to where I am now.

To this room. Darkened, not through any choice of mine, but because it couldn't be any other way. The only visible light was the harsh glare of a streetlamp, filtered first by the rain, and then by the blinds. This empty shell of a room had no curtains.

The bandaged hole in my wrist throbbed painfully as I thought back to the day before yesterday when the three lines indicated, beyond any reasonable doubt, that I really was pregnant. It wasn't just my imagination. It wasn't just the stress of my illicit liaison wreaking havoc on my cycle. It had really happened.

The lightning outside showed me, briefly, my small corner of Windhoek. At least until tomorrow morning, I would be safe in this room. My body heat would register, I was sure, but the sensors in this room would be insufficiently accurate to tell a rat from a buffalo. And nobody at central control would bother to come and check an old, worthless building. Not on a night like this. Anything not webbed in would be assumed to be a rodent.

But someone would be around tomorrow, probably vermin control. By sunup, I had to have a place to go, and a plan.

By my count, I had only two things going for me. The first was that, so far, I was the only one who knew why I had gone rogue. Most likely, the Control Committee was treating my case as a malfunction. After all, less than a day had gone by since I had removed the Identicell from my wrist. The second was that the system itself was designed with the express purpose of keeping track of webbed people. It just wasn't prepared to deal with offliners—the Committee would have to organize a manhunt, without the benefit of electronic localization.

On the other hand, the second point could be considered to encompass all my current disadvantages. It was almost impossible to do anything without an Identicell. Doors wouldn't open. Public transport would not take me anywhere, and even regular traffic would not stop to allow me to cross, or even take evasive action if I happened to walk in front of a bus. And the lights in this room would remain off for the duration of my stay. Not only was it frustrating, it was dangerous. And it wasn't enough for me to just survive. I had to get out of the city. And I had to do it fast.

But the thunder made it impossible to think. I hit the worn carpet with my fists and cried.

The sunlight coming through the blinds meant that I had seriously overslept. I had been exhausted, but now I was in danger. Vermin control could appear at any time.

Out the door and down the steps, I was almost grateful that I had nothing to my name except for the contents of a small backpack: some food bars, a bottle to collect water with and a toolkit. I had been living mostly off the benefits of this last item for the past week.

It's amazing just how useful a screwdriver can be in the right situation, especially since most vending machines are flimsy plastic affairs. What would be the use of making them too strong? It's just not cost-effective now that everyone's webbed in. Vandals can be tracked down in minutes, so armored machines would just be a waste of money.

And who would dream of going offline?

I could already see my objective: a small warehouse just two blocks from my hiding place.

Looking around to make sure that I was unobserved, I moved into the alley beside the building. Desperately needing a side door, my relief when I saw it was enormous. And heightened by the discovery that the door was just a standard-security item. It would identify and log anyone going in, and sound a silent alarm in case of unauthorized access. But, just like my lodgings of the previous night, a door that reported *nobody* going in, in the middle of the night, would be ignored as a malfunction. Such was the power of being offline in Namibia.

I would have some uninterrupted time to work. All I had to do now was wait until dark.

***

Midnight after a day of nerves. Just walking through Windhoek. Avoiding the patrols. Avoiding other humans. Jumping at every noise. And praying, always praying that Timmy, one of my students in the second grade, had been telling the truth about the existence, location and contents of his father's collection.

He had been so delighted to learn that his teacher, always a source of anxiety to him before that day, was interested in the old stuff that I wouldn't have put it past him to have made it all up.

School rules had prevented me from visiting, but I had never forgotten the incident or the details.

No time for subtlety. I simply pushed the screwdriver between the door and the frame at handle-height and put my weight behind it hard. Once. Twice. A desperate third time.

On the fourth push, I felt something snap and the door

popped open.

My flashlight, already at the ready, immediately revealed that Timmy had been telling the truth. Dark mechanical shapes loomed in front of me. I illuminated the nearest, the beam of light falling on a badge: Ford-Namib. A small minibus, twenty or thirty years old at most.

It, at least, was useless to me. If Timmy had been telling the *whole* truth—and nothing so far had indicated otherwise—then all the vehicles were in perfect working order. That, in turn, meant that the minibus, old as it was, would be webbed in. Not as comprehensively as a newer model, but well enough to make it stupidly easy for the Committee to track its whereabouts if I should happen to steal it.

I needed something older. Lots older. Sturdy enough to move across the countryside, but not so new as to be webbed. I moved the flashlight from one form to another, but found nothing usable. Panic was beginning to change from a vague feeling in my stomach to a definite one in my throat as I moved further into the warehouse.

I was soon surrounded on all sides by the hulking metal of the collection, looming menacingly in the dark.

Hurry! It was entirely possible that the authorities were already on their way, although I thought it unlikely. Windhoek might be the social and political center of the Sub-Saharan Confederacy, but Africa was always and would always be Africa in some regards. Bureaucratic sloth was one of these.

Deep inside the warehouse now. The hulking minibuses and mine crawlers had given way to smaller forms, ghostly in the dark under white dust-sheets. I chose a likely candidate and pulled the nylon cover off the front. A tall, vertical radiator grill topped by a graceful statuette and a badge that said "RR".

Despite my situation, I couldn't help stopping for an instant to catch my breath. The vehicle in front of me was a Rolls Royce Silver Ghost from the early twentieth century. Unsuitable for my needs—too old and too slow—it made me wish my father could have been alive to see it. I had inherited my passion for old vehicles from him, and, to this day, I could still imagine the look in his eyes whenever some particularly beautiful or historically significant vehicle would pass us on the road.

But I still had to find something I could use.

Quickly discarding several older cars, I became intrigued by a smaller dust-cover-topped mound. Climbing over an ancient bicycle, I pulled the cover off.

Bingo.

The olive paint, stenciled white palm-tree logo and squat shape told me that I was looking at an old Afrika Corps Zundapp sidecar. Rugged, relatively fast (at least compared to the old Rolls) and proven on African terrain, it also had the one quality I needed most: it was definitely not webbed in.

And the fact that it started, fit through the aisles in the warehouse, and managed to get out the door without generating any immediate and devastating official response caused me to think, for the first time since taking the pregnancy test, that I might survive long enough to actually have the baby.

***

My wrist was killing me. If anyone had asked my advice on going offline, the first piece of wisdom I would have imparted—ignoring the more obvious drawbacks, such as the fact that it carried the death penalty and was very inconvenient when trying to flush a webbed toilet—would have been this: if you're going to remove an embedded Identicell from your wrist with a kitchen knife, it would probably be best to avoid riding motorcycles immediately afterwards, especially on African roads.

Pity I hadn't been able to take my own advice. The pain and seepage seemed to get worse all the time. I ignored them.

Fortunately for me, the camp was just fifty klicks to the north of Windhoek. The way I needed to go. The area was sparsely populated and, despite the time lost in my search of the warehouse, I should still be there before dawn.

It was stupid for me to go, of course. If the Committee had sent out a Rogue/Offline bulletin about me, I would be arrested on sight. I knew that bureaucratic timelines would probably have precluded this risk, but it was still chancy.

But I had to see Nathan before I left. I just had to. To tell him. And not just disappear like so many others. At least he would know why.

A light ahead meant the camp was near. I carefully parked the Zundapp among some bushes, hidden from view of the road. Not good enough to fool a flyby, but sufficient to ensure against casual molestation. I walked to the bus stop to wait for a hoverbus, knowing full well that it wouldn't stop for me, as, without my Identicell, it wouldn't even be aware that I was there.

Forty five minutes. Bandage loosening under my constant fidgeting.

Finally a bus went by. Empty, of course, at this time of morning. It didn't stop, but no matter. The guard at camp would never have noticed that. He'd just assume that I'd been on the bus.

As I made my way on foot from the bus stop to the camp, I reflected on my fall from grace. Just three days ago, I would have enjoyed the ride here on that very same bus, floating on a cushion of air over any imperfections the road could throw my way. In air conditioned, silent comfort.

As it was, though, the buzzing from the two-stroke engine in the motorcycle was still present in my ears. Combined with the dust from the road in my eyes (how unfair is it, I reflected, for this country to be both dusty and muddy?), I felt blind and deaf. And when you add the pain in my wrist, I was almost looking forward to the immediate imprisonment that should result from this idiotic side trip to the camp.

And after imprisonment, death. But I walked on anyway.

Ignoring my foreboding, however, the guard just smiled and waved me through the gate.

"Hi Milly," he said. "In a bit early today, aren't we?"

I could barely hide my relief. "You know us," I said, "when we volunteer, we're not kidding around!" The sun was just starting to make its appearance over the rugged terrain in the eastern distance.

He laughed and opened the second gate, a heavily armored doorway.

I was in!

Two years worth of practice took me straight to Nathan's hut. The lanes between the huts were still clean at this time of day. The crews had probably just been through. But there was nothing I could do about the mud.

I managed not to drown myself getting to the door of the hut. Made of plastic, and just large enough to hold the two of them, it was still a great improvement over the infamous camps of the twentieth century, with their crowded tents and rampant disease. But then, white prisoners had always numbered in the thousands, no more. Most of the white population had been allowed to flee to wherever it was that their ancestors had come from.

Only those foolhardy enough to insist on staying had been imprisoned. Mainly farmers and landowners, who insisted on getting their "rights" from a people that they'd never respected or even treated as fully human.

The fools had paid for their pride. Badly in Namibia, much worse in South Africa. The lucky ones had died in the fighting.

Nathan had not been one of the lucky ones. Pride had kept him on the farm, but his then five-year-old son had stayed his hand when it became apparent just how severely resistance would be punished. Surrender and three years of life in this concentration camp had followed.

I knocked and waited. He would know it was me. I was the

only one who ever bothered to knock.

It was quite a while before the door opened, but I didn't knock again. I could hear them moving inside, although it was suddenly difficult to hear anything other than the noise of my heart, which had decided to imitate a bass drum, and simultaneously move from my chest to my throat. Again. Though not with fear this time.

When the door finally did open, I quickly pushed past him and shut it behind me.

"I've come to say goodbye." I said.

And then I sat on the nearest bed and let it all out. I cried for ten minutes, simply unable to control myself or stop. It was all I could do to keep the sobs quiet. If anyone heard me, the game was up.

He just stood by my side, silently, one hand on my shoulder. His shock, if any, had subsided by then. A deep sadness took its place.

"Why now?" he whispered.

"I'm pregnant."

The silence that followed lasted a few moments, allowing me to look around. Seated behind his father on the opposite cot was Jake. Thin and blond, and so still I hadn't noticed him until that moment. I felt Nathan's hand leave my shoulder and looked back at him. His face indicated that he was struggling to say something, but unable to get the words straight in his head, and unwilling to speak before doing so.

I laughed softly.

"It's yours," I said.

He looked guilty, but nodded.

"I'm going to have it."

"But…"

"Yes, pregnant from a white father. I know. Death penalty for the mother *and* the baby." I said.

He nodded, tears welling in his eyes. He knew where this was going. How it had to end.

"I'm going to make a run for it. I'll try to get out of Namibia to the north. The Unaligned Southern Angolan Front is neutral, and don't like the Coalition much. They'll let me in."

He shook his head.

"As soon as you start heading north, the Committee will be all over you."

I just held up my wrist, with its filthy, gloriously seeping bandage.

"Ouch." He said. His own Identicell had been removed when his citizenship had been revoked for the capital crime of being white inside the territory controlled by the Subsaharan Coalition. It hadn't healed well and keloid scarring marred his wrist.

"I've got a motorbike outside. But I wanted you to know what became of me. Goodbye." I said, suddenly wanting to leave. I got up and walked towards the door, but he grabbed my arm and turned me towards him. His features had taken a hard set.

"Take Jake," he said. Jake looked up from where he was sitting.

"No, it's too dangerous."

"It's more dangerous here."

"No. It's not. The Committee is taking care of him. Feeding and schooling. You know that. That's why I'm here." I said.

He let go of my arm, sharply.

"We both know what's going to happen. As soon as he turns ten, I'll be executed and they'll start brainwashing him. I've seen it happen and I don't want that for him. I know what you're doing is dangerous, but at least there's some hope. You can take him. You're the teacher. Call it a field trip."

I said nothing.

"No, daddy." Jake finally spoke. He was on the verge of tears.

His father just looked at me, not trusting himself to speak, but finally managing to get one word out.

"Please?" he said.

***

As we moved northward on ever-worsening roads, I reflected once again on the irony of the situation: how the technology that would have made this trip a breeze also would have rendered it impossible. Even something as simple as a webbed-in hover-taxi would have been able to move at an easy three hundred klicks. And would have gotten us caught in about ten minutes.

As it was, we advanced sedately, as they would have a hundred and fifty years before, feeling every rut in the road shoot through my wrist, every pothole, every dip, every bend.

I refused to cry out, though, for Jake's sake. He had been told to be brave, and was doing unbelievably well, biting back tears. If he could do that, knowing his father had maybe a few days to live, there was no way I would show weakness. No way.

The drone of the engine made conversation impossible, so we rode in silence as the morning gradually turned to noon, the sun, dimly visible, moving relentlessly from right to left beyond the cloud cover.

I used the time to worry. How would we ever cross the border? A citizen and a white child, alone together. And she pregnant from a white father to boot (I knew that I was being paranoid, it would be months before anybody could even tell I was pregnant, but I worried anyway). Fortunately, relations with Angola were cool, but not openly hostile, and I thought it should be possible to cross over without meeting any bored, trigger-happy border guards, as long as we did so a few miles into the bush, away from the main crossing points. Still, there was always a real danger of getting caught.

And I didn't even want to think of the possibility of not being given asylum…

Being so preoccupied with this brooding, practical matters slipped my mind completely until the engine sputtered, coughed, ran unevenly for about six hundred meters, and finally stopped altogether. I kicked the starter. Nothing. Only a full minute later did I finally realize what had happened.

"Stupid, stupid, stupid!" I screamed.

And stopped when I remembered Jake. Too late. He was staring at me wide eyed, lower lip trembling, still trying to hold back his tears. I immediately went over and hugged him.

"Don't cry, Jake, we're out of gas. It's nothing to worry about. We'll just walk for a bit, and then we'll get to Angola."

So saying, I pried the compass out of the bike's instrument panel with the screwdriver. We would be following the road most of the way, but would turn off soon, needing an empty area to cross the border.

At least I thought it would be soon, by dead reckoning (how stupid was it to assume that the reserve military gas tanks would be enough for any and all mileage? I hadn't even checked to see if they were full!). I had no real idea. The bike was not webbed in. No GPS. And even had it been available, I wouldn't have been allowed access to the system without my Identicell.

Ah, the Identicall. I pulled the broken metal square out of my pocket. 2 centimeters square and wafer-thin, it had been in my upper wrist since the day I turned fifteen. It made civilized life possible. Doors opened for it. Computers computed, showers functioned, buses stopped and vending machines vended. It also told the world that I was a teacher, a respected member of society, a volunteer at the camp.

Without it, I had, in quick succession, been reduced to living on the unguarded fringes of that same civilization, stealing from it and occupying empty, unwanted spaces, and then to crossing the wilderness exposed to the elements, like some primitive twentieth-century explorer.

And now this.

I was walking! *Walking*! Without any food. Insufficient water. And no idea how much further I had to go. Did early humans feel this way all the time? Lost? Confused?

I continued to put one foot in front of the other and glanced at Jake. He was crying silently, streaked face glistening in the weak noon brightness, already covered with muddy dust.

Somehow, his tears justified mine. Surely, falling completely out of civilization, exposed and walking, was sufficient cause for tears. I let them go, in small guilty starts at first, and then with abandon.

And the sky, as if in sympathy, dropped its own water. Softly, timidly in the beginning, and then with equal abandon.

Still, we walked on. Just a little worse off than before the rain.

Ménage à Trois

I know I got naughty with the title on this one, but it's actually a spy thriller set on the moon. As humanity prepares to return to our satellite, people in the West need to understand that there will be many more players in this particular space race than in the last one.

So we have China, India and the U.S. replaying the Great Game a couple of hundred years later.

This story was written for the *Return to Luna* contest created by Hadley Rille Books and the National Space Society and was one of the winners, appearing for the first time in the anthology of the same name.

The man's helmet pressed against mine allowed us to communicate without radio. Radio was a no-no in our line of work, and wasn't necessary in any case. He simply shouted, and the contact between our visors carried the sound.

"Ms. Lombardo?"

I nodded.

"The plans are in the storage drive!"

I pulled back and nodded again, indicating that I had heard, understood, and would proceed as agreed.

He nodded back, dusky face barely visible beneath the tinted visor, even in the full glare of the sun, and bounded back the way he'd come. I admired the elegance of the new Indian suit in action until he was hidden from view by the lip of the crater. I would file my recording of the movement as soon as I had time since sending it out, even encrypted, was not an option. But first, I had to get this drive to Rosemeyer.

The Indian was long gone, but I still waited fifteen more minutes before making my own way. I stood in the shadow of an outcrop, observing the barren, empty majesty of the Sea of Tranquility under the sun of lunar noon. Even though my visor was nearly full-dark to shield my eyes from the reflected glare, Earth hung in the sky like a giant milky sapphire, and I wondered for the millionth time how humanity could have ignored this wonderful place for three quarters of a century.

My rover was parked out of sight nearly a mile away, in the largest patch of shade available—only the solar arrays were in the sun—and I sweated as I walked. My suit had been optimized for daytime temperature, which meant that, though it was lighter and allowed much more mobility than the previous model, it also had the bare minimum amount of insulation—which meant that while I could easily survive the scorching sun, I would not necessarily be comfortable.

The drive back to the High Vegas was uneventful. The guy manning the airlock was surprised to see me because he knew that nobody had gone out that way today, but waved me through without comment. It might be a useless precaution to enter through a different door than I'd used to exit, but one could never be too careful these days. I knew my movements would be recorded and in the hands of both the Indian and Chinese services within a couple of hours.

Leaving the rover in the government-vehicle lot, I peeled off the suit, recovered my clothes and walked quickly past the spaceport facilities and into the main dome, which we referred to simply as "the Strip". Bright lights destroyed the majestic view of Earth in the sky, but the teeming crowds seemed not to care. They were there for a different reason. Maybe to impress others with their off-planet vacation. Or maybe just to mingle with the highest of the high rollers—a good night at the tables could pay for the cost of the flight out. And the casinos would accept anything: cash, jewelry, deeds to property on Earth. The only thing non-negotiable was the ticket back.

I was relieved to turn off the strip onto the deserted side-corridor leading to the government sector. Despite the fact that this base was a critical strategic and scientific outpost, the official area was much smaller and grubbier than the public enclosure, placed in a secondary dome out of everyone's way. The western space programs had, after much pleading, gotten their moon base, but not without some creative pitching to gaming industry investors.

The entrance door had both the NASA and ESA logos stenciled on it and two humorless-looking guards stationed outside. I wondered how they managed to stay alert and grim in the face of no threat more serious than a possible drunken tourist making a wrong turn, but they did. The one on the right wordlessly studied the badge on my suit with both UV and IR light before opening the door.

Brett Rosemeyer's office was the last in a warren of small closed cubicles on the second level. I was amazed how government offices everywhere, even here, were indistinguishable from one another—dull, utilitarian and slightly depressing. Brett himself was my picture of a stereotypical public servant: balding, slightly pot-bellied, and possessed of the moon-dwellers pallid complexion. Only the fact that I knew him to be an extremely creative and intelligent individual kept him from being completely comical.

He looked up as I entered, and gestured towards the seat facing his desk. "So, I take it all went well with our Indian friends," he said, the remnants of a British accent noticeable under the Alabama drawl.

"They asked me to give you this," I replied.

He studied the chip for a few moments and laid it next to a model of a streamlined silver race car that was the only ornament in his office. "Do you know what it is?"

I nodded. "Plans to the Chinese base on the far side."

"Yes. Now the thing is why? Why in the world would the Indians give this to us? It couldn't have been easy to obtain. Getting into that base is nearly impossible. Bribing the Chinese is expensive. So why did they just come over and give us the plans?"

I didn't know. The Chinese and Indians had been playing their chess game on the moon for the last twenty-five years, and looked upon the NASA / ESA base as a bit of an irrelevant Johnny-come-lately. The fact that most of our surface area was used to house casinos and hotels was just another reason for them to laugh at us.

"I have no idea," I replied. "But I suspect it'll come to us when we take a look. Or maybe it's just a play to get us on their side and balance things a bit." The construction of the second Chinese base on the moon had been a serious blow to Indian pride. They would never let the great red nation forget that India had put the permanent base up first, but the Chinese had wasted no time in establishing technical and psychological dominance. This second base had been a terrible blow.

Brett raised an eyebrow. "Strictly speaking, you aren't cleared to view this material."

"We both know that I have to. After all, I'll be the one taking any action that comes from this, and I won't risk it unless I have access to the original plans, not some sanitized version that's been run through analysts on Earth. They'll probably delete some detail that they don't think I need to know and get me killed."

He laughed, motioned for me to close the door, pulled the drive off his desk, lay it on the reader and waited. The big screen on the wall behind him flickered to life, showing a large mess of lines of different colors. It was not immediately possible to make anything out.

"Let's start with what we know," Brett said. "Exterior." This last was directed at the screen. All lines except for the gray ones that marked the contour disappeared. "Overwrite and compare with stored orbital photos."

A second image appeared on the screen: the Chinese base as seen from orbit. The two forms jiggled on the screen a couple of seconds before a new message appeared—'Match Positive'.

"Good," Brett said. "Let's see what else we have in here."

We began to peel back the layers of the schematics, taking notes and saying nothing in order to avoid contaminating each other's observations. Even so, it was impossible to be unaware what Brett was thinking. He had to be thinking the same thing I was. I looked over at him.

"And now we know," he said.

I nodded, but decided to play it by the book. I would probably have to go out there and have a look, and wanted to be absolutely sure that we were on the same page.

He began reading his notes. "The dome is hollow, the only inhabited areas are contained in a ring along the circumference. Strangely, though, the main power lines have outlets in various places along the empty space in the middle, which is forty meters deep. And it's full of air."

I broke in. "Energy readings show that 98% of all their electricity consumption occurs within the empty part of the dome, and that they've been stockpiling very cold liquids there as well."

"So it isn't empty."

"Obviously."

We sat for a minute, both of us thinking the same thing, neither wanting to say it out loud.

"They're building something," Brett said.

"They're building a spaceship," I replied.

Silence ensued. He knew I was right, illogical though it was to build a spaceship on the moon. The design of the dome's interior, the frozen liquids—rocket fuel?—in the hollow area and the energy consumption all pointed precisely in that direction.

"But why?" he said after a while. "It doesn't make any sense. I can understand not building it on Earth, just in order to avoid having to pull a large ship out of that gravity well, but the most logical place to build it would still be in high Earth orbit. Why put it on the moon? You end up having to ferry all the materials all the way over here! It must be costing them a fortune."

"It has one advantage. If you build it in Earth orbit, everyone will know what you're up to in no time flat. Over here, all we know about is that there's an opaque dome. Maybe the Indians gave us a bum steer to make us nervous."

"Why would they do that?"

"Who knows?" I said. "We're new to these little games they've been playing. Maybe they want us to share our intel or just get us all jumpy about the Chinese."

"What do you think?"

"I think it's real. I think that, under that dome, the Chinese are putting together the Mars mission they've been promising for so long, and they've been doing it secretly in order to unveil it at some psychologically relevant moment. They don't just want to win the race for the solar system, they want to do it in such a way as to embarrass everyone else."

Brett nodded, but I wasn't finished.

"The only thing that doesn't add up is why the Indians would just give this to us. There's something we're missing here, and I don't like it."

***

Night suits were less comfortable than day suits. The insulation was thicker, for one thing, and they were also designed with safety margins that daytime suits didn't have. The extra bulk was offset by slight servo assistance. I just hoped I didn't have to make a run for it.

I knew that anyone looking up from Earth today could enjoy a beautiful full moon, but it was no use to me. The far side was as dark and cold as it would be for a few more days. The same darkness that kept me hidden from casual observation also kept the movements of the Chinese convoy murky and difficult to interpret.

I had been watching the approach of the huge balloon-wheeled Han-class trucks for fifteen minutes with the infrared filters on my visor, and was nearly blinded when the station suddenly turned on a pair of huge floodlights. It took my visor a couple of seconds to adjust to the new conditions, and my retinas a couple of minutes to lose the aftereffects.

Once I could see clearly again, I watched as at least twenty suited figures emerged from the Chinese base and began to unload the lead truck. They took their time, carefully removing aluminum-colored drums heavy enough that it took two men to lift them, even at a sixth of the Earth's gravity.

Fuel, I thought, and then chided myself for jumping to conclusions. I was here to gather data uncolored by unconfirmed assumptions. I timed the offloading of the first truck: thirty-four minutes. The second also carried drums.

Things got a bit more interesting at the third truck. It carried only one structure: a large semicircular husk that, had it not been for the fact that I wasn't supposed to be jumping to conclusions, would have looked exactly like half the outside edge of a booster rocket or fuel tank. All twenty of the workers were needed to carry it into the station. The weight was seemingly small enough to allow them to lift it with little problem, but it was amusing to watch them struggle with the inertia. One thing, at least, was certain. The recording would be of great interest to the analysis team back behind the Strip.

The next truck in line held what looked like another booster half. I tried to get some close-ups.

Suddenly, light glinted off something in the shadows to my right. Moving very slowly, I turned to look in that direction, setting my visor to its full-night setting. The illumination from the floodlights was uncomfortable in this mode, but it allowed me to make out the unmistakable figure of a suited human.

He'd chosen a nearly perfect vantage point from which to observe the comings and goings at the Chinese facility unseen: lying in a small depression in a shadow cast in the floodlight glare by a tall rock. Only the fact that I was off to his left and slightly behind him—where he obviously expected not to find anyone—allowed me to see him at all.

So who was he? Not one of ours, I was certain, just from the suit's heat signature. Our night suits had a couple of hot spots around the knees from insufficiently shielded servo motors. This suit seemed to be beautifully isolated—I could barely make out the outline of his form. And I knew he was there. The best bet would likely be someone working for the Indians. The Russians were rumored to be planning a station, but currently had only extremely limited presence on the moon.

So it had to be the Indians. But made no sense—the fact that they had been able to get us the plans seemed to indicate that they had someone on the inside, and wouldn't need to use an outside observer. Something else was going on here. I turned off the camera and began the walk to my pickup point, hidden at the bottom of a crater, miles away.

***

I walked into Brett's office, and was greeted with, "Hi Linda, take a seat." Brisk, businesslike and unlike him. Something on his mind, then.

I sat down. "What's up?" I asked him.

"Trouble. Take a look at this." He handed me about ten printouts. They were, as far as I could tell, photographs of the lunar surface taken with infrared light and processed into monochrome by one of our image servers. Specifically, they showed footprints in the dust.

"I don't get it. It's just a picture of some footprints. What's special about it?"

"Do you recognize the tread pattern?"

"No, should I?"

He rolled his eyes. "Some kind of spy you are. The pattern is from a pair of the boots Addidas manufactures for the ESA and NASA."

"So?"

"So those pictures were taken beside the Chinese base by another of our agents after you left."

"They aren't mine. I was wearing untreaded boots!"

"Exactly. They were taken in the position occupied by the unknown person you filmed when you were out spying on the base."

"But he wasn't one of ours! The suit didn't fit the profile."

"Exactly."

I stared at him silently for a few moments, trying to understand the significance of what he'd just said. It was pretty obvious that someone wanted to make the Chinese think that we'd been snooping around their base. But who? It just didn't add up.

Or maybe it did, when you took into account the strange gift that our Indian friends had given us. I looked over at Brett, who'd been waiting patiently for me to digest the news.

"What would the Indians gain by framing us?" I asked.

"Why would you think it's the Indians?"

"Obvious. They were the ones who put the first piece of incriminating evidence in our hands."

"The plans."

"But why?" he said after the pause had grown uncomfortable. "What do they hope to gain from this?"

"I think a better question would be: 'what do they want us to take the blame for?'"

"And have they done it yet?"

"I doubt it. If the Chinese were mad at us we'd have heard about it. Plus, the Indians would only go to this kind of trouble to hit them hard. Hit them in a way that would hurt. And that means something we'd notice." A thought struck me. "We haven't noticed anything, have we?"

He chuckled, well aware of how much I hated the whole 'need to know' thing. "No, we haven't heard of anything like that. We need to find out what the Indians are planning, how to stop them from doing it or, ideally," he winked at me, "how to let them go right ahead, but without being able to blame us."

"All that worries me is whether you erased those bootprints," I replied. "I'm due some vacation time, and this seems like the perfect time to take it."

He grinned. "Request denied. And the prints were gone as soon as our other agent finished taking his photos."

***

The Chinese and the Indians had been playing the game ever since the Chinese had established their own Lunar base, a mere ten miles from the original Indian base—the first in an ongoing series of insults and provocations of varying sizes kept in check only by the fact that any overt action could lead to a war in which four billion lives and the global economy were at stake.

Strike—the Indians put their base up first.

Counter strike—the Chinese place their second base on the far side.

But neither side really knew how to react to the NASA / ESA installation, or whether even to take it seriously. After all, both Asian efforts were serious scientific and military outposts paid for by the government, while this one, ostensibly, was a casino. At first, they'd just ignored us.

But lately, they'd been trying to use us as pawns in their maneuvers. We could usually tell what they were doing, and went along whenever it was convenient to do so, but there was still a large risk involved.

So here I was, trying to figure out what this particular version of the game meant for our lunar hopes.

The main difficulty with Lunar surveillance, I reflected, lay not in being able to observe your quarry, but in keeping your quarry from observing you in turn. The lunar day was set to last for another five Earth days at the least, so I couldn't use the cover of night. Craters or rocks could hide me from view, but it would also make it impossible for me to observe my quarry.

I lay in the shadow of an outcropping, feeling naked despite my dark-mottle camouflage suit. The Indian base was just three-hundred yards away, and my job was to make certain that nothing left without being logged and recorded. I wished we weren't on such a shoestring budget. Then we could get a couple of satellites up, and dispense with on-the-ground intelligence.

I fought against the slight discomfort of the heat, even here in the shadows, and I had to fight even harder against the temptation of turning my gaze towards the magnificence of Earth in the sky, but I gritted my teeth and kept my binoculars aimed at the base. I had a feeling that the Indians were up to something big.

My concentration was such that the ambush was almost unsurprising. A tap on one shoulder and a sudden pull on one arm brought me to my feet. Four figures in Indian-model suits surrounded me. The fact that I was outnumbered, and that they were armed with shotguns and serrated knives sealed the deal. I doubted the guns held anything heavier than birdshot but, while they might not inflict a fatal wound to my body, it would certainly leave my suit in tatters. And a single large tear in my suit would be as fatal as a bazooka shot out here.

They motioned for me to follow them into the base, which I did, cursing myself. How could they have gotten past my watch?

If I got out of this one alive, I would have the first images of the base's interior, so it wouldn't be a total loss, but I would also get sent back to Earth on the next shuttle, condemned to continue my career behind an analyst's desk in Washington, or, if I was lucky, in Brussels.

Of course, the Indians might just launch me into space with their next load of garbage.

Once through the airlock, my hosts popped their suits and turned to me. I opened my helmet, assaulted by the silly half-expectation of finding myself overpowered by the smell of curry.

The antiseptic reality was vaguely disappointing, as was the purely functional aspect of the truck hangar. Immaculate whites and polished aluminum dominated the chamber, clashing with the single grungy-looking truck, covered with static-cling dust.

"Walk slowly toward the truck," one of my captors, a short, dark man with a thin mustache, said. I thought he might have been the one who'd handed me the data drive which started the whole thing, but I couldn't be certain.

I was disappointed—I'd hoped to be able to see a bit more of the interior of the base—but I complied. I took a final look around, trying to get my autocam to record any interesting tech that might be present, but was once more disappointed. All I really saw was that the truck was a personnel carrier, with an airlock for the rear. The lock was standing at position four—both doors open—so I climbed aboard and sat on the right hand bench.

"This is an outrage," I said. "You have no right to abduct me."

"You were spying on our base."

"I have the right to observe everything, anywhere on the moon. No part of the moon belongs to any nation except for the interior of your bases. This is established by treaty. A treaty that you signed."

"Shut up."

I was sweating now. Were they going to take me out a few miles and space me? Were they going to torture me in the truck? Group rape? I shuddered and looked them over. It really didn't look to me like they were preparing for violence, but I had nothing to go on. No western agent had ever been captured by either of the other powers present on the moon. And neither the Chinese nor the Indians were particularly forthcoming about the fate of their missing people.

Only two of my captors joined me in the rear of the truck, and I relaxed a little. They might still space me, but they weren't likely to try anything too elaborate. The inner lock door closed with a muted thud and the truck began to roll. We moved a short distance before stopping again. A hissing, then a roar, could be heard through the walls of the truck, and then nothing, the silence of space. We'd evidently gone through the airlock to the surface.

This was quickly confirmed as the truck began to move once more, the bumps and judders seeming to signify that the driver was more interested in speed than in smooth transit. I wondered where they could be taking me. Would they simply drive up to our station and knock on the door? I doubted it. Even though I had been watching their movements, the Indians could not openly admit to holding me against my will. They couldn't legally police any part of the surface.

So where, then? The Chinese base wasn't really an option. Unfortunately, that left no other choice within the range of a ground truck. Would they really try to space me? They had to suspect that I wouldn't go without a fight.

The truck bumped its way along for nearly two hours. Despite the way the time dragged on, my attempts to break the oppressive silence were quickly swatted down by my dour companions. I wouldn't get any insight from them, that was for sure.

Suddenly, the truck stopped. By my calculations, we had to be a good fifty or sixty miles from the Indian base. Far enough that they could just dump my body there and go home, with nobody really any the wiser. I tensed to jump them if anyone took even one step towards the airlock.

But nobody moved. The dull drone of the engine was replaced by a high-pitched whine, and I suddenly felt ferocious g-forces take hold of me and press me against may seat. About ten seconds later, the acceleration changed direction, pushing me, albeit more gently, towards the back of the truck.

Now this was something I could turn into a decent report. Most small buggies on the moon had limited rocket propulsion—the one I'd taken to scout the Chinese even had extended range and could fly around the moon, but, to my knowledge, trucks this size were all ground-bound. It was more fuel-efficient to move heavy loads with solar-power during the lunar day, and trucks were no fun at all during the night. It could get cold at night.

At least one thing was certain. They probably wouldn't go to all this expense to space me. It cost fortune to bring canisters of liquid hydrogen and liquid oxygen from earth for rockets, and even though the Indians had, as a question of national pride, given their moonbase program a blank check, they would still have to justify the expense. And simply disposing of a spy a little farther away wouldn't cut it with the bean counters.

Another hour later, the frequency of the sound coming from the engines changed, becoming much lower-pitched. Deceleration tossed me forward, and once again, I prepared to jump my captors, but they surprised me.

"Please seal your helmet," the nearest one said.

"Huh?"

"We're letting you out. Once we open the airlock, you'll have thirty seconds to get clear before we turn the motors back on."

I just nodded. This was ridiculous. They had to know that I could get help from our base within a couple of hours no matter where they dumped me. I would have to break radio silence, but I judged that a small price to pay for my life, court-martial or no court-martial.

Less than a minute later, the truck bounced a couple of times on the ground and lay still. We'd landed.

My captors opened the inner lock, and motioned me into it with the shotgun. I sealed my suit and got inside. The lock quickly emptied of air, and the outer door opened. I briefly debated whether to go or to try to stay in the lock, but the fact that they had shotguns and I didn't seemed to make the choice clear.

I ran as far from the truck as possible, and was well out of the way by the time the blast from the rockets pushed the truck into the sky, quite likely the most ungainly space vehicle I'd ever laid eyes on. But you don't need a streamlined form to fly through a vacuum, and the thing flew well enough.

Now I was in trouble. First off, it was night here. That meant that my day suit's insulation would be even less effective than usual. Already, I could feel the cold seeping in. I had maybe three hours before frostbite, and four before I froze.

That wasn't the worst of my problems, however. I could have an airlift out of here with plenty of time to spare. My main problem was where 'here' actually was.

My suit was telling me that I was about a mile and a half from the Chinese far-side base. If I called for help, I would immediately alert them to the presence of a western agent in an area of the moon that was completely empty except for their base itself. The only conclusion they could reach was: spy, and incompetent at that.

Drat. So I faced two possibilities. The first was to freeze, leaving my body here for future generations to puzzle over, while the second was to radio for help, broadcasting a NASA/ESA presence to the Chinese, who would probably be amused by my bungling.

Or would they? The Indians presumably expected me to radio for help. But why? Why had they been going to so much trouble to get us to look like we were extremely interested in the Chinese base on the far side? Were they playing silly buggers with us? Or was there a more sinister reason? My gut was saying 'sinister', but then I have to admit that there's something about being stranded far from everything on a celestial body that is not your own that makes one a little paranoid.

Well, there was only really one way to find out what was going on without freezing to death. My career was over anyway, so I might as well get something out of it.

I began to walk towards the base.

***

"Go away!" the official said, unmistakably agitated.

"I can't," I replied honestly. "I'm nearly out of air." The suit, of course, would suck air in from the surrounding room, filter everything that wasn't actually oxygen, and refill itself, but would take at least twenty minutes to get me to a tank level where I could be rescued before asphyxiating. The walk to the Chinese base had taken longer than I'd expected.

The functionary hadn't wanted to open the airlock at all, amazed that anyone should appear at their door, here in the middle of nowhere. He wasted more valuable time and air until the lock finally opened. And then he'd brought me straight to this room with featureless white walls and pulled in an interpreter.

"You need to listen to me," I said. "I think the Indians are going to attack this base soon."

The translator gave me a quizzical look but repeated my words to the official, who barked out a laugh and an equally curt reply.

"A likely story." He then said something more, which the translator forwarded to me. "An honorable spy would have chosen death before revealing his presence."

"I'm not a spy, listen to me!" I went on to tell him about the events of the past few days. I hoped he believed me—I had just given him highly classified information that would make my court martial truly unpleasant, assuming I survived to attend.

To his credit, the official looked pensive. Then he left, returning five minutes later with an older man in uniform—as opposed to a suit—who greeted me in broken English.

I retold my story, stressing the fact that I believed the Indians would strike their base very soon.

"They've never taken such a big risk before," the older man said, shaking his head.

"They never had someone else to blame, before," I replied impatiently. Why wasn't it as obvious to them as it was to me?

And then it came to me. The Chinese were thinking in terms of logic. The Indians would not attack them because the repercussions would be on a scale unheard of in human history: nuclear war could, in hours, wipe out two-thirds of the human race.

"The Indians can't let you get to Mars first," I told him.

This proclamation had the desired effect. The impassive demeanor cracked, and I'm certain he almost asked how I knew about that, but caught himself in time.

I had an opening. "Their pride is at stake, and they think they see a solution. They won't let you do it. Think about it, they've been trying to prove to the world that they're your equals for, well I don't know how long, but at least since you put your first Taikonauts into space. They'll hit you with western weapons and leave western tracks, but it will have been the Indians."

"Why should I trust you?"

"Because I'm here. I could have called for an airlift hours ago. My career is over, and sharing this with you will probably mean prison, but I don't care. This is more important. They're probably out there already."

He gazed into my eyes and I felt myself being minutely weighed and measured. Finally, he nodded curtly, once, and barked a couple of orders.

He turned stiffly and walked out.

***

The Indian agent looked very much the worse for wear. It was obvious that the interrogation hadn't gone well for him. Both eyes were blackened and a deep cut was visible over his left eyebrow.

Hearing the approaching footsteps, he lifted his head painfully and watched me. I don't know what I was expecting, but definitely not a smile.

He smiled, showing bloodied teeth. "Well, Ms. Lombardo. It seems you win this round."

"This isn't a game," I replied. I wondered whether he knew that he'd be spending what was left of his life in a Chinese labor camp on Earth. Unless, of course, our communist friends decided to forego the cost of taking him back and putting him on trial and simply spaced him.

He laughed mirthlessly at me, choked, coughed up blood from some internal injury and laughed some more. "Of course it is," he said. "You just don't know it yet."

I looked over his shoulder. His companion was lying ominously still in a small pool of his own blood. Only the slow rise and fall of his chest indicated that he was still alive. Both were wearing standard issue Indian suits, but their footwear was unmistakably western. Beyond them lay a pair of French-built EADS rocket launchers mounted with what looked like miniature tactical nukes. How in the world had the Indians gotten hold of those?

"I'm just happy we managed to get to you before launch," I said sadly.

He must have understood that my sadness was for his fate, and chuckled once more.

"Oh, there was no need for us to be captured," he said. "We'd already decided to abort when we saw that you'd gone into the base instead of requesting backup. We needed that radio message to point to when declaring our innocence. We were just waiting for our pickup to arrive. You ended up getting us killed for nothing."

"You're not dead yet," I pointed out.

"We were dead as soon as they caught us," he replied.

"Well," I said, "I guess those are the rules." I walked off to talk to the Chinese officer about possible asylum. I might have selflessly saved the world from nuclear holocaust, but I had no illusions that would hold any water with the court-martial.

ANCHORED DOWN IN ANCHORAGE

I wrote the next story for a climate change anthology that ended up being cancelled, but I loved it so much that I couldn't just leave it in my hard drive and eventually found the perfect home for it at *Into the Ruins*. It was also a last-minute addition to this collection, but I'm delighted it made it in because it deals with issues that we're all going to have to face very soon.

Phil crumpled the printout. It was from his boss, reminding him that his six months of immersion were nearly up, and that he would have to file the story today or it wouldn't make the *Times'* Great New Cities special edition – and that would make everyone at the paper extremely unhappy. Did he even have a draft they could see?

The draft, forty pages of copy and the photos he recommended paper-clipped to it sat on the desk beside him. Over the past three weeks, he'd almost sent it out more times than he could count. It would have meant his Pulitzer, after all.

But he hadn't. Now he knew he wouldn't. So no prizes would be forthcoming, but at least he'd chosen the lesser betrayal.

He walked out of the hotel, knowing he wouldn't be back. He hadn't actually been living there for weeks, anyway, but since the *Times* was footing the bill, he still used it as a base of operations and makeshift office.

'The New Río' was the title he'd envisioned; an article drawing parallels between social and physical characteristics of the Brazilian city of seventy-five years ago and the American city of today. But, brilliant as the concept was, it would never see the light of day. He couldn't do that to Anchorage, couldn't do it to Soledad.

He headed up the hill, sweating in the unseasonal pre-monsoon heat which presaged a night of rain. He was late, but knew he'd still get there before her.

***

It was hard to believe that he'd already been there six months. Where had the time gone?

The Alaskan Airlines seaplane that had brought Phil in from Seattle landed on the water just a few hundred yards beyond the submerged buildings. The old airport was, like most of the old commercial sector, under five feet of water. Anchorage hadn't had enough money or political clout to get dykes built in time – the city had been too far down on the Army Engineer's priority list – so the population had migrated to the hills.

Phil descended from the plane and boarded a large motorboat with glass-sided walls and roof. The uneventful trip to the pier allowed him to get his first glimpse of Anchorage. He'd already seen thousands of photos of the semi-submerged office buildings, so his attention was drawn to other things – the numbers of airplanes moored to the piers, to buoys or simply anchored in the sea, the fishing fleet behind him, plying the surprisingly calm sea in an attempt to get a few final harvests in before the acidification process made fishing a thing of the past.

Most of all, he was surprised at the temperature. It was very early spring, and he really hadn't known what to expect – he'd half-expected it to be as warm as summer, but then he'd also half-expected to freeze. The reality was cold, but not too cold. Good, that would be the first data-point for the article.

On leaving the boat, he was accosted by a flock of rickshaw drivers, a product of the migration from the lower forty-eight, and from at least three or four south Pacific islands that no longer existed – relics of the days when the government thought that populating Alaska was something that would have to be done through opportunistic treaties.

Phil selected a smiling, dark-haired youth at random and let him load the large suitcase onto the long poles – notched to keep baggage in place – and took a seat in the rear.

"Where to, sir?" the kid asked. Southern accent, but not too extreme – maybe Kentucky. Definitely not from Vanuatu, then.

"The Hilton. But if you want to make a few extra bucks, I'd like a tour of the city."

"Can we drop off the suitcase first?"

Phil smiled. An Indian driver would carry an elephant on his poles all over Kolkota for a few rupees. But this wasn't India, this was America. Overcrowded, dirty, underpoliced, but America. A real life twenty-first century boom town.

"OK," he replied.

They checked him in to the New Anchorage Hilton – the old one, though still standing, had been deemed structurally unsafe when the water reached a couple of feet. Anyway, guests had been avoiding the water-logged hotel for years. The company had accepted its losses and built from scratch far enough up a hill that they wouldn't have that particular problem again for a few hundred years.

The city had the raw, unsafe feel of frontier towns everywhere. Phil wasn't particularly worried. His time with the Marines in the euphemistically named 'Police Action' had put him in worse cesspools than this one on a regular basis – and back then, any time the Chinese army wasn't shooting at them had been considered R&R.

But it still felt weird to be riding a rickshaw over a muddy dirt street winding its way through a shantytown of wood and corrugated houses on American soil. There were plenty of migrant slums in the lower forty-eight, but nothing like this.

"So, who's the big dope dealer in town?" Phil asked the kid.

"I have no idea."

Yeah, right. "I can pay for the information."

"Money ain't no good to me if I'm feeding the fish, mister. You some kinda cop?"

"A reporter. I'm doing a story about Anchorage. I'm going to be here six months. I'll find out eventually, you know, so you might as well tell me."

"You'll end up dead. Not a lot of cops here to protect you."

"I'm tougher than I look," Phil replied. "Survived a couple of tours down in China. Drug enforcers don't scare me much."

"Yeah, well they scare me. You'll find out anyway, so leave me out of it, will ya?" The kid was panting by now, the hill had taken it out of him.

At least, Phil knew, he'd managed to get a little bit of info on the state of affairs in the city. It was obvious the drug lords did, as speculated, control the lives of at least the lower classes. And in a town one step removed from being a tent city, that meant mostly everyone. His assignment was to expose the dual government in Anchorage, and bring it to the notice of the surviving middle-class in the Midwest, so they could be properly appalled at it.

The upper hill had a few decent-looking restaurants and a couple of nice houses.

"Stop here," Phil said. The view over the city was uninspiring, and the wind was cold, but the Pacific Ocean was magnificent, as always. He turned back to the kid. "What's your name?"

"Reilly."

Sure it is. "Well Reilly, do you think you can take me to one of the farms?"

"Farms?"

"You know the ones I'm talking about. I have satellite photos, so it's not much of a secret."

The kid didn't look happy, but he nodded. "I guess."

"Good. Pick me up at the hotel tomorrow at ten."

Phil paid the kid enough to ensure his appearance the following day. The *Times* would have sprung for a car, but after spending nearly four years in the military destroying fossil-fuel infrastructure to keep the Chinese from spewing more greenhouse emissions into the sky and getting shot at for his trouble, he wasn't much of a car person. Out here, solar power was years from becoming a reality.

***

She didn't fit his image of an opium farmer even remotely. Not too tall, thin and maybe thirty five. Dark haired, light skinned and pretty enough without being a classical beauty.

She had opened the door to the farmhouse without asking who was calling, which meant either that she was oblivious of the current social conditions outside her door, or that she had some kind of concealed security system that allowed her to judge the threat posed by visitors. Evidently, she didn't consider a single man and a rickshaw puller to be much of a threat.

Her eyes, however, spoke of a no-nonsense personality and of no time to waste. Although what else she might be doing with her time at this time of year, Phil couldn't imagine.

"Whatever it is," she told him as soon as the door was fully open. "I don't want any." Seeing that he wasn't holding anything that might be considered samples or sales material, she went on, "And I'm a raging atheist without any chance of conversion. My soul was lost years ago, and no matter which religion you represent, no amount of prayer will save me." She moved to close the door.

Phil smiled and held out a hand, gently, but placed in such a way that, in order to close the door, she would have to push back his arm. "I'm not a missionary. I'm a reporter."

The relaxed, slightly bored air she'd been affecting vanished. Her eyes immediately locked down and she studied him intently. The first thing she tried was ignorance. "You must have the wrong address. There's nothing about me or my farm that could possibly interest a reporter."

"We both know that isn't true," he replied calmly.

She looked him over again – he could tell that, now that she could see him at close range, she was regretting having opened the door. He was a big guy, and had stayed in shape even after leaving the Marines – and the small scar just beneath his longish brown hair could be seen here. He could never quite decide if it was sinister-looking or not, but hoped it was.

"Where's your camera?"

"What?"

"You say you're a reporter. Where's your camera?"

"At the hotel. I'm not a regular newspaper reporter. I'm doing an article about Anchorage for a special magazine edition of the *Chicago-Detroit Times*. They want to do a full article about the new boomtowns, both in America and in other countries." He shrugged. "I got Anchorage."

"You still haven't told me why you didn't bring a camera." Her arms were still crossed, her expression skeptical, but at least she wasn't trying to close the door.

"Oh, yeah, sorry." Her no-nonsense demeanor had finally gotten to him. "That's because of the way we research these articles. We aim for full cultural immersion. Which means I'm going to be here for the next six months. My method is to get to know the people who are going to be the main characters of my story before writing anything or taking any pictures."

"And you've decided that I'm going to be one of these main characters?"

"Well, no, not yet. I just asked the kid back there to take me to the nearest opium farm, and he brought me here. I would need your OK for that, anyway."

She laughed, short, curt and to the point. "Yeah, I'd hope so. You can imagine how happy I might be at having you follow me around and take pictures while I cultivate a plant that is illegal except under strict pharmaceutical license everywhere in America. Do you really think I'll let you do something like that? Go away."

"*National Geographic* does it all the time!"

"News for you, man. I'm not a naked little African or South American running around in a desert that wasn't there a few years ago. Or even some Oklahoman in a dust bowl whining about how the government has let half of America dry up. I'm a successful businesswoman. And I don't need you here to ruin it." She gazed at him, stonily, for a few seconds before proceeding. "And another news flash: you're not the *Geographic*."

She shut the door, pushing him back. He let her.

***

The next couple of farms were run by people who were cagey at first, but then strangely honored to be included in the article. One of them actually said that he wouldn't mind giving his name and posing for photos. He called his wife and five kids to the sitting room to meet Phil. The girls curtsied cutely and he was offered coffee, lunch and more coffee.

But he left those farms with mixed feelings. Yes, he could write the story as a contrast between the traditional farming values of the old American heartland – these were farming families as Phil had imagined them – and the criminal distribution system they were feeding, and have the article meet all the criteria his editors could want. And he could add a heartwarming, hopeful note about a place where families could still feed children – five of them! – which would truly touch the feelings of people in the lower forty eight, where professionals could, if careful, raise one child, and the slums were home to starvation and sensationalist rumors of cannibalism.

Or, he could go for the real story. The story of people who'd grown up as something very different. How people who weren't farmers or rugged frontiersmen were getting along, changing the rules and turning Anchorage into a place that was completely different from the rest of the country. After all, the millions living in shanties on that hill had arrived in the past five years. And they'd been able to afford the ticket. They probably weren't farmer types. That was the story that would get him the awards.

And he had a feeling that *she* was the key to that particular story.

***

He spent the next few days attempting to nail down the distribution side of the equation, and quickly discovered some surprising facts. While opium was the biggest game in town, the price and profit margins were nothing like what you got with any natural drug in Chicago. Back in the lower states, the demand to escape from reality was enormous. And the supply of anything – even drugs as obsolete as heroin – was limited, heavily policed. And the synthetic alternatives were a bit like playing Russian Roulette. They were still popular, though.

The whole system was different here: the price of heroin was so low that almost everyone, from rickshaw drivers to executives, could afford their own brand of happiness. Winter, though not as harsh as it once was, was still a serious affair, especially if you lived in a house made of cardboard. Heroin demand went way up in winter. In winter, *everyone* on those streets was in an opiate stupor.

Why did the process work? From what Phil had been able to discern, there was basically one distributor who controlled the drug supply. That, logically, should have meant a high price.

But it didn't. The same heroin made from the same Alaskan opium that was reaching the lower forty eight with astronomical street values was dirt-cheap here in Anchorage. Something simply didn't add up.

Research and bribery had gotten him as far as a mid-level distributor in the supply chain. The guy was an MBA, and his "protection" was essentially an elderly woman at a desk who screened his calls. When Phil, having been unable to get through to him, simply appeared at his office one day, prepared for a showdown with the goons that Reilly was so afraid of, he was met by a smiling red-headed man who'd offered him coffee.

"Where's your muscle?" Phil asked bluntly after exchanging pleasantries.

The guy chuckled softly. "You only need protection when

you're running a criminal activity in which large amounts of money are generated. The money from the opium trade in Anchorage, while large, is just enough to cover the expenses of the people working here."

"So why the thugs at street level?" Phil had had run-ins with a couple of them, but nothing too serious.

"They're only there to keep the general population from asking questions. And they're specifically kept from using lethal force. We don't want to start any vendettas – not good business practice."

"So are you going to tell me what's really going on?"

"No. And I'm as far up the chain as you're going to get. So write your story about some other aspect of city life."

He was right. Phil had been effectively stonewalled in every subsequent attempt to go through or around the guy – he wasn't going to get information that way.

He went back to the hotel and sat thinking for a while. He knew that he'd have to find another angle if the story was going to work correctly. He thought he knew what to try tomorrow. And, besides, the girl was pretty.

***

Same door, but this time it was around seven o'clock, and about a week later. The wind was biting, but he could hardly feel anything other than the unexpected knot in his stomach. He laughed ruefully at himself. *So much for the hardened soldier, the veteran reporter.*

He knocked. And waited. And knocked again.

The door opened a crack. The woman he'd spoken to earlier could be seen in the soft glow coming from inside.

"You again," she said. "What do you want now?"

"Just wanted to see if I could buy you dinner."

"Dinner?"

"Yeah, you know. Like with food and stuff. Maybe candles on the table." Phil had done his research, and knew that she was unmarried and currently unattached, but that her tastes ran towards men. He told the butterflies in his gut that he was only doing this to see what info he could get from her. They didn't believe him.

"I don't think I'm dressed for it," she said, as the door opened. She wasn't – sweat pants and a man's coarse shirt. But then she smiled. "I know you only want information, but nobody in America would ever turn down a free meal, even here in Alaska. Give me five minutes." She turned to go, leaving the door open.

"Aren't you going to tell me your name?"

"You're a reporter, which means professionally nosy. You probably already know my name, my background and the names of my high school sweethearts. I'll go to dinner, but don't bullshit me."

Ouch. She was right. He knew her name and her father's. But that was about it. She'd moved to Alaska six or seven years before, depending on whom one believed, when her father, who'd been there for years, died. Where she'd been before that or what she'd done was anyone's guess.

Fifteen minutes later, she was transformed. Low-riding jeans, a designer t-shirt, hair let down and just the tiniest touch of make-up had Phil reminding himself that, no matter what happened, he couldn't get emotionally involved with an opium farmer who would be central in his article about the pervasive drug culture in Anchorage.

Never fall for the bad guy.

***

He went all out. Not only had he rented a car, a real petrol-burning, bad for the atmosphere car, but he'd also taken her to the restaurant at the top of the Plaza, one of those slowly rotating jobs that was reputedly the best place in Anchorage. If he'd only wanted to get her to fall for him, he wouldn't have spent the money, but since his ultimate objective was to write the story, and that meant getting the information he needed, it was of the utmost importance to *seem* sincere.

So he asked her about her father.

She smiled. "Everyone thought dad was completely nuts when he bought the farm on the hill. It wasn't a farm back then. Alaska was still too cold to cultivate much of anything. It was just a chunk of rocky ground that spent half the year frozen solid. They basically gave it to him for free."

"When was this?"

"Oh, back before I was born, must have been about twenty-fifty or so. And the land just sat there. Remember, this was when everyone though that the temperature had gone as high as it would, since we'd gotten the US to cut back greenhouse emissions enough that there was no more growth. The way he used to tell it, my dad was the only one pointing at China. Of course, no one understood atmospheric inertia back then."

Phil nodded. Having gotten her started, he planned to play the 'really interested' card for all it was worth. And yet, over the previous hour, he'd discovered a woman of intelligence and spirit notably lacking in the 'screw everything – nothing's really worth it' attitude so prevalent down south. He found that he actually cared about her past. Which was something he was going to have to work to avoid.

"So when the drought hit LA, my parents were on the first plane here. They didn't even bother to sell the house. I still have the deed, although it's worthless now – in the middle of the desert."

"So you were born here."

"Yeah. Back then, you could still drive ten minutes into the countryside and pretend humanity didn't exist. My name, Soledad, means loneliness in Spanish. It was probably a mistake to give me that name." Suddenly, tears welled in her eyes, and the cool competence was replaced by a suddenly vulnerable look.

Phil barely managed to avoid leaning over the table to comfort her. "Why?"

"Mom never got used to the emptiness. She was from LA for Christ's sake! Remember that these people," she gestured at the slowly rotating shanties visible on the hills outside the window, "started arriving in the last ten years. Back when my parents moved here, Anchorage had maybe a quarter million people. And then she got word of the LA riots, and the flooding – she told dad that she wanted to go back, to help her family. Dad refused. Then one day we got word that her parents and her sister had tried to leave the city. Their car was ambushed by water-raiders to the west, and I don't even want to think about what happened, but in the end, all three of them died."

She paused to wipe her eyes. "Why am I even telling you this? You either want to pump me for information or get me into bed and then disappear. Either way, you don't care."

Ouch. A bit too close to home. "That's unfair. I've been listening, haven't I? You're just prejudiced against reporters." He smiled crookedly and this time he did clasp her hand in his.

She shook her head and pulled her hand back. "Mom was distraught. There was nothing we could do to calm her down. Dad thought she just wanted to be alone, so when she said she was going for a walk, he let her."

She took a deep breath. "They found her body washed up on the shore the next day. Coroner said she didn't drown, must have fallen off a cliff. Everyone knew she hadn't fallen, and dad never forgave himself for letting her go. That's when he started drinking." She looked Phil straight in the eye. "I was six years old when this happened, and seventeen when I last saw my father. Went down to Columbia, got a job at an ad agency and worked my way up the ladder. By the time he died I was an account director."

"So what are you doing here?"

"Came to sell farm, saw the flooded city down there, and realized that dad had been right when he bought this land. And the emptiness, even with five million people, has a call that's in my blood. I never went back to New York."

She looked at him again, as if wondering how much more to tell, and then shrugged. "And besides, I knew that I wouldn't be able to go back and live behind the dykes and in the tunnels again. New York might have managed to hold back the water, but you still get the feeling of living in a cave, with nowhere to go. Here, on the other hand…" her voice trailed off. "Well, it just feels like we're actually building a future."

He took her home in his rented car, and asked her one last question after walking her to the door and telling her how much he'd enjoyed himself. "And the opium? Was your father right about that, too?"

Her laugh was a light, pleasant tinkle. "Of course not." Her eyes twinkled at him. "The opium was my idea. It's been there for about five years. Pleasant dreams," she said as she closed the door behind her.

But it was too late. The hook had been set by her charm, her intelligence and the fact that she was certain that there was a future for America. She was going to be big trouble.

The drive back to his hotel was a somber one.

***

Five months after their first dinner together, Phil had all the information he needed for the article, and dozens of good photos. He knew the angle he currently had wasn't Pulitzer-worthy, but it would be a competent, interesting article that would be no better or worse than the ones appearing beside it in the issue. How life had changed irrevocably when oceanic expansion caused by increased water temperature, plus melting icecaps had threatened downtown Anchorage.

How the town council had begged the army engineers to place them higher on the priorities list for the dykes, and how they'd been ignored, and could do nothing but watch and grind their teeth as first the big cities like New York and Miami and then cities doomed by the drought in the Southwest were put ahead of them. Nobody had believed the water would run out in San Diego, no matter what the scientists said.

He would tell how they'd had to abandon the city center to the rising ocean. Desolation.

Then hope. The Alaskan Miracle. How, from despondency, hope had arisen when the rising temperatures and changing weather patterns had transformed the cold Alaskan countryside into beautiful, well-watered farmland. How the port city of Anchorage had become, over the course of just a couple of decades a farming hub where everyone had plenty to eat and lots of water.

He'd wrap it up with a look at what was to come – a mix of hope and trepidation. He would describe Anchorage's future as one of the brightest anywhere in the world, but would temper it with a word of caution regarding the lack of facilities to deal with the exploding population, and the rampant, universal use of drugs derived from the dirt-cheap opium being grown with impunity right here in the countryside surrounding Anchorage.

The whole thing would be illustrated with the life stories of the local protagonists: a farmer, an unemployed addict, a social worker trying to avoid a humanitarian catastrophe. A textbook article.

Bah, he thought. It would be textbook all right, but it wouldn't tell the world what was really happening here. But what was he missing?

The article was ready to write, the notes compiled, and he knew which photos he would recommend to the editor, but he had no intention of leaving just yet.

He lay awake wondering at how completely the last few weeks had changed his life. How the woman beside him had made him view society's morality in a completely new way.

Suddenly, a few lights blinked on the computer screen and a soft alarm chime sounded. Soledad was awake immediately. She jumped out of the bed and began to pull on her jeans.

"What is it?" Phil asked her.

"Perimeter breach in the poppy fields."

Phil knew the ripe poppies could be scored, the lacerations emitting a fluid that, when dried, was the base for heroin. The fluid was always a target for junkies and opportunists.

Soledad typed a couple of commands into the computer, and the screen split into four rectangles, each displaying the feed from a security camera. She quickly took stock of the situation. "Five of them."

"Junkies?" Phil asked.

She looked at him suspiciously, unsure whether he was still trying to get information even now. "Yeah. The dealers would never do this."

"Why not? Sounds like a great way to get free dope."

"We have an agreement," she said, in a voice that meant that further argument would lead to a fight. "These are just some of the people from the shanties trying to get a free fix. One of the few problems with owning the farm nearest the city. We need to stop them before they do something irreversible. The drugs sold down there are very watered down. Now, the essence of the poppy is far from pure, but if they stay long enough…"

"Well, I was in the police action in China. I can probably deal with five junkies. Do you think they're armed?"

"Of course not. And don't be silly. You're not going out there. We have ways to deal with this." She picked up the phone and dialed a short number. "Hi, Beth? Soledad here. I have uninvited guests. Five of them. OK, thanks." She hung up and turned back to Phil. "Now we just sit tight and wait."

"What if they come after the house?"

"It's never happened before, but they'll find the doors are stronger than they look. So are the windows – my dad was a bit paranoid. And there's a shotgun under the bed. So just sit, they'll be here in a few minutes."

"Who will?"

She looked guilty for a second, but said nothing.

He just sat, watching the monitor and tensing every time one of the junkies walked toward the house, then relaxing when it turned out to be a false alarm.

Suddenly, the monitors were filled with more people – uniformed people.

"What's going on? Are you being raided by the police?"

Soledad shifted uncomfortably. "Not exactly."

Phil watched the confused milling as the uniformed officers mixed with the junkies in the field. It took a while before he understood the situation. The officers were escorting the junkies off the property. They weren't being too gentle, but they weren't being too rough either. Five minutes later, they were all gone.

Click. The final pieces locked into place, and the potential story went from a competent piece of journalism which would not stand out from its peers to a potential scandal-breaking, Pulitzer-winning bombshell.

"So *that's* why I couldn't get a single lead on the top drug lord in this town. Because the police are in on it too! No wonder they all played dumb no matter how many rounds I bought. And here, I stupidly thought the cops would hate the dealers! So, who is it? The commissioner? One of the captains? Who?"

Soledad looked miserable. She started to speak, then stopped, then started again, but was unable to continue. A single tear rolled down her face. "Look," she said, "it's not any single person. Everyone knows about this."

"And they all turn a blind eye?" Phil's bemusement was beginning to turn into righteous anger. "Everyone in the city's addicted and the whole police force is in on it and nobody does anything?"

"It isn't like that! You're a southerner. You'd never understand."

"Of course not. We try to keep corruption out of public circles down there."

"This isn't corruption! It's for the public good. No one is making any money out of this."

"Sure. I imagine you're giving the heroin away."

She glared at him, hurt. "As a matter of fact, I am, you bastard." Soledad pulled away, refusing to look him in the eyes. "And so is every other poppy-farmer around Anchorage."

"Huh? Why?" Phil was confused. He'd just assumed that everyone was making millions off the stuff, just like they had in southeast China when he'd been there. "Hard to believe, when all the farmers live like kings."

She laughed, an ironic bark. "Have you seen the price of *food* these days?" Crying freely now. "Look, when Anchorage began to grow, we began to have a problem with drugs. Real bad stuff, from the labs in Miami. I had just come in from New York, and the mayor had been a friend of my dad's. He came to dinner, and we got to talking about the problem. He explained that drugs cost a fortune, but that the early dark in winter gave a lot of depressed people living on the streets two choices: drugs or suicide. We had the highest per-capita murder rate in the US. And most of it was drug related."

Phil nodded. The same had happened in the southwest when public order had finally become too weak to control the trade coming in from Mexico.

"So I proposed a solution," She concluded. "We would grow our own, fine-tune it to give the user a mild sense of oblivion, enough so that the users would forget their problems, and sell it for peanuts. All we needed was to find the right drug. Eventually, they discovered a genetically modified strain of poppy that could survive the new Alaskan climate from an American company that claimed to only sell it to the pharmaceutical industry. So I became head of Anchorage Pharma, and here we are."

"So you're the drug lord?" Phil couldn't believe it. He'd been with her for months, and had never seen her doing anything not related to work on the farm.

"No. I'm just the name on the papers, because my experience let me pull off the jargon at the meetings. The drug-lord, as you call it, would be the mayor."

Phil was stunned beyond words.

She went on. "Look. We've got crime down to negligible levels, no one is starving and the job openings are actually growing at a faster rate than the population for the first time ever. We're in a transition and the drugs are a necessary evil. Even now, we're working on the plan to wean the people off the dope."

"So the ends justify the means, huh?"

Her eyes flashed. "They do when the end is to save lives, yes." The ensuing silence dragged on for minutes. Finally, her red-rimmed eyes looked into his, and she said, "If any of what you said to me over the past few months is true, then you'll never file that story."

He nodded silently. He was a journalist, this could be his biggest ever scoop.

He would have to think about it.

***

As predicted, he'd been late, but still arrived before Soledad.

A sunset was a sunset, no matter where one was in the world. But something about looking out on the Pacific from an open-faced bar in Anchorage Heights, over a late dinner made it special. Poignant, but eerily beautiful.

The office buildings of Old Anchorage jutted out of the water like some cubist version of Venice, the red-tinged water covering streets and most of the lower stories. But these buildings, unlike those in Italy, had not been built to survive in the sea. Especially not in this sea, with its monsoon-driven waves.

And yet, Phil knew, they were inhabited by tens of thousands of migrant workers – people who'd come for the harvest and the planting of winter wheat. Handymen and mechanics had been coming for the past twenty years, but now, with the price of fuel being almost prohibitive, many of the tractors would stay in their sheds – it was cheaper to bring workers in from the south and do everything by hand.

"Phil," Soledad said. "Are you with me?"

"Sorry, just thinking about the people in those buildings."

"What is it with southerners and the shanties? I mean we don't go down south and obsess about your slums, do we?" She smiled to take the sting out of her words, but he knew she meant it. Alaskans were just getting used to the reality of having a city of five million on their coast, and just learning the realities of the migration – they were still sensitive about the poor who lived in those warrens that had once been the old downtown of a much smaller city, and the shantytowns that papered the hills.

Phil smiled back, "I'm from Detroit, you can't really call me a southerner, can you?"

She said nothing, but her eyes twinkled, and he understood that she'd scored on his sensitivities. "Touché," he admitted.

"So, eat your crab. You won't get any better in the lower forty-eight."

"We don't get any at all in the lower forty eight. The acid's killed them all off."

The bar was just a hole in the wall, peeling yellow paint over plank walls; it looked like something from another century, maybe Key West in the time of Hemingway. But its view of the Pacific from halfway up the hill was simply breathtaking.

"So did you find what you *were* expecting?" Soledad asked him, knowing she was about to lose him once more.

"Quite a bit more, actually," he leered at her. "Amazing hospitality of Alaskan women. Above and beyond the call of duty."

She smiled. "I mean in the city, you pervert."

"Just this," he said, showing her the sheaf of prints and photos in their manila folder.

Her face fell, and the meal was finished in silence, and in both quantity and quality, he had to admit that it was one of the best he'd had in years. And the check came, for both of them, to less than half of what he'd have paid for much poorer fare for one person anywhere in the lower forty-eight.

Finally, she asked him the question that had really been on her mind all through dinner, the one that had burned in the awkward silences, and made their small talk, normally so natural, feel strained.

"So, when are you going to send it in?" she asked, trying to make it sound nonchalant, offhand.

He wasn't fooled. Looking her straight in the eyes, he replied. "The deadline is in a couple of hours. I don't think I'm gonna make it."

She was well aware what that decision meant. What it meant for his career. The sacrifice he was making. "Do you really mean that?"

He nodded. He'd made his choice.

She took him home, tears in her eyes.

OLD MAN OF THE FOREST

This is a weird one. It's spiritual and a bit teasing, almost dreamlike. At least that's the space it occupies in my head. Your mileage may, of course, vary. It's an Indian story, based loosely on one of the tales in the Mahabharata. I had a lot of fun writing it, and it's probably the story in this book furthest from the typical Western canon.

It was originally published in *Aurora Wolf*.

"They can't really see us, you know."

"Yes," the wrinkled creature replied with the infinite calm of advanced age. "I've known that forever. Only the truly worthy can spot us for what we are, and even then they can't truly understand what they see. They all think they see me." Hanuman laughed, and his features, so severe when he was at war, showed the marks of too much laughter: tiny lines, fine creases in the leathery skin. "Can you imagine if it were truly me they were seeing? Even when I was young, I couldn't have been in all those places at once!"

"They believe in you. Maybe if you talked to them, something could be done to bring us from our exile."

"We are not in exile, my young friend. We are privileged to observe without being seen, judge without being evaluated. Only when the language of the gods is spoken once more on Earth shall the vanara race once more speak to humanity. They are not worthy of us at present."

The younger vanara seemed on the verge of rebellion. Frustration oozed from every pore and was visible in every movement. "That isn't fair. They don't even know who we are. They think we're just monkeys, animals."

Hanuman sighed. The young were never swayed by his wisdom, but it never hurt to try to impart it; after all, they wouldn't be young forever. "They do not know we're still here. Is it their fault that they cannot see us as we truly are, cannot interpret our actions as we wish them to? No. The gods have decreed that it be so, and we must serve the gods in this as we do in everything. Humans may be blind, but they are not ungrateful. See how their temples hold idols to us; they even worship members of our race."

"They worship you, old one," the young woman spat. "There is nothing for any of us, no glory to be gained at all. And if what you say is true, then the gods will return before we have a chance to gain immortality."

"What do you think you can do? We no longer live in the age of heroes. Gods walk the world no longer."

"I will find my path to immortality, even if you are unwilling to help me on my way."

She turned and left, half-walking, half-swinging through the branches, the traditional vanara mode of locomotion. Hanuman was left shaking his head gently. Over the years, many of the conversations he'd had with his descendants had ended this way, but at least he knew that he could generally trust in their good judgment, and not have to worry about their bringing too many problems onto his head.

Besides, humans were accustomed to seeing them as monkeys, and monkeys were supposed to be funny, and near-intelligent.

***

Harshini fumed. The Old Man would never be able to understand her. Though every vanara ever born heard of the exploits of Hanuman, and knew that the only reason Rama had managed to survive his battle with the demon was because of their help, she had trouble believing it had ever happened. It was impossible that that old tyrant would ever have felt the need for adventure, and even if he'd been young at some long forgotten moment, it was inconceivable that he'd ever have let himself be swayed by hot-blooded impulses.

No, he'd probably presided over a treaty meeting or something, boring and stuffy, and time had embellished the details, turning a diplomatic session with no action whatsoever into a poetic saga worthy of the gods.

Well, she would show him that a vanara could take part in heroic deeds, but most of all, she would show him that there was no need for them to continue living in their self-imposed exile. The legends said that, once, vanara had lived in palaces. They would do so again, but humanity first had to see them for what they were.

The nearest village was a small, nameless collection of huts and shacks just at the bottom of Hanuman's mountain. The huts were just high enough on the slopes to avoid damage from the annual flooding, and some of them were practically buried in the foliage. Harshini was able to approach unobserved, near enough that the acrid reek of human filled the air.

Finally, taking a deep breath, she walked, upright and regal, onto the main path between the houses. She tried, by force of will, to communicate that, under the spell that kept the humans from seeing her as she was, there lived an intelligent being, a member of an allied race.

But the humans ignored her, going about their business as they always did. One of them kicked out at her half-heartedly, obviously not intending to hit her, but wanting to clear the path ahead of him. She tried to look into the man's eyes, but he moved on, oblivious that he'd been selected as an ambassador between two great peoples.

Harshini shrugged and kept walking; if the man's burden, whatever it had been, was more important that creating understanding between humans and vanara, then he would be the one to regret it, not her. And she certainly wouldn't beg for his attention.

The next person she encountered was useless for her

purposes: a child of about seven, rail thin, with huge brown eyes and skin so dark as to be nearly black. She shrugged past, looking for someone with a little more authority.

The waif, of course, followed her.

"Go away," she said, turning quickly. "I'm here on the most important of business." She knew the humans were enchanted so that they could understand none of what she said, but experience with the children of her own tribe had made it abundantly clear that children could understand a tone, even if the words themselves were beyond them.

It soon became apparent that she'd gotten a defective child, however. She'd taken a few more steps toward the cluster of houses nearest the river when she realized that the little boy was still following her, eyes just as wide as before, and with the beginnings of a smile. She picked up her pace, soon coming to a tiny square formed in the hollow between some houses. It wasn't much to look at—even the modern vanara who could boast no palaces had better meeting places than this—but years of watching the humans from the forest had shown her that this was were all the important events in the village happened.

The square was empty, save for one old blind woman sitting in a ray of sunlight in the corner furthest from the river. Wrinkled like a prune, she seemed oblivious to the fact that she wasn't alone, and even more so to the dictates of common sense, which would have kept her to the shade on such a hot and humid morning.

She paused in the square for a moment, trying to decide what to do next. It certainly wasn't the type of reception she'd been planning on, but then again, she had to admit—now that she was alone—that the whole quest had been driven more by anger and the rush to leave the Old Man's presence than by any sort of forethought. She would push forward, even if it meant moving on to a different village. In fact, that was just what she would do. There was another cluster of huts just around a bend in the river, less than an hour's walk away. She would find what she sought there.

Satisfied, Harshini set her shoulders and, being very careful not to stoop or succumb to the temptation of using her forelimbs for walking, she strode proudly towards the river, intent on using the path along the bank to reach her destination. Adding insult to injury, even the little boy seemed to lose interest in her at this point and wandered off on some mission of his own.

But, when she passed the final house, she found the path blocked. A young woman, no more than sixteen or nineteen—it was difficult to tell the age of humans with any accuracy—stood dead-center on the path, facing away from the village. The half-saree she wore was a clue that she might be a little younger than she looked, but again, Harshini found herself unable to age the girl with any precision. But she would rather have died than admit that maybe, just maybe, she was out of her depth not just in this, but in the whole undertaking.

She strode up behind the girl, making no effort to hide her approach. The girl jumped visibly and turned suddenly. Her posture made it obvious to any creature of the forest that she was ready to flee, but Harshini wasn't what she was afraid of, because the girl relaxed when she saw the vanara.

"Oh, hello, little one," the girl said.

Harshini's heart nearly burst from her chest. Could this one possibly see her for what she truly was? Was that why she spoke? "Good morning," the vanara replied, solemnly holding out one forepaw, hoping the woman would understand the gesture. The girl took it, but dashed any hopes with her next phrase.

"Aren't you cute? Sometimes I wish I could live like you do, in the jungle, doing whatever you please, without a care in the world."

The girl could have been the little boy's sister, with the same dark skin and large brown eyes. But then again, Harshini admitted to herself that all humans looked alike to her. Yet another thing Hanuman would have pointed at to show her that she was too inexperienced to do anything.

But even an inexperienced vanara knew that when a human dropped water from her eyes, it was a sign of sadness. "What is wrong?" Harshini asked. She knew that humans, even this human who'd seemed to see the truth, couldn't understand a word any vanara said, and heard only the mindless chittering of tree apes, but maybe by an earnest effort of will, the spell could be broken.

But the girl just turned and walked a few paces further down the path, away from the village, making convulsive sobbing sounds while her shoulders moved up and down. The girl seemed to have forgotten that she was holding Harshini's hand, and the vanara followed her. The sadness that afflicted this one must have been powerful indeed.

Coincidence was on Harshini's side that day, because the girl decided to unburden herself. "I wish I'd never even set eyes on that dirty tradesman's boy. Then I could have married my Abhayaprada and no one would have complained. But now all I hear is that a fisherman's boy is not good enough for me. Hah! Fishing has been good enough for our family forever, but suddenly, at the prospect of someone moving up a tiny bit in the world, we remember that not everyone is equal."

She sniveled a bit while Harshini considered the stories she'd heard of humans. From what she knew, the girl should be delighted at the possibility of marrying above her station. Many of the tales both from these people in the south and the people of the mountains who lived north of the forest and looked a little different told how every girl-human wanted nothing more than to marry above herself. But asking questions would have been worse than useless, so Harshini settled herself on the grass beside the girl, to listen. Off in the distance, the river bubbled to itself, but the vanara's sense of urgency had subsided. She decided that there was no need to go all the way to the next village. This girl seemed on the verge of understanding that the vanara were more than they seemed.

Harshini listened.

"But my parents…" the girl paused for a few moments to snivel, to dry her nose on the sleeve of her choli. "My parents have set the misri for today. It is my old grandfather's birthday, and who knows what those merchants find it auspicious for. Probably the anniversary of fleecing some poor villager and driving his family to starvation. I won't be there! Let them see whether that's an auspicious start. My mother should have known that giving me my ring so I could give it to that little monster was a mistake."

The girl pulled a ring out of a fold in her stole. It was a small thing that glittered in the sunlight, a trinket that would have kept vanara girls fascinated all month; how lucky human girls were.

"I should throw it into the river," the girl said, pulling her arm back. Harshini, alarmed at the potential loss of such a treasure, pulled her arm back. The girl hardly resisted, and smiled. "You're right. This is half the wealth of my family, and I shouldn't discard it so lightly, even if it means my doom." Then she looked at Harshini and patted her head. "Look at me, talking to a monkey this way, as if you knew what you were doing instead of just playing. Well, come along if you wish. It's not much good running away if I only walk this far."

The girl replaced the ring and set off down the path, forcing Harshini to hurry and even, despite her best efforts, to use her forelimbs for added purchase on the ground, hoping the girl wouldn't turn around and see her.

The sun climbed higher as they walked.

***

Time seemed to pass more slowly as they followed the bank downstream. The warm sun beat onto them, and the humidity seemed a live thing, clinging in a way that it never did in the cool, leafy shadows of the forest. Long before they reached the next village, Harshini was concentrating on putting one foot in front of the other, as if in a dream.

She lifted a foot, dropped it, lifted another, and put that one back on the ground. Every third step or so, she would lower her right forepaw and use it to propel herself a little more.

So absorbed was she in this task that she almost failed to realize when the girl who'd been leading the way suddenly disappeared.

There had been no warning other than the rustle of reeds that grew between the stream and the bank, and then a slight yelp as a dark, half-naked figure swept in, pulled the girl off her feet and onto his shoulders and ran off again. A splash told Harshini that the assailant had carried her into the river.

She followed, pushing aside the reeds, only to see a man with a black mustache looking back at her as he poled a boat into the current while keeping the girl subdued with his legs. In moments, man, girl and boat disappeared around a bend.

Harshini stood by the bank, panting in the sun and paralyzed with fear. What could she do?

The answer came to her with crushing finality: nothing. Even if she ran back to the village, the villagers would simply laugh at her, calling her a monkey and, eventually chasing her off with brooms and possibly even stones. She sat down on the path, beating her fist against the ground in frustration.

A sudden glint caught her eye. Lying in the path, forgotten in the struggle was a small band of yellow metal. The ring. It had obviously been thrown clear in the struggle, and Harshini picked it up and studied it. She felt the weight of it in her hand, and knew that it was a treasure the likes of which hadn't been seen among her people since the time of her grandmother's grandmother.

But with the certainty of a communication from the gods, Harshini knew that she couldn't keep the ring. It belonged to the girl on that boat, blind as she was to the true nature of the creatures that lived in the forest deeps, and needed to be returned. In fact, perhaps it might be the key to saving the girl's life—for though the young vanara might know little of the ways of humans, she was wise enough to know that the girl had been taken against her will, and would be found in or near the next village.

But which way to go? Harshini knew that her hands were little match for the cunning knots and locks that humans placed on their dwellings, but she still almost ran off downstream, to attempt a rescue, or to attempt to trade the ring for the girl herself. But the image of Hanuman, chiding her for foolhardiness, came to her, unbidden. She knew that to rush off without thought was to invite catastrophe—and worse, to struggle in vain.

She turned back towards the village she'd come from. The long minutes that they'd covered to get there now stretched out eternally on the way back, the distance never seeming to end despite the fact that she was running twice as fast, using all four legs for speed.

Finally, the cluster of wooden huts came into view, and the rushed headlong into the central square to find the village out in force and a shouting match in progress.

"If the girl isn't here at noon, there will be no wedding," a large woman with lighter skin and a heavily made-up face was shouting. "I knew that boy would only bring shame to us by marrying beneath himself."

The boy in question was standing beside, and slightly behind his mother, pouting lips showing no expression that Harshini could read. The upturned lips and half-smile said he was enjoying the spectacle, but the situation demanded that he be angry or frightened. She cursed her inexperience once again.

A young man burst into the circle, heading straight towards the groom, but was restrained by the strong arm of one of the villagers. "You! You took her. You knew she didn't want to marry you, so you took her anyway." He kept screaming words at the other man, words Harshini had never heard before, but which caused the groom's family to murmur darkly.

"Hush now, Abhayaprada," a second woman said in soft tones. "We must not waste time now. We must find her."

And into this cauldron of recriminations, Harshini walked. "I know where she is," the vanara said.

No one looked her way. They were too intent on glaring at each other. Besides, she knew they couldn't understand a word she was saying. They were only human.

She would have to think of something else.

Harshini looked around. One of the problems, possibly the biggest one, was that the humans were all much taller than she was. This meant that even if she jumped around, she could only put herself level with their eyes for tiny fractions of time. If she could find somewhere to stand, she might make them pay attention long enough to show them the ring.

The log sections that served as benches were all occupied by old humans, and long experience had taught Harshini that tugging on a hand would only get her kicked. And then she saw the little boy, the same one that had followed her on her first pass through the village.

He wasn't paying any attention to her either, but at least his eyes were level with Harshini's own. She strode quickly, erect, to where he stood and tugged on his nose, which captured his attention immediately.

"Ow," he yelped.

"Oh, be quiet, it was just a tiny pull," she said. He looked on uncomprehending, so she sighed and placed the ring in front of his face, where he couldn't help but see it.

The little boy's first reaction was to try to look around the vanara's hand, to see what interesting turns the adults' argument had taken, but as Harshini thrust the metal band insistently into his line of sight, an expression of confusion crossed the boy's face, followed shortly by a look of astonishment.

"Mama!" he cried, taking the proffered ring out of her unresisting hand, "Mama, look!" He ran to the distraught mother.

Harshini had a moment of satisfaction when she realized that the missing girls actually was the little boy's brother, but that moment was short-lived, as all eyes turned on her, as if expecting her to tell them all. She stood straight and said. "She's been kidnapped. I'm sure it was a man from the next village. I can show you where it happened."

But the villagers were quite clearly unable to understand. The milled about in confusion, some prodding her, others going back to arguing among themselves. None of them followed up with any questions. "I can show you," she said.

But when the girl's mother took two steps toward her and said: "Where did you get this?" Harshini knew it was a lost cause.

Instead of answering, she swept the ring out of the mother's hand and, passing between a sea of legs, ran down the path, with half the village in pursuit. She was surprised at how quickly they forgot about the girl to chase her with cries of: "Stop the monkey!" and "Come back here, you little thief!"

Once again, Harshini set her dignity aside to create speed. Using all four limbs, she propelled herself along the riverside path just fast enough to stay a couple of steps ahead of the group, led by the enthusiastic youngster. She certainly didn't want to lose them.

When she reached the place where the girl had been kidnapped, she laid the ring on the ground and stood aside. The villagers piled around it, but there were many fewer than in the meeting. Of the groom's family, there was no sign, but the other youth, Abhayaprada, was there, panting in his exertion. He picked up the ring and turned on the vanara.

"Where is she? Where is my love?" he asked.

An older man, who, by the look of him could have been

the youth's father, was looking around, studying the damaged vegetation beside the river. "She's been taken onto a boat," the man said after a moment. "See? This is where someone dragged something heavy into the river. Look at the footsteps."

"She must have been taken!"

The older man nodded grimly. "And I think I know who did it." The man looked at the girls mother, sadly, it seemed. "I don't think the merchant's son will want to marry your daughter now, even if we can prove that her honor is intact," he said.

The woman looked around. "I wouldn't want her to marry someone who wouldn't move a finger to recover her, anyhow. But if there are doubts about her honor, I doubt anyone will ever want her." The dam burst then and the tears the woman had been holding back flowed freely.

The older man looked down the path where Abhayaprada was already disappearing in the direction of the next village and smiled gently. "I don't think you will have to worry about that. I really don't."

The villagers moved down the path en masse.

***

"So they got the girl back, shaken, but not overly damaged. I hear the wedding is going to be in less than one moon."

Hanuman smiled at her. "That was a truly great deed. You should be proud of yourself."

"You aren't angry that I disobeyed you?"

"Of course not. You did enormous good. Your praises will be sung far and wide."

"Please don't make fun of me. The villagers I helped were insignificant. Even the village doesn't warrant a name."

Hanuman just gave her an enigmatic, irritating look. "Perhaps. Or perhaps not so much. And how did they thank you afterwards?"

Harshini felt the blood rush to her face. "They called me a thieving monkey and ran me off with sticks. You were right, there is no way to get humanity and vanara back together. Far from seeing great deeds by a noble race, they see mischief by vermin."

The Old Man of the Forest chuckled. "Again, perhaps. Give the story a few hundred years. In my experience, these things get better and better with each retelling."

And he walked off, leaving Harshini's head full of questions that she knew the infuriating old fool would never answer.

DEFENDING FIORDLAND

"Perimeter breach in area seven," said the kid. He calmly turned off the alarm, a small, glowing circle on the map on the monitor, and bent over his laptop, typing quickly. A new window opened, which would allow him to track the progress made by the hunter-killer machine. Debbie and French crowded in behind him, trying to get a better look.

"I can't see anything," French complained. The new window was dark and tiny.

"I'll switch to infrared in a minute. Just let me get the final calibrations done. It's the first time we're going after a live target, after all," the kid replied. "And would you mind moving your beard? I think it's inside my ear."

French grunted and moved half a step back, taking his foot-and-a-half long black and gray beard with him. The kid nodded his thanks, still typing. He looked at his readouts, typed some more, and paused, watching.

By this time, even the normally unflappable Debbie was moving impatiently from one foot to another, anxiety getting the better of her.

"Well?" she said.

The kid started, his concentration broken. "Oh, right, sorry." He typed in a command, causing the small window to turn from a vague black-on-black morass into a green and gray display easily identified as the feed from an infrared camera. Now they could see what the hunter-killer machine was seeing.

The view was, unsurprisingly, low to the ground. The machine was built for stealth, and part of that was the need to keep potential victims from seeing it coming. In consequence, the leaves on the bushes at the side of the path rushed far overhead as the machine raced down the track.

"How come it doesn't hit anything?" asked Debbie, who had flown in just two days before from a fund-raising meeting in Auckland, and hadn't been kept abreast of the progress on the machine. Both French and the kid knew that she had her qualms about it, but she'd been outvoted. "Can it react, like a real robot?"

"No, of course not," the kid replied testily. "That's only on TV shows. It reacts that way because I put the position of every bloody tree, bush and rock into its GPS system by hand, and programmed it not to run into them. Why do you think it took so long?"

New information flashed across the screen.

"Our intruder seems to have tripped another motion detector. Now Rocky'll adjust his course." Rocky was the kid's pet name for the hunter-killer.

Sure enough, the image in the window showed a small correction in course, to the left of the screen, and a sudden absence of undergrowth overhead.

"Hmm... seems our uninvited guest is down on the beach."

"You think he was brought in by sea?" asked French.

"We'll have a look after we take him down."

The infrared monitor showed movement ahead: the unmistakable heat signature of something alive, which disappeared almost immediately.

"So, what do you think we're dealing with?" asked Debbie.

The kid looked back at them.

"Cat," he shrugged.

"You could tell just from that quick look?"

"No. Call it an educated guess. The fact that it came in from the seaside makes a cat the most likely candidate."

On the green screen, things suddenly got lively. The hunter-killer accelerated, jostling the camera, making it very hard to see what was happening. They got a vague sense of the heat signature, reacquired now, centered in the window, and saw two faint points shoot from the machine and impact the brighter blob on the screen, which moved drunkenly for a few more seconds and collapsed.

The kid stood up, stretched his arms, and reached for his coat.

"So, want to go see who our uninvited guest actually was?" he asked, but too late. Debbie and French had already donned their jackets and were heading for the door.

Stopping only to pick up a flashlight, shaking his head at the way his elders often forgot to do anything practical in their enthusiasm, he followed them out.

***

Fiordland National Park in New Zealand is not an easy place to take a relaxing hike. Like the fjords in Norway, it consists mainly of a series of sharp inlets and steep valleys connected by goat paths. This terrain made the heart of the park almost completely inaccessible by land, with only the most hardcore campers even making the attempt, which suited French's team just fine.

Entry by sea was less difficult, but only slightly. Here on the southwest corner of New Zealand, the capricious mood swings of the Pacific Ocean could make landing in the narrow, steep inlets a tricky proposition.

As the kid ran down the path towards the beach, he was given a sharp reminder of why it was always better to be careful on these slopes, tripping over a bush and badly twisting his ankle. He didn't notice, being too excited by the fact that that they had been able to test the machine, and that it had worked! He continued to hobble after Debbie and French, finally catching them about halfway to the site. His injury made the going difficult, but he had a light and they didn't.

French supported his weight the rest of the way down, and ten minutes later, they reached the machine, which, having fulfilled its directives was in standby mode: powered down and waiting for instructions. Ignoring it, they made for a point a couple of meters further ahead, where the light picked out a small, furry lump, completely immobile on the floor. Two pale elements protruded from the shape. Darts.

"Nice shooting, kid," French said.

"Not my shooting. All I did was program the machine. The rest was automatic."

"Nice programming, then. Both darts, right on target." French prodded the furry lump with his foot, turning it over. It *was* a cat. A lean, mean-looking one, too.

French grinned evilly in the dim light. "Well, that's one cat that won't be having a Kakapo dinner tonight," he chuckled. "Or ever again." He pounded the kid on the back in glee.

"Trouble," said Debbie unexpectedly. While the men had been congratulating each other on the effectiveness of the attack, she had gone down on one knee and given the cat a quick once-over. Her trained eye had immediately identified it as a slightly undernourished tom, a bit scarred but tough-looking. This was the first clue that made her think it had been pulled off a back alley in the nearest town. The second indication didn't require a veterinarian's eye. Wrapped around one foreleg was a GPS locator ring, one of those that included a heart rate monitor, usually used by biologists and conservationists to track animals in study populations. And only one group would want to track a cat in this National Park.

"ARoE!" spat French.

Animal Rights on Earth purported to look after all animals, and they had the impeccable public image to go with that. But, in reality, they were more concerned with cuddly things like rabbits and white mice, things that could be used effectively to touch the public's heartstrings and pocketbooks. In consequence, they made a big fuss about animal testing and fur, but ignored most endangered species completely. Until a few years before, French had regarded them, even the fringe elements who really believed in the cause, as useless but essentially harmless.

That was before he tried to reintroduce the extremely endangered Kakapo to mainland New Zealand. Now they were his sworn, and potentially deadly, enemies.

Debbie and the kid waited for his decision.

He looked at them, shrugged. "I'm not really sure what this means, other than the fact that it can't be a good thing. One thing is certain: we won't get any answers standing out here in the cold in the middle of the night. Let's go to bed and see if the other shoe drops tomorrow."

Shaking his head, he started wearily back up the hill towards the cabin.

On a different hill, a Kakapo boomed majestically, the sound echoing in the dark valleys.

***

Despite the previous night's proclamation, French didn't wait for the repercussions of the incident. At four-thirty in the morning, Debbie cheerfully roused the kid for his early-morning Kakapo rounds. Since Kakapo were nocturnal creatures, the best time to observe them was very early in the morning, while there was some light to see by, but before they went to sleep.

The kid hadn't really signed on to observe Kakapos—he was more interested in using technology to defend them—but

French had told him in no uncertain terms that on a station as undermanned as this one, and in the middle of nowhere to boot, he would have to do his part of the watching if he wanted the job.

The kid had agreed, so, soon after being awoken, he was sitting on a mountaintop watching a male Kakapo trim the grass around his track-and-bowl system, feeling a little awed by the whole thing.

His awe wasn't directed at the track-and-bowl system, which was merely a couple of dirt paths and a small depression in the dirt, built by the Kakapo for acoustic reasons to help project its booming mating call, nor was he impressed by the Kakapo itself, a small, gray-green parrot which had almost become extinct because it couldn't fly.

No. The reason for his awe was that the Kakapo was there at all. There on mainland New Zealand, the original home of the species. Three months into his informal internship, he still hadn't gotten over the enormity of that single fact.

Like most of New Zealand's flightless birds, the Kakapo had found itself instantly out-evolved when humans arrived bringing dogs, cats and rats with them. Unaccustomed to predators of any sort, the Kakapo had become extinct almost overnight. Soon, only really remote areas like Fiordland and small islands off the coast had any Kakapos, then only the island, and, finally, just *one* island, Codfish Island, which was turned by conservationists into an impregnable fortress. The last bastion of the Kakapo.

But then French, a wealthy inheritor who was volunteering at the New Zealand Department of Conservation, had had a dream. More importantly, he'd also had the money to pull it off and the bloody mindedness to bend a few laws and not care whom it might offend.

Five short years later, the kid was watching a Kakapo go peacefully about its business on the mainland.

The kid shook his head and kept taking notes.

***

"Mr. Phillips, is it true that your parrots are clones?"

Debbie and the kid winced, exchanging a significant look. The other shoe had taken a few days to drop, but when it did, it left no doubts. The weekly helicopter had disgorged two suspiciously well-informed reporters and a quiet man from the Department of Conservation.

And despite the fact that French was a loose cannon, his hatred of reporters being even more notorious than his hatred of being called "Mr. Phillips', they were all aware that the man from the DOC was the more immediate danger.

"In the first place, they're not my Kakapos. They're wild animals, we only study them and protect them from exotic predators," French said abruptly, obviously ill-at-ease in front of the TV camera. "And yes, they are clones." He paused, holding a finger up to avoid further questions while he gathered his thoughts. "It wasn't the ideal solution, of course. Ideally, we would have used a diverse genetic selection to create our colony. Unfortunately, there wasn't enough diversity on the Codfish Island reserve, so we took genetic material from the healthiest male and female, and cloned each of them six times."

"So they aren't *real* Kakapos," the reporter, a typical blond media woman, went on in her typical matter-of-fact media voice. The fact that she had no idea what she was talking about didn't really seem to faze her much.

"Don't be daft, woman. Of course they're real!" French exploded.

Debbie made a face, knowing that any sympathy for their cause in that particular channel's audience would disappear after the interview was edited and aired. But then, that was French for you: much more comfortable around parrots than people.

"But they're clones?" Still unperturbed, the reporter pressed her advantage.

"That only means that they're identical to each other and

genetically similar to the original couple. They're perfectly good Kakapos."

"The public doesn't see it that way. What they see is that you're killing real animals to protect these clones. Don't you think that's a bit of a contradiction?"

French glared at her and turned around abruptly.

"Goodbye," he said, storming towards the cabin.

The reporter called after him.

"What about the reports that you stole the original female to start this colony? Are they true?"

His only reply was the slamming of the door.

Debbie sighed. "That went well." She turned to the kid. "Get inside and try to calm him down while I fetch Mr. Webber."

She strode over to the man in the DOC windbreaker, exchanged a few pleasantries, and walked him to the cabin.

The kid had succeeded in bringing only relative calm, although the debris of a wooden chair marked the tranquility as recent. French was sitting in another chair, muttering darkly into his enormous beard.

"Hello, Ed," he growled at Webber, "come to cut my funding?"

"You know it's not that simple."

"Answer my question."

Webber just nodded, but at least he had the good grace to look embarrassed about it.

"Typical," said French.

"Oh, come on. You know you're not making it easy for us. We *want* to keep funding this project. You know we think it's important. It's just that you're getting the public against us with your overbearing attitude. That's not the best way to get government funding, you know. And neither was stealing that female Kakapo. The island team was sick with worry."

"I didn't steal anything. I borrowed it and I returned it in better shape than it left, and with a fertilized egg inside, so don't give me that."

"And killing all the cats in the National Park didn't help either. Rats or stoats were fine, but you know people are partial to cats. And also to Rabbits."

"The rabbits were eating the podocarp fruit," grumbled French. Both men knew that the podocarp, which flowered once every two years was the Kakapo's main source of nourishment during mating ritual.

"Well, it's all moot now, anyway. Without funding, you'll have to pull the plug."

French looked at him and laughed heartily. "Did you really think that your funding was keeping us going? Oh, it didn't hurt, but it was only covering about ten percent of our costs! Did you really think that we could be this effective in cloning the Kakapos and defending their territory without a real investment, as opposed to the pittance the DOC was sending us? Fortunately, I'm rich enough that I can take the hit. We aren't going anywhere."

Webber actually looked relieved.

"Good," he said. "You know you'll still have our chopper available, only you'll have to pay for pilot time and fuel. And, of course, your permit to use this land is still valid." He walked to the door, looking back one final time. "We really want you to succeed, French. It's just that we can't justify sending you money. These AroE people are really good with the PR, and, well, you're a PR disaster."

"Bugger off, Ed."

Webber shrugged, closing the door behind him.

***

The weeks immediately after the interview were enormously quiet, as if the world outside the reserve had forgotten about them completely. The kid was particularly bored, since his machine had had only a few exotic rodents for target practice during that time.

So he was caught completely unprepared when four of the

motion detectors on the beach went off simultaneously, indicating separate breaches at each.

"Shit!" he exclaimed, typing furiously to get the hunter-killer online.

Debbie looked up from her book. French was out Kakapo watching, but on that chilly April night, he hadn't been able to cajole or bully either of his teammates into joining him.

"What's up?" she asked, looking over his shoulder at the monitor.

"Multiple non-kakapo life forms along the beach. At least four of them," the kid replied.

"What kind?"

"No idea. They caught me snoozing, and Rocky hasn't caught up yet to make a visual. It can't be too big though, because I'm having trouble getting them on infrared."

"OK, get the machine on the job and see if you can take them down. I'll get French and move to the area. Try not to hit us with the darts." This was a running joke among them since the machine had done exactly that during calibration, hitting French in the boot with a—fortunately empty—dart, despite the kid's assurances that anything the size of a human would be ignored by the programming. Debbie paused to pick up a radio handset. "Call us when you bag something so we can recover." She left.

The kid got to work. *This* was what he'd signed up for. Electronic perimeter defense in an important cause, and damn the torpedoes.

Despite being caught unprepared, the combination of the machine's mobility, the motion sensors placed strategically along the beach, and his own programming ability, the hunter-killer was quickly in the area. A couple of minutes later, he finally had a scurrying heat signature on the monitor. *Too small for a cat*, he decided. *A rat maybe?*

The machine shot after the rapidly receding heat signature on full automatic. The kid was along for the ride, and he watched the intruder take a sharp left and climb a rock, evidently feeling safe at a distance of two meters. A single dart brought it down.

One down. He used the central radio to call Debbie's handset and indicated where the body lay. Then he concentrated on the screen, ready to lend a hand in the unlikely event that the machine should need further instructions.

An hour passed, two. The kid giving commands, the hunter-killer he'd designed and built executing them. By the time Debbie returned, grim-faced, to the cabin, they'd managed to get three intruders, but could find no trace of the fourth.

Debbie cursed softly to herself at the table, arousing his curiosity and prompting him to tear himself away from the keyboard to go have a look.

On the table was a rat. Dead, tagged, and somewhat strange-looking.

"What's wrong with it?" he asked.

Debbie grunted in disgust. "It's been altered genetically, and I'm guessing that the external changes you noticed are actually the less important modifications. I think this rat got a behavior mod."

"But wouldn't genetic modification take a long time?" At least a few generations of rats?" he asked.

Debbie gave him an exasperated look.

"Computer engineers," she said, shaking her head in mock disgust. "You're all the same. You think the field of cybernetics is the only one that has advanced in the last hundred years."

"Yeah, cute. Now can you answer my question?"

"OK. Genetics has advanced as well. If you want a particular characteristic, you take normal donor DNA and fiddle with the molecules until you have the configuration you need. And then you clone off a few copies. Hence our friend the superrat, abilities as yet unknown."

"But why?"

"It's just a guess, but it seems to me that the nutty elements in

AroE have it in for us, and they've decided to forego the passive activities they've been using up to this year. They seem to have decided that, while this program exists, their precious bunnies and cats won't be safe roaming around New Zealand, so they've decided to take us out directly, having failed to do so through public pressure," she said.

"And the rats?"

"Oh, I guess they're modified to attack Kakapos," she said, but then seemed to think better of it. "No, they're too small to attack Kakapos. Probably built to go after the eggs."

"That," said the kid, "is truly messed up." He knew that some eco-groups fought over public funding, but to deliberately go after critically endangered animals? That was *nuts*.

Debbie winked at him. "Now do you understand why we needed a roboticist on the project?"

"You mean you knew this would happen?" said the kid.

"Well, French was actually the one who was convinced from the start, but he's always been a bit paranoid. I just humored him, but, as usual, he got it right."

They sat on a couple of chairs, smoking some old cigarettes and studying the poisoned rat until, five minutes later, French returned.

"They're off the coast, on a big speedboat or a small yacht," he reported, placing his binoculars on the table next to the rat. "Not even bothering to run without lights. They want us to know who ruined us. Those *pricks*. They know those waters are off limits to boats. How much do you want to bet that they'll be gone by tomorrow? The Royal Coastguard will never even know they were there."

"A boat, huh?" said the kid. He thought he might have an elegant if not particularly innovative solution to their problem, but would have to work on it a little before asking their opinion.

***

Summer gave way to a relatively mild autumn, but the rat

attacks did not abate, falling instead into a sort of pattern. There would be a frenzy, five or six rats appearing at once, followed by a couple of weeks of nothing, which had the kid in a constant state of alert, nerves frayed, never sure when the next assault would come, and, even worse, never completely certain that all the rats had been accounted for after each one. That was true torture, not knowing if, somewhere in the wilderness, one or more of the rats were waiting to catch an unsuspecting bird or eat an unwatched egg.

Until, one day in June, they found out. French entered the cabin that morning following his dawn Kakapo watch and simply sat down in his old leather armchair. Completely silent, he looked out a window, toward the ocean and ARoE's ever-present boat. A single tear rolled down his cheek.

Debbie and the kid exchanged a look. She motioned that he should stay where he was, and be silent. He nodded, bowing to her greater familiarity with French's moods, and watched with interest as she unobtrusively positioned herself in front of the door.

Fifteen minutes later, French seemed to pull himself together, and sprang into action. Saying nothing, he opened the closet and pulled out an old Steyr rifle complete with scope and a box of bullets. He turned around, and made it as far as the door, where Debbie stopped him.

"Where are you going, French?" she said, taking his hand in hers. It was the hand holding the rifle.

"I'm going to kill those bastards," he replied woodenly. Even to the kid, who had never seen French act this way before, it was obvious that he was in the grasp of a very deep sorrow, a sorrow that the taciturn French could not adequately express any other way.

"What happened?" she said, still standing in front of the door.

"They killed Marty," he managed, in a cracked voice. "Four rats."

Debbie looked stricken. Marty had been a male Kakapo living a full two miles from the beach who'd recently began booming for a mate. That bird had been one of the main hopes for the project.

French hid his face and tried to push past her. Debbie stood firm.

"No," she said. "I won't let you do it. Even if you manage to hit one of them at this range, the rest will simply come back with the authorities. All you'll achieve is to get yourself thrown in jail forever, and the rest of the birds will be as good as dead."

"This is my life. You know that. There's no way we can stop this rat invasion, so they win. At least let me take some of them with me!"

Debbie said nothing, but she didn't move out of the way either. The silence stretched out, growing tenser by the minute.

"There might be another way." The kid, silent until that moment, finally made his decision. He had completed his new project a few weeks before, but had been too afraid to bring it up. He thought they would reject it out of hand, report him to the authorities, and throw him off the project. Now he saw that he'd been mistaken. These people truly *believed*.

French and Debbie looked at him, saying nothing, but clearly surprised that he'd spoken. Taking this as a positive, or at least a neutral sign, he quickly cleared his worktable and reached into his tool chest, producing a foot-long tube with a rounded end on one side and what looked like fins on the other.

"What's that?" Debbie asked him, "It looks like a stubby rocket."

The kid looked guilty, but shrugged. "A torpedo."

"*What?*" She didn't look happy, but French already looked more animated, laying the gun down on the nearest chair and approaching the kid.

"Will it work?" French said.

"I've tested I in the breakers. It works. And the payload is fertilizer and some other stuff. Pretty basic, and infallible."

"No," Debbie said again. "You're talking about killing human beings. You know as well as I do that if you sink the boat out there, they won't make it ashore in those currents."

The kid laughed. "I seriously doubt that this will sink a boat that size. The payload might damage it a little—hopefully enough to get them to leave—but that's about it."

"Are you sure?"

The kid looked a little uncomfortable. "Well, there's always a chance that it might go wrong, but I'd say ninety-five percent sure."

French took her hand in his and looked into her eyes.

"Debbie, you know what this project means to us. It's our life. And you know that we can either stop them or lose everything that we've worked towards for the last twenty years. You know I'd do anything to save them. *Anything.*" He paused, another tear escaping. "But, even so, if you tell me, now, not to do it, we won't do it."

Debbie stared at him, started to speak once, twice, but said nothing. Tears brimmed at the edges of her eyes as she opened her mouth one last time, before finally looking away in silence.

French hugged her close for a long time.

"Kid, how long do you need to get it ready?" he asked.

"I can have the batteries charged in six or seven hours."

"Well, then, tonight you're going to get your chance to see if it works. If the kakapo survives on the mainland, you'll be a large part of it, a very large part." He clapped the kid on the back.

***

Rose-colored dawn illuminated French's forehead, below which two dark, expressionless eyes watched the scene on the water. The boat was about a hundred meters off the coast, easily visible from their chosen vantage point on the nearest cliff.

They were all aware that time was running short. The boat's crew would have to leave within the hour to avoid detection by the Coastguard's regular patrol.

Consequently, the kid found himself typing furiously, getting the final systems online. The fact that he'd had to run up the steep path from the beach, after placing the torpedo in the water wasn't helping at all. He tried to regularize his breathing enough to be precise with the keyboard.

The torpedo wasn't equipped with a camera, so he would have to guide it by sight, and trigger it when he felt it would be most effective. Fortunately, the dawn was bright enough—he could clearly discern the white tube on the surface of the dark sea.

There. The last command was keyed in. They could now watch the torpedo approach the motionless boat. The kid swallowed, throat dry, armpits moist, as the scene unfolded, inputting small course corrections, hoping nothing went wrong, and that he could guide the weapon to its target without losing precious time in turning back around for a second run. The future of the kakapo could, conceivably, depend on his aim.

To his immense relief, the torpedo emerged from the savage breakers still heading in the right direction. Now, despite the strong current pulling towards the left, he was confident that he could hit the target on the first try. There were less than thirty meters to go, now.

Twenty. Ten. The torpedo was barely visible at this distance. He waited a couple more seconds, armed the impact detonator, and waited.

He'd cut it pretty close. Almost immediately, they saw a stubby geyser erupt amidships on the starboard side of the yacht, followed instantly by the muted thud of the explosion.

French looked a little disappointed by the lack of any impressive fireball or other large display, but said nothing. He simply studied the effect through his binoculars.

"There's a tear in the side," he remarked noncommittally. "Not too severe, but they'll have to head back to port soon."

Almost as if the boat's crew had heard him, at least two people appeared on deck to inspect the damage, immediately followed by the sound of the engine coming to life. The boat began to move away from their position.

"Perfect," French said, satisfaction reaching his eyes for the first time.

The kid sighed, relief, combined with the lack of sleep, causing him to sag. He was happy. At the very least, the ARoE people would know that they'd have to be more careful in any future covert operations.

Debbie whimpered. The kid turned to see her pointing, a stricken look on her face, towards the sea.

The boat was listing slightly, but that wasn't the reason for her worry. Two figures could be seen on the deck, flailing at something unseen. Another's head could be seen bobbing up and down in the water.

"What's happening?" the kid asked.

French raised the binoculars. "The people on deck seem to be under attack from something. Some kind of small brown things. Lots of them."

Another of the figures jumped into the water.

"They'll drown if they don't get back on the boat. That's not a sea on which you want to take a swim!" Debbie exclaimed, gripping French's arm. "What's happening?"

"The rats!" the kid said, suddenly understanding. "The impact must have sprung their enclosure, and you told me they were bred for additional aggression. They must have panicked and attacked the crew!"

The last human figure jumped overboard.

"Can't we do anything?" Debbie asked, agonized.

"No way. We'll never make it in time. Look, one of them has gone under already, and they're being pulled towards the rocks. And the boat's going, too."

"But we have to try!"

"I'll call the Coastguard, but I think it's already too late." He chuckled. "Fitting, in a way, don't you think? If they hadn't been so hell-bent on killing the kakapos, they'd be at home with their families instead of on their way to the rocks."

"How can you be so callous?" Debbie asked. Her pallor spoke volumes about what she was feeling. "Those are human beings out there. People with dreams, lives, families! And we killed them!"

French put his arms around her once more. She sobbed into his shoulder.

"We didn't kill them, their own rats killed them. You have to remember that. Look, the boat is still perfectly afloat." He turned to the kid. "You'd better get the hunter-killer going again, I think we're about to have an infestation of soggy rats."

He pushed Debbie away and looked into her eyes.

"I'm going to call the Coastguard, to see if they can actually rescue someone. But I don't want you to get your hopes up. I saw the last one go under a few minutes ago, and haven't seen any sign of life since."

He turned and walked down the hill, leaving the stricken Debbie and the kid alone in the pale dawn light.

Off in the distance, a kakapo boomed majestically. One last call before going to bed for the day.

Happy Hour at Lilu's

In the course of my career, I've done many things. One of the most interesting was to manage the Middle East for one of Argentina's mate companies. Mate is an infusion similar to tea, and it was introduced to the Middle East via Syria in 1946 by people who'd fled the oppression that Syria suffered under the Ottoman Empire and settled in South America who then returned to the newly independent country.

One upside to this time was that I logged a ton of time on the ground in Syria (pre-ISIS, thankfully), a wonderful country full of interesting stuff and biblical connections. I chose one of the oldest for this tale.

It first appeared in *Demon Minds*.

The end of that particular chapter had humble roots. It began at a McDonald's in the stark industrial city of Volgograd in southern Russia. The man placing his order had had a very long day and was running almost completely on automatic but, luckily for him, and, as it turned out, even luckier for his mother's continued prospects, he hadn't quite descended into that state in which he noticed nothing around him.

And it was that last spark of attentiveness which looked into the girl's eyes as she handed him his change and recognized her spectacular beauty, disguised under the uniform and visor, but quickly apparent to his trained eye.

Maybe seventeen or eighteen years old, he thought, and altered his plans for that night. Instead of heading straight to the hotel after dinner, he settled himself at a table to wait for the end of her shift, despite knowing that it might be a while.

And it was. Three hours later, the girl emerged from the bathroom dressed in baggy civilian clothes, with her blond hair sensibly drawn into a tight pony tail. Another uniform, this time designed to avoid notice on the dark, dangerous streets.

But now, even more than before, he could see the potential in her, in the grace of her movements.

"Excuse me," he said, careful to catch her just as she left the restaurant, wanting her to feel that she was close to a safe, familiar haven, but not to have to worry about losing her job if someone took it the wrong way that she was talking to a stranger inside the premises.

She stopped, stepping instinctively back towards the interior, but held her ground after she'd had a chance to look him over. He didn't look at all threatening, dressed impeccably in a dark suit of conservative cut, still spotless even at this hour of night. He certainly didn't seem like the type who would try to rob her, and there were just too many witnesses present for him to try abduction or rape. She relaxed slightly.

"Yes, can I help you?" She cursed herself for saying it, but her training just kicked in automatically.

He smiled and fished inside his jacket, pulling out a business card which he handed to her.

"My name is Asher. I represent a talent-search agency based in St. Petersburg. We look for new models."

"Talent-search?" She was instantly back on her guard. In post-communist Russia, "model agency" and "talent-search" were too often euphemisms for the Mafiya's prostitution rings. And the poorer areas of industrial cities were a prime recruiting ground for the brothels.

He smiled again, apologetically this time. Unless a formal meeting had been arranged, this was the reaction he got from every girl in every Russian city. The only exceptions were the really rural villages, where the bumpkins were too unsophisticated to know how the real world worked, and were immediately flattered to have been noticed.

"I'm sorry," he told her, "I know what this looks like, but we're a legitimate agency with a large and famous list of clients. All our information is on our the card. Investigate us if you like, call our office. Call the police in St. Petersburg if you really need confirmation. If that satisfies you, give me a call—I'll be in town for a few more days."

He paused as she looked the card over, knowing that the info was genuine, and that she would call him. After all, how great could her life be in this town, with this job? All he had to do now was set the hook: "I'm the scout that discovered Irina Vostoyeva, and I think you could be just as popular. You have the potential."

She still didn't look convinced, but mumbled, "Okay, I'll call you, maybe." She started walking toward the bus stop.

"Wait," he called after her, "what's your name? So I'll know who's calling."

She hesitated, and then decided that it would be all right. "Ania."

"Ania. That's Polish, isn't it?"

"Yes, my father is Polish, but I was born in Vilna," she said, then waved an walked away.

He watched her go. The daughter of a Polish pipeline worker, unless he missed his guess. A childhood of hardship spent following whatever oil or gas work her father could find.

Yes, she would call.

***

Ania's eyes were red, swollen. Her rage at the injustice of it all was clearly visible. There was no way she should have been left off the model agency's staff. She'd been much prettier than two of the three girls chosen, although she had to admit that the third had been simply gorgeous.

But the other two? Why were they destined for a life of fame and riches while she was to remain part of the unwashed masses?

Asher sympathized, although he suspected he knew the answer. One of the girls had gotten in because he, himself, had bribed the gatekeeper. She might have made it in on merit, but he couldn't take the risk. Daughters of important Mafiya captains needed to be pampered.

The other one? Well, he had no proof, of course, but likely that she'd given a good account of herself on the casting couch. Even real modeling had its sordid side, and nobody would question the day's recruiting. They had netted at least one superstar today, a beautiful Siberian girl with mixed mongoloid and European features, stunning black hair and green eyes. The other two would be accepted as bonuses on a brilliant day.

He was disappointed for Ania. He'd expected her to make it, and to get the commission for the discovery. Adding her to the agency's portfolio would also have increased his own prestige.

But there were other ways to recover his investment in her.

He patted her arm sympathetically.

"Don't cry. Look at it as a life experience. There are other modeling agencies, and at least one more casting scheduled before you have to return to Volgograd," he lied. "And you came very close this time. You'll make it."

She dried her eyes, a tiny speck of hope returning to her features.

"And what's more," he continued, "how often are you going to have an all-expenses-paid stay in St. Petersburg? Visit the Hermitage, enjoy the nightlife! I'm invited to a party tomorrow, why don't you come along?"

And she did. It was a glittery affair for Russia's nouveau riche, full of oil barons and actresses and soccer players.

Asher soon managed to get four or five sweet-tasting, innocuous-seeming drinks inside her, and then a line of cocaine, and then one of the soccer players.

She was quickly reeled in after that.

***

A desperate father's inquiry had mobilized a jaded St. Petersburg detective into a half-hearted search. What he'd uncovered had eventually pointed to the Mafiya and the cop had dropped it like the proverbial hot potato, but not before calling a contact of his in the middle east.

The contact, a Beiruti policeman had promised to look into it and he'd had some success, but had eventually had to ignore the case because of a high-profile political assassination that he'd been assigned to investigate. After all, the girl in question was just another whore in just another whorehouse in a city that was full of them. Rich Arabs had to have *some* place in the world where fun was allowed after all. If not, how would anyone know they were rich?

Nevertheless, he'd felt guilty enough about it that he'd told his priest about the case in confessional, and that led to a phone call to the embassy of the Order of Malta. The Maltese had been very specific about what they were looking for.

Another phone call, long distance to Los Angeles this time, had resulted in Tim Birkin's current situation.

He was the seated in a bar overlooking the Lebanese Mediterranean coast. It was a beautiful place caressed by a soft spring breeze, and he didn't really want to be there. He'd been woken up in the middle of the night, ordered by a complete stranger to board the first flight to New York out of LAX and had, eventually, after connections in New York and Amsterdam, landed in Beirut. He'd been met by a driver who'd dropped him off at the seaside café, left instructions that he wait for a policeman named Bassam and then departed.

Exhausted, jet-lagged and plunked in a country where everything could go (and, historically, had gone) to hell without warning, he consoled himself with the thought that he'd known this day was coming ever since he'd turned eighteen and inherited his birthright. It had been fun, but a reckoning had always been due.

Damn.

Bassam finally arrived, looking precisely how Tim would have imagined: dusky, fiftyish and slightly overweight with hair already more gray than black, and a moustache to match. One notable thing about him that immediately caught Tim's attention was the way he smiled: it was a guileless, open expression that expressed honesty and invited the same.

By the time introductions and pleasantries had been exchanged, Tim found himself liking the man despite his mood.

"So," Bassam asked him, "do you have any identification?"

This wasn't completely unexpected, especially as Tim suspected that his new Arab friend was probably as new to the international cloak-and-dagger set as he was. Birkin handed over his passport, which Bassam inspected.

"And the other?" Bassam asked.

Tim tried to avoid rolling his eyes, but wasn't quite successful. Even so, he pulled a signet ring out of a pocket in his luggage and handed it over for inspection.

It passed. Bassam smiled at him and shrugged before wordlessly giving Tim the folder he'd been carrying.

Tim inspected the papers. Ania Wolkowicz was, or at least had been, a beautiful girl, judging from the photos included in the file. Most of them were culled from the talent-search agency's book, but some, more recent, were from the website of the escort service where she'd worked immediately before her disappearance. The accompanying text gave ample biographical information which told a depressingly familiar story of the type that ended with so many Russian girls working in Lebanese brothels for Saudi petrodollars.

Nothing in the file would have concerned the Brotherhood of Hethel, one of the more obscure Maltese brotherhoods, were it not for one small anomaly. The man who'd recruited the girl was Asher, a suspected long-time associate of the Brotherhood's most ancient enemy: the demon whose destruction was the central reason for the order's existence, and who had been out of sight for almost six generations.

The fact that the brothel itself was called "Lilu's" left no doubt in anybody's mind as to the identity of the owner, and even less as to the arrogance of the demon. She was hiding in plain sight behind a tacky neon sign.

Tim Birkin's instructions had been concise. He had to get inside the brothel, confront the owner, ascertain that she was, in fact, the demon Lilith, and take measures in accordance with his hereditary position of Knight-Commander of the Holy Brotherhood of the Flower of Hethel.

It was ridiculous, of course. He was a building contractor from L.A., not some crazy Crusader type spurred on by religious mania, and he certainly didn't believe that demons were walking the earth, no matter how disgusting this particular woman's profession was. Technically, he wasn't even Catholic; his family had let the practical aspects of the matter slide since at least the time of his grandfather, resulting in no baptism ceremonies for quite some time.

But one didn't go around saying no to a job assigned by a group of people willing to pay a hundred thousand dollars a year to maintain a hereditary position that never actually did any work. The ridiculous signet ring and vials of consecrated water were an easily suffered indignity.

So he would confront the owner of the brothel, prove that she wasn't Lilith, and let the Beiruti police deal with the charges of white slavery in the Ania case.

He'd be home in three days.

***

No matter what the western world believed about Beirut, there was money there. That was because its mix of Catholic and Muslim Arabs had created a cosmopolitan atmosphere where attitudes were a lot more relaxed than in the neighboring states, which drew revelers and partygoers in search of alcohol and women. And also a lot of money.

The hotel was a typical five-star belonging to an international chain, and it was booked full enough that Tim decided to forego the crowds in the restaurants and order room service while he thought through his next steps. He wanted to have the situation completely wrapped up by the following day.

Bassam had hinted that the police could get in touch with the brothel's management and get him an interview, which gave Tim a little insight into how things worked in that city. Cooperation evidently purchased leeway, and the blind eye of the law was everywhere.

So he'd go see the woman tomorrow and fly back home the very next day.

Why was he in such a hurry? Beirut, when not being shelled by insurgents or Israelis, or being invaded by Syrian armies, was a great city for a holiday. The *joie de vie* of the inhabitants was incredible, belying the tormented history of this Mediterranean settlement. And the women he'd seen on the streets that afternoon were beautiful.

And still, all he wanted to do was leave. Why?

He supposed it was simply the fact that the very first knowledge he'd had of the place was the unpleasant certainty that it was the whorehouse for a whole continent. And that was so quickly followed by the reality of one particular girl's descent into white slavery that he'd simply been unable to shake off the sick feeling despite spending the rest of the afternoon sightseeing.

It wasn't that he was an innocent. He was perfectly aware that every major city in the world had its prurient underside. Hell, L.A.'s was pretty damn visible. But here, he just couldn't ignore it.

It was Ania's face, Ania's eyes. They haunted him as he imagined the way a young girl would make her living at a place like Lilu's.

He studied her face in the file photographs, studied her beauty, knowing full well that if he chanced to see her, she would have aged decades from those glamorous photos of an aspiring model.

In his rage, he actually found himself wishing that the owner of the brothel really was the demon Lilith. His father had taught him the Brotherhood's lore regarding how to deal with that particular scourge, at least.

But it wouldn't be, he was certain. Demons were just something you used to scare your children into behaving or to frighten them beside a campfire. No, this would just be a human predator, growing fat through the results of other people's poverty and desperation.

He studied the photo of the girl, memorizing the features, until dawn began to break and the room service people refused to bring him any more whisky. His sleep, when it finally came, was fitful and haunted.

***

He woke with a start at four PM, jet-lag having combined with alcohol to insure that he felt like he'd been dragged through a combine harvester. It took him a long soak in the tub, gallons of water and rather more than the prescribed quantity of ibuprofin for him to feel anything close to human, but when Bassam arrived to pick him up, he was, at least, presentable.

The red light district was inland from the city center, looking decidedly less high-class than the neighborhood that housed the hotel. It wasn't an obviously unsafe area, as he'd expected, but the change was visible. Modern high-rise apartments and offices gave way to traditional Mediterranean Arab houses, the outer walls unfinished and unpainted, as was traditional in the region. Not poor, but not trying to impress the Europeans.

The neon lights, however, would have been right at home along any seedy avenue in L.A.. And they were all on, even at seven-thirty in the afternoon, much too early by local standards. Even for dinner.

Surprisingly, the area was jumping. Some locales even had small crowds of well-dressed men chatting unconcernedly out front.

Tim turned to Bassam, who recognized his surprise and chuckled.

"It's happy hour," he explained.

"What?"

"Just like at any bar. You go in, pay for one drink, get two. Only with naked women dancing around on poles."

"But aren't these prostitution dens?"

"That's optional, of course, but it's a little too expensive for this crowd. The women on this street are all European girls who work for US dollars or Euros, mainly making house calls. The men who come at this hour are just in for a couple of drinks with their friends before dinner. Most of them are probably office workers here with their colleagues and the boss."

"They let their bosses see them at these places?" Tim was amazed. Some things were fine for a Saturday night with your friends, but better kept from people with whom you needed to maintain professional credibility.

Bassam laughed, "This isn't America, Tim. And most of what goes on before midnight is pretty tame. It's mainly just a way for the brothels to cash in on a time of day that would otherwise be dead, and for the less-expensive girls to get something in the way of extra tips. Although most of that goes to the house too."

They drove in silence for a while before Tim spotted the red neon that announced Lilu's and Bassam pulled the car over and parked in an adjacent, unpaved, alley.

Tim got out and stood, just staring at the sign. If the owner really was Lilith herself, she had more courage than he'd believed. Lilu was actually one of the original names she'd claimed, dating from Assyrian times. And the red neon wasn't subtle at all.

And despite being a modern, secular individual who was superstitious about nothing, those letters gave Tim the creeps. They were too red, too bright, too evil. The vial of holy water in his pocket, which he'd felt completely idiotic for bringing along, now gave him comfort which he badly needed.

The sun was setting gloriously over the Mediterranean as they entered the brothel.

The interior quelled Tim's anxiety, however. Just another smoky, dimly lit strip club with a couple of pole-dance areas and topless waitresses. A scene so bad-movie familiar that it seemed ridiculous to feel any sort of apprehension. Plenty of men in their twenties and thirties filled the seats, eyes riveted on the nearest dancer, while they lied about their sex life with their coworkers.

While Tim looked the place over, Bassam was in deep conversation with the bouncer. The discussion took place in Arabic, but it was obvious that the policeman, having met with initial resistance, was applying pressure in order to meet the owner. The bouncer eventually shook his head and went through a doorway behind one of the stages.

"Are we in?" Tim asked.

"Yes, but they have to put up some kind of fight. I think we will meet with a middle-level man first because they like to stall authority figures."

Bassam could have been a prophet. He was forced to reenact the scene with the bouncer for the benefit of a short, greasy man who claimed to be the manager. Much heated Arabic ensued before they were finally led backstage into a paneled office. And even there, their host's pride dictated that they wait a further twenty minutes.

A woman finally entered the office. Dark-haired and dusky, she was dressed in a conservative gray suit that didn't manage to hide the fact that business at the bar would probably triple if she replaced the girl at one of the poles.

The first thought to cross Tim's mind when he saw her was that this woman was too young to be anything even remotely resembling what he was looking for. But she was also too young to have been running this club for the last three decades as well.

She didn't look much over thirty.

But then he saw the eyes.

Her eyes were of a brown so dark as to be almost black, but, behind them there was no spark of emotion, no sign of humanity, no life. They made Tim feel like a frightened little boy caught doing something naughty.

Bassam was made of sterner stuff; he hesitated only a moment before spouting Arabic at her.

She looked at Tim, "Mr. Birkin," she said in Oxford-perfect English. "I'm pleased to make your acquaintance. My name is Lilith. I am the owner of this club."

"I thought your name was Lilu."

She smiled, "I have been called many things in my time. I think, perhaps, Lilith is the right name when dealing with you. It will be more comfortable, or at least more familiar, for you if you are who I believe."

Tim said nothing, just looking into those ageless black eyes, fighting to beat down the feeling of dread and reminding himself that, no matter how disgustingly evil her profession, the woman in front of him was only that, a human woman. She was probably a hard, dangerous bitch, or she wouldn't have reached the upper levels of the Lebanese underworld, but that was all. If he was careful, there was no reason to be afraid. He did have a police escort, after all.

"Are you what I believe?" Lilith asked at last, breaking the silence.

Tim started, "What do you believe?"

"I think you're a member of the Brotherhood of Hethel."

She took one look at his startled face and laughed. Tim felt himself turning red. So much for his dreams of being the next James Bond, only with a supernatural foe.

"So, you finally found me again," Lilith sighed. "Well, I guess it was about time. It's such a nuisance that sometimes I wonder if it's even worth running away any more."

Now, Tim finally had something to say, "Don't give me that. I don't really believe that you're Lilith, the demon. All I want is for you to drink this, so I can prove you're just a woman and I can go home again." He pulled a vial of clear liquid out of his coat and presented it to her.

Lilith eyed it suspiciously. "What is it?"

"Holy water."

She laughed. "Do you really expect me to believe you? How do I know you're not just trying to poison me with something else?"

"I'll drink before you do. It's harmless. It's just water unless, of course, you really are a demon, and I don't think you are. So prove me right."

Lilith Laughed again, the tinkling of breaking glass. "I'm afraid I'm going to have to disappoint you."

Tim stared, not understanding.

She went on, "You see, I really *am* that Lilith." Seeing the look on Bassam and Birkin's faces, a mixture of disbelief and disgust at this waste of her time, she clarified: "Most of the stories about me, and demons in general for that matter, are greatly exaggerated. We mainly can't change shape and, as far as I can remember, I've held this same shape for seven thousand years. I can't remember my childhood, so if you need a description of hell to verify my story, I can't help you at all. And all the dark magic I've been accused of over the years is a fabrication. My magic mainly lies in being able to compel people to do things they wouldn't normally do, things they feel are wrong, or dangerous. But it mainly works on children. Adult males are easy where sex is involved, but I'm not really certain that that's actually my magic." She chuckled. "The rest was just invented by people who can't understand why I don't grow old and why I follow my driving passions. They call my passion "hungers", but that's just because they fear what they don't understand. To summarize, other than the fact that I haven't died, and that I have some vague hypnotic quality, I'm just like everyone else. I'm not even sure there's a supernatural reason for it."

Tim, who had been feeling a vague apprehension, which waxed and waned in intensity since receiving the assignment, but was always present in the back of his mind to some degree, suddenly found it utterly absent. What this woman was postulating was so outrageous that he found himself completely at ease. It was obvious that he was the butt of some elaborate practical joke. Probably one of his friends who knew about the Brotherhood of Hethel was responsible. Or, he thought, with sudden dread, he might be the central figure in some enormously complex reality show. Perhaps millions of people all over the world were laughing at him right now, present by way of hidden cameras in "Lilith's" office.

Only one thing was certain: Bassam was in on the joke. He gave the cop a black look.

To hell with it, he thought. *I might as well play along and try to trick them into letting me get home early.*

He looked at Lilith suspiciously, "Even if all this were true, why would you admit it? Wouldn't it be easier for you to have your bouncers throw us out and run for it while the police brought backup?"

"The police probably aren't involved. It isn't illegal to be a demon, even if you run a brothel. I think your friend Bassam here is on his own. But, to answer your question, the reason I'm telling you is that, after five hundred years of being hounded by your brotherhood, I've grown weary of running. While I can't say that I look forward to death, I must admit that it sometimes looks like the more restful of my alternatives. So I've decided to come clean."

Now Tim was certain of his role as the central figure in a prank. No screenwriter, regardless of his qualifications as a no-talent hack, would have written Lilith's previous lines. He rolled his eyes.

"Come on," he said, a slight smile creeping into his features despite his determination to play along. "Do you really expect me to believe that you'd just give up immortality without a fight? That goes against human nature, and I'd be willing to bet that it goes against demon nature as well."

"You'd lose," said Lilith, fire burning in her eyes. The anger was the first emotion she'd displayed during the conversation. "Eternal life is the consequence of something much deeper, not an objective in itself. I will never be able to die in peace without getting my revenge."

"Revenge?"

"Have you ever heard the legend that I was really Adam's first wife?"

Tim nodded. All the accumulated facts and rumors about this supposed demon had been drilled into him at an early age. Most were typical biblical fare and most contradicted each other. Only the Assyrian and Babylonian legends were somewhat coherent, and even they differed in certain aspects.

"Well it's true. I made him happier than any woman has ever made any man since that time. Our life together was perfect, and paradise really was paradise."

"That's not what the legends say," Tim noted. "They say that you never really got along and that he finally asked God to make him a woman of flesh and blood."

Lilith sneered, "Typical. You actually believe the stuff set down by the men who came after? The truth was that I was perfect for Adam, and he knew it. God had given me to him in his eternal wisdom because he wanted the mother of the race to be immortal, an eternal loving companion to oversee their future. He, though, was mortal and he couldn't stand the fact that, in this one aspect, I was so superior to him. He got what he wanted: a mortal woman to die alongside him."

Lilith paused, held Tim's eye and continued, "And I got a

reason to keep existing: to get my revenge on her children. To watch them suffer and, eventually, to watch them die. Only Asher, my only surviving son by Adam, has stood beside me all this time, although his devotion is more to me than to my cause."

"It doesn't really seem like you've had much success," Tim told her. "There's six billion of us on Earth today, by last count."

"Oh, I've done my bit. Most of those six billion have pretty miserable lives, and none of the rest are really happy. I've even started my share of wars over the years."

"I get it. You were Helen of Troy!" Tim teased. He was really getting into the spirit of things. What did he have to lose, anyway?

But Lilith didn't rise to the bait. "Among other things, which is why your order was created in the first place," she replied calmly. "But that wasn't my biggest coup." She gestured to the office around her. "This brothel is."

"A bit of a slide, compared to the sack of Troy, don't you think?"

"Not really. There's more to this story, and I shall tell you. But first, would you like something to drink? Here I am, a professional hostess, and you two without even a glass of water in your hands as you listen to my story. What shame!"

She quickly took their orders and called the bar. Only moments later one of the waitresses arrived, carrying a tray. She distributed the drinks.

"Thank you, Ania," Lilith said.

Tim recognized the name immediately and took another, closer look at the girl, reflecting on how often waiters and waitresses were invisible, hidden behind their jobs. It was obvious that this was the girl in the pictures, the girl that he'd obsessed about all last night, the girl whose suffering had solidified his determination to enter this dive.

He saw her young body. He saw the old eyes. There was nothing fake about this girl's suffering. He suddenly wanted nothing more than to board the next plane back to L.A.. This game simply wasn't fun anymore.

"Ah," Lilith said, "I see you recognize our little angel. Yes, one of our most valued and profitable assets."

Seeing that their hostess was gazing at the girl, seemingly lost in thought, Tim took advantage of the situation and poured the vial of holy water into her drink. Bassam saw it but, to his credit, said nothing.

Lilith looked over at them.

"Cheers," she said, taking a drink.

They imitated her, and Tim took a long pull, watching her drink and swallow though his mind was focused on Ania, on those old eyes in a young face. He was about to denounce Lilith as a fraud when she spoke, smacking her lips together.

"Hmm," she said, looking at Tim. "A certain tangy zest to this. Holy water, right? Well, the thing about holy water is that, while it probably isn't good for me, it can't really hurt me. I've the very been around since first human was created. Holy water, like Christianity itself, is a relatively recent development. The water works against evil Christian things like vampires and such. But I am not a Christian thing. I am not even particularly evil, just very angry."

Tim had had enough, and made as if to leave, but found, to his horror, that his body refused to respond.

Lilith Laughed, "The poison you drank, on the other hand, is perfectly effective against humans. The police will eventually find your bodies far away from here, giving me the time I need to disappear."

She shook her head, "I'm beginning to get really annoyed with the Brotherhood of Hethel. You always manage to find me in the end. I might have to do something about your leadership," she sighed.

"In the meantime, you'll probably be conscious long enough to hear why this brothel is my greatest achievement." She paused to take another sip of her doctored drink, making a face.

"Well, it goes like this. In the mid seventies, the world was a swinging place. Antibiotics and the pill had eliminated the risks involved in recreational sex, and people were taking advantage of the situation. I was able, in the middle of it, to convince a Soviet bioweapons developer to sell me a strain of a particularly nasty little retrovirus they'd cooked up.

"So I bought this place and injected my girls and boys with the virus, telling them that it was a mandatory gonorrhea inoculation. And, every day, dozens of men came in, and were infected. And I've been doing it for thirty years.

"In case you haven't guessed, that little bug is what you've come to know as the HIV virus. I suppose you can reason out that, even without your interference, I was going to have to close this place down anyway, since AIDS has created its own paranoia, becoming less effective.

"And, anyway, I've gotten hold of something even better. An airborne virus that's almost 100% contagious just by being in the same room with a victim. And death is slow, painful and certain. I've already purchased a shopping mall in Shanghai as my next base of operations—a mall with a very effective ventilation system. More than effective enough to deliver a few billion airborne virus cells every day." She rubbed her hands theatrically, "And there are a lot of people in China."

Bassam had already blacked out, and his head lay on the table, his breathing ragged. Tim struggled against the effects of the poison. He needed to get out, to tell the world, to stop this monster.

But the darkness got him first.

PRIMAL

This came to me on a flight to Brazil, on approach to Sao Paulo airport. It occurred to me that despite the presence of one of the world's largest cities, the jungle looked like it was barely kept at bay, that if humanity blinked, it would take back what had been taken from it.

Well, in "Primal", humanity did much more than blink. The story is a veneer of science fiction over something much deeper, greener and darker. Appropriately, it was first published in *SciFan*, a mag that combined the science fiction and fantasy genres.

Gunfire thudded against the armor plating, eliciting a muted cheer from the helicopter's crew. One row behind him, a couple of volunteers hugged each other, unable to believe that, after the fruitless months of scouring the countryside, this one last desperate ploy had actually worked. There were people down there.

He was their leader, the obstinate visionary who had refused to give up. Who had pushed them beyond the limits of endurance, always wanting to investigate one more clue, one more possibility. This victory was his, more than anyone else's.

And yet, he barely heard the cheers, hardly felt the friendly pats on the shoulder. His eyes were riveted on the scene below, where he knew that one of the world's largest cities had once stood. Where more than ten million souls had once lived and worked and struggled and loved.

But now, all he could see was the meeting of two extreme colors: the dark blue of the ocean dying against the unreal emerald green of the jungle. Only the fact that he was expecting it allowed him to make out that some of the smaller vegetated hills were a little too rectangular and that some of the depressions were a little too straight. But, other than that, he was hard-pressed to recognize that the ravenous flora covered what was once a city.

Until the chopper cleared one of the hills and the statue came into sight. Once a huge white figure of Christ whose open arms dominated the skyline, the statue was covered in vines, with long tendrils hanging from one arm. The other arm had long since broken off and been swallowed by the jungle below.

"Dan! Are you listening?"

The shout in his ear and a sharp tug on his arm pulled him out of his reverie. He raised his head to see Claudia crouching beside him in the helicopter's cramped aisle.

"Yeah," he shouted back, to be heard above the roar of the engines. "What's up?"

She favored him with a look that expressed doubts about his sanity, but decided against making an issue of it at that point. "We're picking out a landing site, and wanted your opinion."

"We need to land near the source of the gunfire, but far enough away that we can see them coming if they decide to come after us. Preferably on some stretch of open land."

"That's what we thought. We'd picked out that piece of beach, over there." Claudia pointed at a stretch of white sand slightly wider than the rest. The area between the jungle and the sea gave them maybe seventy meters to work with. They would have at least some warning if the natives tried a hostile approach. The armored camp facility folded and stored in the chopper's cargo hold would have to do the rest.

"Okay," he shouted, "Take us down."

***

The only thing he recognized from ground level was the humidity. His clothes, under the kevlar armor, were stuck to his body five minutes after leaving the chopper. But that was it. He couldn't believe that, a mere twenty years earlier, he had spent endless afternoons playing volleyball on this very beach. There had been a bar that served the world's greatest Caipirinhas and catered to some of the world's friendliest women. And behind the bar had been a city of ten million people.

But now, there was no bar, no city. Only the jungle.

"Penny for your thoughts?"

Dan found himself smiling at the anachronism.

"Just thinking that if we hadn't flown in just now, I would never have recognized this beach. Never have recognized Rio."

"Had you been here? Before?" Claudia didn't say before what. There was no need.

"I used to come down on holidays when I was in college. You wouldn't believe what the parties were like." He shook his head wistfully. "And the people, they were so alive! So happy. I can't believe they're all gone."

Claudia looked him over and shook her head critically. "Come on, Dan, it's been like this everywhere we've gone. The death toll in Sao Paolo was much higher."

He ignored her, and just looked out into the dense green, but she wasn't going to be put off that easily. "And besides, they aren't all dead. Someone out there was shooting at us just now, from somewhere not too far away. So we should get inside the camp. And that way, we can lose this armor."

The rest of the team had erected the four lightweight fiber-sandwich walls which formed the bulletproof outer perimeter.

But he just stood there, knowing she wouldn't leave until she understood what was eating him. That was Claudia through and through—always ready to mother the team members, even the thus far unflappable leader of the expedition.

He sighed.

"Listen," he said, "when I was young, I used to think that the city was living on stolen land. That the jungle was always on the edges, just waiting for a chance. Always pushing at the concrete. Ready to overrun the city. I used to imagine how it would look, the jungle rolling off the hills and tearing the streets apart. And now, here I am. I just can't believe it."

She put a sympathetic hand on his shoulder and spoke softly. "Come on, let's get inside before someone decides to take a potshot at us." She turned back and walked into the camp.

With one last look at the nearest foliage, he followed her.

***

"So, what will the side effects look like?" asked Willoughby. Slight and short, she was nevertheless the single most dangerous individual on the team. Her short-cropped hair testified to her military background while the grey that streaked it had been earned through twenty-five years of combat experience, the first five in the Royal Marines. She'd been fortunate enough to be stationed in the Middle East when Europe collapsed and Britain starved, and had spent the rest of her career fighting for different warlords in Asia. Dan had recruited her over two years before, and she had proved to be as effective in protecting the humanitarian mission as she had in killing the enemies of various short-tenured dictators.

"The survivors will likely have visible scars on the face and arms, in the form of deep pockmarks similar to the scarring from serious acne. Uninfected people will not present these marks," Claudia told her.

"And the mental issues?"

Claudia was silent a moment, collecting her thoughts before responding.

"There's no way to know. The strain prevalent in this jungle is completely different from the bug that came out of the African rain forest. Its nearest known relation was found in the Philadelphia infection."

"So we shoot first and ask questions later."

Claudia said nothing, but the whiteness of her clenched fist spoke for itself. She looked over to Dan, a pleading expression on her face.

"Willoughby, we're here to save lives, not kill even more people. That's what the Khalifa's citizens are paying us to do, and that's what the Reconstruction Union expects of us. So, to answer your question, we need to ask questions before we shoot," Dan said.

"With all due respect, Mr. O'Sullivan," Willoughby replied, "the Philadelphia strain was one of the worst with regards to victim dementia."

It was true. Contemporary accounts spoke of human beings acting like rabid dogs, but that had been in the throes of the infection—and the whole process had taken less than five years.

"That was fifteen years ago. Anyone alive in this jungle will have long since recovered or was immune in the first place."

"We're not immune, sir. We've never been exposed to live hosts, and we haven't been inoculated against this strain. We can't really risk violent contact with any of them. A torn containment suit is not something I want to contemplate. And you're paying me to think of those details for you."

"True, but I would rather risk it and see how it plays out." Dan paused to see Willoughby's reaction. When she nodded curtly, unhappy but accepting, he went on, "Claudia, please continue."

"The locals will probably be well-fed, since both fish and fruit are plentiful and at least some of them should still speak Portuguese. It's also likely that local predators will have learned to be wary of humans, so that's one thing less for Mahmoud to worry about."

Everyone laughed. Mahmoud's armor still bore the scars of a jaguar attack in a part of Central America which had not been inhabited by humans for years, and the crew still occasionally played the radio recordings of the attack. A man that size screaming for his mother had been one of the few funny things his fellow team members had been able to find in the whole grim voyage.

Willoughby spoke again, "so do we take our suits or our armor into the jungle to go look for them?"

Everybody shifted uncomfortably. The containment suits

couldn't be worn under the armor, but, while they were proof against direct contact with live hosts, they weren't bulletproof. The armor, on the other hand, was virtually impenetrable but not airtight or waterproof. When wearing armor, it was critical to stay out of physical contact with infected mammals—and all mammals were assumed to be infected until tests proved otherwise.

"I don't know about you, but I'm taking my suit," Claudia said. She would willingly risk her life to save even one survivor—and not having to shoot them if they approached her was part of that. She, even more than Dan, was totally committed to the purpose. After all, doctors were always more committed than mercenary administrators.

Dan chuckled.

"We'll take our armor and stand in front of you," he said.

***

They didn't look particularly healthy or well-fed.

The eyes that stared back at them from the undergrowth looked feral, they looked scared, and they looked young. The oldest, a girl with dirty blond hair, and shocking green eyes couldn't have been more than twenty-two or twenty-three. The rest, a mixed group of mulatto urchins were even younger. Too young to remember when the city was still alive.

They weren't armed, so Claudia took a few steps forward, making soothing noises in her best approximation of Portuguese.

The children turned and disappeared, swallowed up by the jungle.

***

Hours later, they finally found a small village. Huts made of braided leaves were placed in an area cleared of undergrowth in the shadow of the trees. The huge, mutated trees that had come into being a few years after the long-anticipated global climate change had raised tropical temperatures by a few tenths of a degree. The trees that had, in a mere twenty years, grown taller than anything around them. The trees that had plowed a city of ten million under the ground and made it disappear. Some were variations of old, familiar species, while others…

Others were new. Red trunks and purple leaves often meant poisonous fruit. And it was in these new species that new viruses had formed, mutated, and suddenly sprung out at humanity. All over the world. And all at once.

The village was empty.

Willoughby and her team moved in cautiously. They circled the village clockwise, checking the huts one at a time, one soldier entering each as the rest kept watch over the surrounding huts and forest. Under ten minutes later they declared the area clear.

"But they were here half an hour ago," Willoughby declared. "They heard us coming and ran for the jungle. I can almost feel them watching."

"Do you think they'll be back?" Claudia asked anxiously.

"I doubt it. Not as long as we stay put."

They waited, but, by late afternoon, there was no sign of the inhabitants. Not wanting to be caught in the jungle after dark, Dan ordered the return to camp.

****

The night was hot and humid, the darkness illuminated only by the dancing flickers of torches set in the clearing.

But she was unmistakable. The unkempt blond hair, the deep green eyes which looked as if the jungle itself had taken up residence in her irises. The delicate features under a layer of grime. Even dancing wildly to the beat of unseen drums, Dan would have recognized her anywhere.

Suddenly, she became aware of him and turned to impale him with her mesmerizing gaze. Her body continued to move wildly, but her eyes never moved from his, calling him to her with a hunger that transcended humanity.

He couldn't—and didn't want to—resist. He approached her with every intention of being devoured, and devouring her in turn. His feet joined the rhythm of the drums and he danced towards her.

She moved away, gyrating into the undergrowth, into the deeper shadows where the flicker of light was nearly absent.

He followed. Longing to touch her skin, to take her into his arms, to become one with her body. He reached out, desperate, and found her moist skin feverish, hot to the touch.

And woke in his tent, sweating and seated, with one arm outstretched, trying to caress a girl who wasn't there.

***

They went back to the village the next day, but this time they weren't going to risk having the villagers escape. Willoughby and a small team struck out along the beach to the north, then turned inland, going around the village and approaching from behind.

The rest of the team milled about and pretended to be busy, hoping to lure any observers into a false sense of security.

Despite not actually doing any work, the heat and the tension of waiting for word from the scout team, coupled with the nerves from the certain knowledge that someone in that jungle was armed with more than just makeshift spears had Dan sweating profusely. He was immensely relieved when the radio receiver hooked to his ear crackled to life.

"O'Sullivan, can you hear me?" Willoughby's voice.

"Loud and clear."

"We're at the village. Villagers are still there. What should we do now?"

They hadn't really believed that the villagers would be caught out by the maneuver, but they'd discussed possibilities if it came to pass. Trying to have the rest of the team make contact in the village was out of the question. If they started towards the village like a troop of elephants, they would find it empty.

So they could either let the security team make the initial

contact, or have the main expedition move towards the village and let the security team try to follow the inhabitants to wherever they hid from strangers.

Neither option was perfect. Claudia was against having the security team make initial contact. She believed that Willoughby was perfectly capable of initiating a massacre if any of the villagers got too close for her comfort. But the other option could mean a lengthy chase through the jungle—a terrain that the villagers knew much better than they did.

"Make contact now," Dan said.

Claudia, who had been surreptitiously listening to the conversation, gave him an anguished look, but Dan just shrugged. It was his job to weigh the risks. Her job was to cure the villagers.

The good news was that two members of the security force spoke fluent Portuguese—which was why they'd been selected, and they all had tranquilizer guns in addition to their more lethal options. Things would have to go very wrong for Claudia's massacre scenario to come true.

The next ten minutes were hell. Between the heightened tension and Claudia's accusing stares, Dan just wanted for it to be over with. He became aware of the fact that he was straining to hear something over the sound of the surf, and realized that he was waiting for the sound of gunfire—a certain sign that everything had gone to hell in the village. He forced himself to relax and at least give the rest of the team an appearance of calm confidence.

"O'Sullivan?"

He jumped. "Yes?" Even to his own ears, his voice sounded strained. So much for the fearless leader.

"We've made contact, and the situation is stable. Four of you can come up to the village."

"Four of us?"

"They asked that no more than four come up. They don't

trust us yet."

Dan wasn't surprised. How long had these people lived in complete isolation from the rest of humanity? How would their society have evolved in the meantime?

He pondered these questions as he led Claudia and two other suited volunteers—a doctor and a nurse—along the path they'd followed the day before. It was a much quicker walk now that they knew where they were going, but the oppressive heat of the dark jungle made him feel a slight sense of claustrophobia. He felt that, at any moment, the jungle's mouth would close around them, swallowing them up forever.

The village was just as they'd left it, save for a small cooking fire set up inside a circle made out of large, jagged chunks of concrete obviously salvaged from the ruins of the city from which the jungle sprouted.

A group of villagers faced the aid workers—obviously not the entire population of the village. They stood in a circle, as if proximity might protect them from these unexpected invaders.

Off to one side, alert but trying to maintain a non-threatening attitude, stood the security team. Claudia caught Willoughby's eye and smiled gratefully. She received a curt nod in return.

One man from the group stepped forward. He seemed to be in his late forties, with a wiry frame that spoke of a physically demanding lifestyle. His mulatto skin was pockmarked with the telltale scars of the virus.

"Hello," he said hesitantly. He looked at Dan's group as if asking for approval. It was obvious that he was uncertain of his English.

Claudia smiled reassuringly. "Hello," she replied.

The man relaxed visibly, and even went so far as to smile, revealing yellowed teeth, several of which had long gone missing. He said nothing more, however.

Claudia took a slow step forward, being careful to avoid

startling him, and said, "My name is Claudia." She placed a hand on her chest. "Claudia. What's your name?"

"Name Joao." The man smiled, delighted to be able to show off his language skills. He no longer seemed to be worried about the threat they posed, and seemed more fascinated by the novelty of the situation than anything else.

That caught Dan's attention. In the enthusiasm for meeting these people, they had momentarily put aside thoughts of the potential danger they represented. That they might be healthy immune hosts to a disease that had, only twenty years before, wiped out most of humanity, and that had only been controlled, never quite eradicated, was something that they were prepared for, thanks to their biocontainment suits. But they also had to take into consideration the fact that someone in this forest was armed with firearms of some kind.

And where, exactly, were the rest of the villagers?

Dan imagined that they would be circling around, invisible in the impenetrable forest, waiting for the right opportunity to strike the group from behind.

He began to scan the jungle, certain that, at any moment, gunfire would rip into them out of the humid darkness. He imagined movement in every shadow. And then he was certain that something was moving behind the villagers, off to his right. Focusing all his attention on that spot, he held his breath and waited.

A face appeared there, staring hungrily into his eyes, terribly beautiful and unmistakable in its blond frame. He took a step forward, unintentionally startling the lead villager who stepped back with a gasp that brought Dan back to his senses.

Claudia gave him a dark look as she moved into the silence and tried to soothe their reluctant hosts. Dan shrugged and looked back towards the edge of the clearing.

The face was gone.

✳✳✳

That night was party night. All the villagers had been painstakingly tested for each end every one of the known strains of the doomsday virus. And each had tested negative. Even the scarred survivors were clean.

An agreement had been reached with the villagers, who, once they overcame their shock were overjoyed to have been rediscovered—the time of human supremacy had been legendary among them, passed along to the children who'd been born in the years after the cataclysm. The team had called in a transport ship from the nearest inhabited city— Puerto Madryn, in Patagonia—which would take them to Jordan, where most of the associations that dedicated their time to the repatriation were based. A single, ancient Remington bolt-action rifle had been confiscated by the security team, accounting for the earlier gunshots.

So now, a huge bonfire burned on the beach and the members of the team celebrated their success, bootleg beers in hand, dancing and laughing and casting endless flickering shadows into the jungle and the ghostly breakers.

Uninvited but infinitely welcome, other shadows detached themselves from the inky darkness of the jungle to join them. First to arrive was a young man, a villager who hadn't even been born when the plague struck. He walked hesitantly towards the circle of light, as if in awe of the rescue team and afraid to break into such a holy gathering.

Claudia saw him approach and, detaching herself a the other doctors, took his arm and pulled him into the midst of the revelry.

Soon, the entire village was there, and the party turned into a batucada, with everyone moving to the rhythmic motion of the native drums, brought in by the villagers when they realized they were welcome.

When the heat of the night and the movement became too much for Dan, he joined Claudia and Joao outside the circle. Joao was near tears.

"…we heard the news reports," he was saying. "It was terrible. They showed us that millions of people were dying. And then we lost the satellite television channels, so we watched the local TV, which gave us so little information. Only instructions. Don't drink water except bottled water. Don't go outside. Everything will be all right. The army has everything under control. Listen to your local authorities." His English, while still heavily accented, had improved with constant use over the course of the afternoon.

"But then the army stopped coming. No more bottled water was available. The radio, even the ones from far away, went dead. I got very sick and I had to stay inside. I watched my parents and my brothers die. My father lay and rotted just outside my room, and I was too weak to move him, to bury him. I thought I would soon join them in heaven.

"But I survived. I just woke up one day, and I could move again, the pain in my head was gone. I walked out of the apartment and onto the street. I never went back. I thought everyone else in the world was dead, that I was alone."

"You were very nearly right," Dan told him. By this time, he'd seated himself next to them on the dry sand. "The bug was something we'd never seen before. The scientists of the time speculated that it had been born deep inside some rain forest, where the plants had mutated in response to ten years of climate change, giving new gene structures to the viruses that lived within them. Others speculated that radiation coming in through the depleted ozone layer had speeded the normal mutation rate of some strain of Hanta in Patagonia, although that seems unlikely since the infection rate in the extreme south of south America was lower than elsewhere. But before they could pin down the cause, the scientists were mainly dead. Either from the virus itself, or killed when the northern hemisphere collapsed."

"But you survived. And still have radio, and helicopters and beer." Joao said the word beer reverently, as if it was the true proof that civilization had survived.

"Some areas survived completely untouched. Mainly desert areas, where the bug was defeated by the climate. I was working for the United Nations in eastern Syria, as an observer along the Iraqi border. We were based in Palmyra."

"I was in North Africa," Claudia said. "We never even saw the bug, but I witnessed thousands of people dying when we ran out of water. It was every village for itself. My parents were murdered by looters." She stopped. Dan knew that her adolescent years had been difficult. As a white teenager from Spain, she'd been prized as a slave. Fortunately for her, her cruel and scarring captivity had been brief. Two weeks after the death of her parents, the slavers had drunk from a poisoned well. Only the fact that she was always last to receive anything had saved her.

"Some other places survived. A few towns in Texas and New Mexico formed the new United States. Alaska and Northern Canada look about the same as they did thirty years ago. Eastern Russia, most of the Middle East, Central China. There's maybe five hundred million of us still alive. Of course, the big superpowers are Australia and New Zealand. They sank every single ship that came near them once the virus was discovered, and shot down every plane. Not one person died there. The rest of the world lambasted them for it, but I think they were right to do it. And very effective, too."

A few moments of silence ensued, as Joao reconciled the new reality with what he'd known as a child. A world population a tiny fraction of what it once was.

Dan was also lost in thought, but for an entirely different reason.

"We saw some kids the other day," he said to Joao. "But they weren't in the village. Their leader is a blond girl, maybe twenty-something, thin and tall."

Joao's face showed a mixture of sadness and fear. "O bruixa," he said. The witch. "Os filhos da jungla." The children of the jungle.

Dan waited for him to continue, and, seeing what was expected, Joao reluctantly went on.

"After I recovered from the disease, I found others in the wreckage. Some of them walking around dazed, others recovered from the disease, but too weak to move. I managed to save a few, but most of them died. Those who lived are the core of the village we have today.

"For the first couple of years, we lived on the lower floors of a luxury building on the beachfront. But then it became obvious that the jungle had changed. It wasn't the companion we'd learned to live with. It was dark, it was dangerous. And it was hungry.

"The jungle ate the city. It took only five years."

Joao opened his arms, taking in the invisible ruins around them. "A single crack in the pavement was enough for the jungle to take root. And each root made more cracks and more roots. The buildings began to collapse after about three years, so we moved inwards, up the morros to where the favelas used to be. There was nothing left there but trees. The jungle had eaten the bodies of the poor, and overgrown their tin houses a long time ago.

"But in the jungle there were other dangers."

"Animals?" Claudia asked.

"Human animals. People who had survived, but who had given in completely to the hunger of the trees. They had forgotten their language and the species. They used to raid our village, and we learned to guard against them. O Bruixa is their leader, the oldest survivor. We never see her except as a shadow in the forest, ever watching us.

"But, despite our constant vigilance, we found that, every

once in a while, one of our younger children, invariably one that had little experience with the jungle, or had just come back from some of his first hunting or gathering raids outside the protection of the village would simply disappear. At first we believed that the Filhos were taking them, but we soon realized that they were leaving on their own. And if we tried to stop them, they fought us. And if we succeeded, they forgot the language and died within a few weeks."

He made a complicated sign towards the forest, a mixture of the sign of the cross with a two-fingered gesture of some kind.

"Their souls were eaten by the jungle. That is why we are so happy that you have come. If we do not leave this place, all of us will be taken out of God's light forever."

Claudia put a hand on Joao's arm, a comforting gesture.

"Everything will be all right, now," she said.

Off on the edge of the firelight, Dan could have sworn that he saw a motion. The tiniest of reflections of dancing firelight on long, blond hair, which disappeared immediately, making him doubt whether it was real or just a trick of the light.

***

This time the drums were even more urgent, and she was undulating wildly, an obviously sexual invitation that he couldn't resist. That he had no interest in resisting. He walked towards her again, and again she danced off into the jungle. Fast enough that he couldn't catch her, but slowly enough that he could always see her.

The night was at body temperature, and the ever-present humidity was so thick that it seemed to Dan that he was walking through a pool of amniotic fluid.

Leaves brushed his face, the unexpected sensation causing him to wake into inky darkness. He was momentarily disoriented, and when tried to find a better position to get back to sleep, he discovered he was standing. The sounds of the jungle confirmed that he was no longer inside his tent.

Panic welled inside his stomach, before it was overcome by a smell. A musty, humid smell of decaying leaves and growing vines and a living explosion of wetness, with a musky scent underlying it all.

And suddenly he wasn't alone in the darkness. Hair brushed his chest as a hand was lain on his face. A naked body pressed against him. Her naked body, he knew without seeing.

And he wanted her, hungered for her. Now.

Even as he pulled her towards him, the last piece of humanity within tried to stop him. It was a tiny voice that was quickly drowned out in his complete surrender to the jungle.

PROTEIN

We return to Africa in this one, but we do so through an imported mythology. Originally published in *Residential Aliens*, this story deals more with religion than with anything from off planet. It's a story that starts off in a refugee camp… and then things get worse.

"Don't do it. Just stay here," Kombe said, holding his arm in an iron grip.

Tim's fists clenched in fury as he watched the men load the truck. Bags of rice with the UNHCR logo stenciled on them, bags of grain with American flags. He knew that, although the men possessed all the necessary clearances and permits, the food would never make it to anyone who truly needed it, to the people starving inside the refugee camp. It would feed fat shop owners in Maputo and cattle all over Mozambique.

The people on the truck were taking no chances. Although it was unusual for starving refugees—or enraged aid workers—to attack a food truck, it wasn't unheard of. The hard-looking men toting AK-47s weren't just for show.

Tim raged as he watched them, powerless to do anything about it, simply observing from the shadows. The men were Asian, probably Pakistani, or maybe Indian. There had been a huge glut of people from that area moving into the region lately, fleeing the latest round of religious violence. These certainly fit the bill, too dark to be European, too light to be local.

Where they were from was of no consequence. What mattered is that they were stealing the food, and the government of Nsanje would keep turning a blind eye as long as their pockets were lined. Who cared about a few dead more or less? They'd just feed statistics that no one was looking at too carefully anyway.

Tim cared. His mother cared. That's why they were here in

the first place. Tears rolled down the thirteen year-old boy's cheek, and Kombe put his arm around him. "Don't cry. You're doing what you can. We are in a fight against nature, and this is just human nature doing its work."

Kombe knew all about this battle. He'd been a schoolteacher in the camp for three years. He's seen firsthand how his students struggled to learn despite the effects of malnutrition, how his most promising pupils were raped in the muddy alleys between the tents. He'd lost more students than he could count. But still, he did what he could, and was the most respected man in the camp, native or otherwise. A gentle man, king among people forced to live as savages.

Tim allowed himself to be led away, towards the center of the camp, the hill where water didn't pool and mud wasn't all-pervasive. That was where the command tent was.

As they walked, they received greetings from those who were able, smiles from those without the energy needed to move in the heat. Tim knew that any cordiality was directed at Kombe; whenever Tim walked these alleys alone, all he received were flat looks from people afraid to be openly discourteous towards his pale skin and full belly.

The tent was marked with the symbols for the Red Cross and UNHCR and, by unwritten rule, no one was allowed inside except for the people who administered the camp. Although there was no air conditioning, the tent always felt cool. Electricity was available to run a pair of floor mounted fans.

Tim's mother looked up as he entered. She must have seen the look on his face, because she immediately walked over to them. "Is anything wrong?"

Tim said nothing, so Kombe filled the silence. "We happened to pass by the loading area," he told her with a shrug. "They were loading a truck."

Her eyes flashed, but she too knew that there was nothing they could do. The other side had the guns. She just pulled Tim into a hug and held on hard.

***

Rivers flowing lazily toward the sea, breezes playing among the leaves of the trees. Green, but not Africa green. A brighter green, a wetter green somehow. The green of a cold land buffeted by strong northern winds. And yet this was a gentle place, and fertile.

Tim flew over untamed wilderness and mourned its loss. His vision showed the land as it had been before the great waves of foreign invaders had stolen it from its rightful owners, and then bred like rats, replacing the forests with tame, cultivated fields. Replacing the wild boars and even the tame pigs with sheep, goats, cows.

Fury welled up inside as he surveyed those lands he once ruled. He wasn't quite certain why he'd once ruled those lands, but the feeling that they'd been his was overpowering. Even the men, fickle creatures that always wanted something for nothing and expected to receive it just because they asked for it, recognized that his powers were useful, necessary, suitable.

He zeroed in on one particular patch. It was already cultivated, even in these lost and nostalgic times. But it was redeemed by the fact that the tiny cottage of undressed stone was occupied by a man who knew how to call him, knew how to coax life, fertility and even food from the only god he believed in.

The man looked thin, too thin to be healthy. He had graying, shoulder-length hair cut in a ragged line, and was chanting ancient words, powerful words. One word was repeated over and over again. Moccus. Moccus. Moccus. He worked as he chanted, burying a small amount of food where any animal that dug for it could find it. Only one kind of animal would be rooting for it in that particular place.

But Tim knew that these victuals would remain hidden for hundreds of years. Such was the power of the words.

He looked around and his attention was immediately

absorbed by the wall that separated the tiny plot of cultivated land from the encroaching forest. It was brand new.

And Tim suddenly understood. He knew that wall. He'd seen it countless times when, as a child, he'd played in the village meadow. It was no longer new. It was old and crumbling and overgrown and missing blocks. He'd been told countless times that the wall was a thousand years old. He'd laughed at the notion.

Now he knew.

And he also knew that he was meant to rule there, meant to restore the order. Perhaps that order could no longer mean countless boars roaming the forests undisturbed, but there were other ways to achieve the goal. Roaming forests was not the only thing pigs did.

He would rule again. But he had to move now—his land was far away, too far to be felt clearly.

Tim turned onto his back, his eyes wide open. He often had dreams like this, but this time, he wouldn't wake. Or rather he would, but he would no longer be Tim.

Far to the north, a slight breeze blew over a sparsely wooded hill, and a bird called to its mate across a long distance that seemed shorter on that day. There had been no physical change to this fertile island in the North Sea, but somehow, it felt different, as if something long gone had been recovered.

The very ground, the air, even the water smashing itself against the shores felt alive once again.

***

He stirred, uncomfortable in the muggy, humid air. There was a wrongness here. In the soil, in the air, everywhere. Things simply didn't feel the way they should—there was plenty of life, of course,—he could feel it in his limbs the way a sailor feels changes in the wind—but it was the wrong kind of vitality. A softer, slower, tropical life which would never survive a real winter.

Where was he?

He opened his eyes and saw what must have been some kind of sleeping chamber with cloth walls similar, yet different from, the tents he remembered from earlier times. The cloth was thin enough in places that daylight filtered through, adding to the copious illumination entering through the seams.

The bedding itself was made of some material he couldn't quite identify. Not a natural material—he could only sense the barest signs of life within it, as if some component of the cloth had been alive an unimaginable time before—even before his original incarnation—but had undergone tremendous changes since. He shuddered at the feeling, of enormous pressure and death and decay, and threw the sheets from his body.

At least he could stand, and move. Alive! Alive again after hundreds of years. He made exploratory movements with his arms, took a few tentative steps, and knew that locomotion would present no problems. The body was young, strong, virile—even more so, now that its destiny had claimed it. He stood naked, feeling the slight currents caressing his skin. Too hot, too humid, but full of life.

Another step took him to a flap in the tent wall. He could almost feel the life calling to him from the ground—although muted by the floor, which was formed of the same material as the bedding. He wanted to be outside.

The flap took him a while to understand. He was forced to call on the memories held within the body in order to manipulate the tiny mechanism, a small metal protuberance that unsealed a toothed groove. Sunlight poured through the opening, unrelenting, yellow, powerful. Tim's body stepped into the blinding glare.

The entity inside, controller of life and fertility, stopped short, just enjoying the feeling of contact between his bare feet and the dry earth below. He could feel the vitality, deep beneath him and all around him, an explosion of sensations that only he could fully understand. Through the earth, connections could be made to the people born in this place. He called to the sons and daughters of the land, tugged at them, took them by the gonads and pulled. He could hear them responding to him, as all animals did, as all animals always had.

Silence fell among the throngs around him as he strengthened the call. The people wouldn't know why they were being called, but would be unable to resist. The power of their native soil would be behind the summons.

The faces around him were black, but it made no difference. They would serve, as the pale red- and black-haired folk had served before. As long as the animal instinct lived inside them, they would do.

The thing that had been Tim paced unhurriedly, feeling the sun beat down on his naked flesh towards the large clearing he could sense ahead of him. His people, heeding the call, walked beside him, none coming within an arm-length of him even though they jostled each other unmercifully. They flowed, like digested food through a living thing, towards the only place among the tents that could accommodate their number.

The presence inside Tim's body basked, enjoying the feeling of that flow. A strong current of humanity, a wave poised to sweep away all before it. However, there was something wrong, and he struggled to understand what it was. A weakness, not in the flow itself, which was pouring into the empty space like the unstoppable tide he needed it to be, but in the individual components—although they seemed strong and unstoppable as a group, the people within it seemed weaker than he remembered people being. There was something wrong with them, bodies underfed, spirit… absent.

Finding out what had caused it could wait, however. He'd arrived.

The "square" he'd chosen was really just the intersection of two broad dusty avenues between the tents, and the people who'd congregated there were massed more along the byways than in the intersection itself but, in the end, he'd called and they'd answered his call. That was all that mattered.

The empty space around him had expanded, the crowd forming a circle about ten arm-lengths away. They seemed to know what he expected of them, and waited, still and silent.

"I am Moccus," he said. The words, neither in his body's native English nor in the Gaelic he preferred, caught in his throat. The clicks and glottals seemed completely unnatural, inhuman even, but the sounds were dictated by the land. He could feel the truth of this language in the earth between his bare toes.

The crowd responded immediately. On hearing their native tones, even the ones who'd been born in the camp and only spoke the local pidgin reacted. A muted whisper—awe and awakening—rippled through his audience.

"I am here to lead you. I am here to use you. You are mine, but I am also yours. I feel the weakness in your bodies. I can feel what has been done to you, the weight of history pressing down upon your shoulders." He sent a wave of feeling into them, and felt them breathe out collectively, with pleasure, with longing. Another wave, and the longing was fulfilled. "I will destroy you and you will give me your children. And they will give me theirs. Eventually, the descendants will live in plenty. There is a land we must take, and it is to the north." His voice was barely a whisper, yet they all heard him as well as if he'd shouted from the highest mount—he could feel it.

The people around him were little more than animals. They were willing to do whatever he commanded, completely under his sway. There were few sparks of individuality left in that crowd, and less of intelligence. The hard life they'd led had beaten it out of most.

But he could still detect, feel, sparks in the crowd. Flares of individuality, wolves among the sheep. Millennia of experience had taught him to respect these sparks—used correctly, they could create the fire with which to forge the rest of his tools. But if such embers were allowed to fall in the wrong place…

A single man stepped into the cleared space in front of him, a man his body's memory immediately identified as Kombe. This man showed no signs of weakness, no signs of being resigned to a fate worse than death. Here was a reed that had felt the wind and bent, but never broken, always snapping back into place.

Moccus knew that such men were often necessary, to give strength to the mass. "Kombe." The name was one the body had said countless times before, but the sound was different, earthier, real. "You wish to speak."

Kombe stopped two arms away, as if blocked by a physical wall. And yet he spoke. "Tim, what is this? I mean, I can feel it, but I don't know what it means. How are you doing this? Have you drugged us?"

"Tim is dead—or rather the person you knew as Tim was not a true person. The human was a larval stage, and I am the fulfillment. I am Moccus."

"Tim, listen to me—"

Strength was well and good, but some things were not permissible. It was always best to establish ground rules as quickly as possible. Moccus immediately halted the flow of low-level ecstasy he'd been sending into the man, and replaced it with a feeling of pain. Deep, penetrating pain. A pain that raped the very soul. Kombe fell screaming to the ground.

"Tim," he gasped. "Moccus, whoever you are, whatever you are. For the love of god…" Anything else he might have said was lost in a whisper as he writhed in the dirt.

Moccus stopped the pain, allowing the man to breathe. Perhaps this man would become his sharpest blade. Perhaps he would have to be put down. Time would tell. "What am I? You may ask. I am what you are at your core—I am humanity stripped of its veneer of civilization. I control what you lust for, what you hunger for. I control the hunt, and yet I also give form to the prey."

The man on the floor spoke up again. "What do you want from us, with this talk of hunters and prey? Are we to be the prey? Because we certainly aren't fit for much else."

Moccus felt the truth of the man's words in the weakness of his followers. They wouldn't survive the long journey, much less the violence that would await them as they crossed the intervening land to the promised island. But he had an answer in its very nature. "Kombe, all of you, listen. Does anyone know why the pig is one of the most successful animals? Why they never starve? Why you almost never see a thin, underfed boar?"

He waited to see if anyone would answer, but was unsurprised when they held their silence. "It's because pigs will eat anything. They are the true omnivores. Humans are a pale comparison."

"But there's no food here," Kombe said, now standing again, if a little unsteadily. "We wouldn't have let any escape us."

"There's plenty of food here, and I'm not talking about the bark on the trees. I'm talking about real food with protein. Food that has come here, but that is not native to this land. It is just a question of breaking through the barriers that have kept you from taking it for yourselves."

He let them think about it for a few moments. He could feel their confusion, and it was a short while before some understood him and tiny foci of horror and disgust burst into being. Whispers followed, and he let them whisper. The understanding spread quickly, but the horror was more muted. It seemed that some where willing to abandon themselves to what was needed. Good.

A commotion to one side prompted a look from Kombe. "Well, whoever you are, it seems you will have the chance to prove yourself."

A vehicle approached the intersection, stenciled letters and large red cross on the side declaring that it belonged to the camp's medical team. The people in the crowd moved aside to let it through—automatic deference to camp authorities was deeply ingrained among them.

The car reached the center of the clearing and a woman descended. Moccus immediately felt a pang. This woman looked how he felt people ought to look, how his memory showed him they should. Her skin was extremely light, and only avoided being completely white because it had been darkened slightly by the relentless sun, and her hair had once been jet black, but was now streaked with gray. He could almost feel his kinship to her. This, then, would be the leader of his forces.

But when he attempted to communicate with her, to transmit his will, he was balked. The woman before him had no connection to the land, no need to follow what it ordered. She was from another land, from his land, but it was too far away for her to feel its call. He was powerless.

The woman knelt in front of him, and he felt yet another emotional tug. His body was reacting to this person. The feeling was one of love, of security—his body somehow felt that, with this woman here, everything would be all right.

Moccus, however, knew that it was just a glandular sensation, nothing real. She could affect nearly nothing in a positive way, and could conceivably be a roadblock. He ground the charitable feelings inside him to dust.

"Tim. Timmy," the woman said. She tried to put a hand on his head, but he pulled away. "What's happening here? Is this about the truck, yesterday? You know we can't do anything about that, but we're helping here. We're doing something good, and making life better for people who need us. I thought you understood."

Moccus hesitated for one second, then another. He knew beyond a doubt that this woman would try to stop him, that she even had some power over his body. He could feel his glands screaming to go to her, to let himself be held, comforted.

To let this woman blunt his drive.

He didn't speak to her, avoided her gaze and turned to face the crowd behind him. "We need our strength," he said in the whisper that reached the most distant of his followers. "Hold them."

The crowd surged forward, immediately overpowering the few red cross volunteers, men and women who were unconnected to the land, and Moccus was sorely tempted, for one moment, to use them as they should be used, as a source of food for his followers. But the final vestiges of Tim were still within him, struggling to be heard, and Moccus regretfully decided against it. They might not be in contact with this land, but soon Moccus would be moving into territories which they were in contact with—and he might be able to use them, especially the boy's mother.

Nevertheless, all was not lost. With the camp effectively under his control, Moccus knew he could begin the second part of his quest. In order to take power, his people needed to feed, to gain their strength, but the rift, the sickness that affected the land, also needed to be cured. Only if the rifts were removed could the land lend him the strength he needed.

He felt wrongness approaching. Scavengers in human form held sway just beyond the camp's borders. He ordered his followers to move in that direction. The thousands advanced like locusts, tearing down tents and wire fences and shrugging off the poor, confused pale-skinned volunteers—men and women whose lack of connection to the soil kept them from understanding what was going on—who tried to stop them. Moccus himself advanced in the middle of the throng.

It was an hour's walk to the place where the wrongness made its presence felt. Many of his people simply could not make the effort, and they fell away, dead branches dropping by the wayside, making the tree stronger.

A burnt-out vehicle, riddled with bullet holes marked the border of the diseased area. A group of men met them there, holding weapons, but showing no fear. Their connection to the land was tenuous, sick. They had grown fat on their neighbors, abusing the bounty of the earth, and had withdrawn from it.

One of the men, a fat man with a scar down the length of one cheek, stepped forward. "Well, if it isn't the poor scum from the camp. Here for a handout? Or have you finally grown tired of begging for your livelihood?"

Moccus stepped forward. "Actually, we're here to feed."

There was a slight shifting of weapons in grips. "Is that so, little boy?"

"Yes."

"And what makes you think you will find food here?"

Moccus, in full possession of Tim's memories, could have pointed to the ill-concealed truck under a tent of camouflage netting, the same truck that had been at the camp the previous day, being loaded with stolen supplies. But that would serve no purpose. There was more at stake here than just getting food into starving bellies—there was an illness to be cured.

He turned back to his followers, buzzing with the ecstasy that came up through the soles of their feet. They were unarmed—but they also outnumbered the enemy a thousand to one.

"You may feed," he said.

The crowd surged forward. Hundreds were cut down by the first volley, and still they advanced. Soon the screams of the bandits mixed freely with the gunfire. Then the gunfire became sporadic. Soon, there were only screams, and then the screams stopped.

Moccus could feel the protein flowing into his followers, the strength returning to his army. He nodded with satisfaction. They would need their strength for the long march north.

At least feeding them would not be a problem. Humans,

though perhaps not as perfect as pigs, were omnivores. They could eat anything and, if properly motivated, they would.

RAIN OVER LESSER BOSO

Stories come from the strangest places sometimes. "Rain Over Lesser Boso" was inspired by the woodblock print by Hiroshige entitled *Sudden Shower Over Shin-Ohashi Bridge and Atake*. If you look at the story and view the painting, I think the connection is pretty obvious.

It was originally published by Third Flatiron Press in the anthology entitled *Abbreviated Epics*, and is another of my very favorite stories.

Mariko swore like a sailor as another drop of scalding wax dropped onto her forearm and immediately looked around to make certain that no one was present. All her dreams would be forfeit if she were deemed unworthy.

We wouldn't want that now, would we?

The work was nearly done. Acid-resistant wax covered the entire surface of her umbrella. It was better workmanship than any of the other girls would ever be capable of, but the sight of the thick cloth and ungainly, drooping dome made her understand just how much had been lost. The brilliantly-dyed bamboo-and-paper wagasa, so popular before the breaking survived only in the ink drawings on the Samurai's wall and in Mariko's imagination. She carefully wrapped the umbrella in soft cloth.

The afternoon was sunny, and the younger village girls could be seen chasing one another around the dusty square in a way that would never have been permitted when the island still pretended to follow established protocol. She watched them absently, waiting for the call that was imminent. Doubt suddenly assaulted her. What if the promised summons never came?

Do not fret. It will come.

"Mariko?" The voice was imperious and hesitant at the same time, as if knowing that obedience was owed, yet unsure how to react if it was withheld.

"Yes, Mistress?"

"I have wonderful news." The dour look on the woman's pale features gave lie to her words.

"I am listening."

You already know what she's going to say.

"You have been summoned. The Samurai himself wishes an audience with you."

"That is wonderful news, mistress." Actually, most interviews with the local lord ended in punishment, disgrace, sometimes even in death. But it was obvious in the woman's unhappy expression that none of these fates awaited Mariko. "I thank you before the spirits for bringing me these tidings."

Mariko's mistress made a warding gesture with her fingers. "Do not mention the devils to me, girl. I'm not some ignorant village brat who simply can't accept them for what they really are."

No, you're not, but we know what you did to get yourself exiled from Edo.

The woman's eyes flickered, but if she heard anything, she didn't acknowledge it. Mariko, of course, would never allow her features to betray her in that way; the difficulty lay in avoiding laughter.

"I'm sorry, Mistress."

"You should be. Now you need to do something with that hair. Such beautiful long hair, bedraggled because you refuse to tie it down." They fussed in front of a mirror until the older woman, whose grey-streaked locks were anything but beautiful, proclaimed herself satisfied. "Now come. We have a long way to go, and we do not want to be out after dark."

The woman led them on a roundabout path through the sparsely wooded lowlands. Any time they came upon a slight movement in the trees, or a the soft sound of an animal scurrying away from them in the underbrush, the mistress would turn in the opposite direction, even if this meant having to climb over rubble strewn by the big tremor, the legendary event that had broken this small island off the mainland.

And yet, on the one occasion when they did come across a spirit, a dark cloud of smoke that looked almost solid in the path, the woman simply turned around, lips pressed tightly together. Mariko was disappointed—she'd been hoping her beloved mistress would faint.

In much more time than was strictly necessary, the Samurai's palace came into view: a couple of large wood and paper houses in the classical style surrounded by pleasing gardens and a not-so-pleasing wall with huge gaps in the stonework. The gate was open, and only when the path led over a bridge that crossed the stream in the garden, did the older woman relax. "Come girl. We have wasted enough time."

Mariko, still on the far side of the stream, nearly rebelled at the words. She wondered what the frightened mistress would do if her charge ran out into the sulfur fields where spirits roamed by the dozens. Would the woman follow, or would she take the only other honorable path open to her and throw herself down a fumarole?

This is not the moment to play games.

The young woman bowed her head and followed the mistress through the garden and up the steps leading to the front door. A guard who attempted to send them to the woman's entrance was rebuffed. "The Samurai will see this girl right now. That is his will."

The guard stood aside with an expression that conveyed that, though the decision could not be questioned, he would take enormous pleasure in executing them if the words proved false.

The two women entered the waiting room, where a long-whiskered attendant came over to greet them. Mariko was surprised by how foreign the interior of the traditional building looked. Books in exotic languages were laid on two shelves, a strange portrait of a round-eyed lady, pale and forbidding, adorned the back wall, and a long wooden musket hung on a specially reinforced paper panel.

She shouldn't have been surprised. The island, considered unholy since the tremor which had split it from the mainland, opened deep gashes in its fields and filled its air with demons, was the only part of Nihon open to foreigners. Most of the villagers had some trinket or tool brought from some faraway port and given as a gift by sailors or exchanged for some service or good.

Perhaps what jarred was that the Samurai himself, that all-powerful emissary of Imperial Edo, should openly use his house to display so much that was alien. But it wasn't her place to question her betters.

The attendant rushed them through a single, flimsy door of traditional construction and, without further ado, they were in the noble presence. Both women bowed deeply.

"Please, we aren't in the Imperial court. You may face me."

Mariko looked up. This Samurai was a new one, arrived on the island some four months earlier, and the way he looked surprised her even more than his taste in decoration. Previous viceroys had been stern, dark-haired men, lean and menacing and clearly on the way to greater things than policing the empire's accursed island. This man, on the other hand seemed well past his prime to Mariko's young eyes. His jowls hung to an almost obscene degree, and his hair was streaked with white.

She tried to imagine him riding to war, but was unable to imagine any horse large enough to carry him. Even his dark robes were unable to hide his girth. If he'd ever been one of the warriors of legend, that time was long past. At least his eyes seemed kind enough.

Mariko pulled her gaze away, settling it on a small jade figurine at a table by the Samurai's feet.

"We are here as requested," her mistress said.

"So I see, so I see." There was a hint of laughter in his voice. "Do you know why you are here, girl?"

"I am to be sent away."

"Yes, and do you know where?"

Mariko trembled. "To the pleasure cities. You would make me a yujo."

The Samurai's eyes opened wide. "No, no, no," he said. "Not a yujo, never a yujo. You have been trained, you have been educated, you have achievements. You will be oiran."

Mariko nearly snorted, but held her temper. She didn't know what oiran meant, but what difference would it make? She would only be concerned with the pleasure of others.

But it was the only way off the island for anyone who had the misfortune to be born there. Boys didn't even have that option.

Something of what she was thinking must have shown on her face, because the Samurai went on. "There is a difference, you know. An enormous difference. You will have an honored position, servants. From what the mistress informs me, you have the potential to earn respect for the women of Lesser Boso, manage to convince Edo that you are not all mad."

Mariko heard the mistress take a sharp breath.

The Samurai went on. "You alone among the girls born before the breaking have shown yourself immune to the devil ghosts. Your mother must have been a remarkable woman."

"My mother was a fishwife who tore out her hair and threw herself into the sea to drown out the voice of the spirits."

The Samurai seemed nonplussed, both at the information and the way it was delivered: matter-of-factly, respectfully, yet in much too forward a manner. "Even so, you have survived the plague, and you alone can show the court that Lesser Boso has people who are not possessed. It is in your hands to make the travel restrictions disappear."

"But what if I am possessed? What if a spirit walks over the bridge inside me?"

He laughed at the village girl. "The devils cannot pass over the water. They are earth-devils, whose world was opened by the tremor, and the energy over the water sends them up—not only the dust we see, but also their essence—to be dispersed by the winds and destroyed. That is why streams surround this house, and also why your 'spirits' are unable to attack the people of the mainland."

"Then why are we kept apart from the empire?"

The old man sighed. "Even people at court fear what they do not understand. All they know is that the earth shook, destroying half of Edo. And when they recovered, there was an island where there had once been a peninsula. Imagine their shock when they learned that everyone on the island was mad, seeing ghosts and hearing their call."

"The ghosts are real."

"Yes. And so is the madness. There will be no safe passage to Edo until that is vanquished. Yours will not be the final step, but it will be the first. You will take that first step."

"What would happen if one of the devils crossed over?"

"No one knows for certain. Perhaps, being so far from its own place, it would shrivel and die. Perhaps it would be alone forever. And then again, maybe it would open the portal to thousands of its kind, hungry to drive the Imperial Capital mad and to feed on that madness, and to end the Nihonjin way of life. But let other minds worry about this. You must do your duty."

Mariko nodded, allowing herself to be led from the presence by her mistress, who was shaking with rage. "You must never again speak to any noble in that way again. Not all of them have as much patience as the Samurai." She sounded bitter, and Mariko felt close to her for the first time. Could her exile have had something to do with this?

The attendant interrupted. "An honor guard will be waiting at the far end of the bridge. The young woman must cross immediately."

"But that cannot be. I cannot reach the bridge and return before sunset."

The man didn't even blink. "And yet it is your duty to lead the girl there and make certain her feet are set on the path."

Mariko could see the muscles moving in the mistress' jaw. Wordlessly, the other woman turned and stormed out of the foyer. Mariko followed.

The skies outside were painted red with sunset, but darkened also by cloud. As they crossed the garden, Mariko began, for the first time, to believe that everything she'd been told was true. Even as they crossed the wooden bridge over the stream, the first drop of a shower bounced off her nose.

Did you truly doubt the rain would be here?

The mistress made no comment, simply taking an uncharacteristically straight path to the bridge. Mariko struggled to keep up while opening her umbrella. The mistress, oblivious, didn't even seem to notice that she was getting wet while her ward was dry. It was obvious that all the older woman wanted was to get back across the stream, to the Samurai's house and silence in her head.

They were making good time, carving through the open fields as if there were no such things as spirits, when the inevitable happened. The mistress, despite peering as hard as she could into the failing light, almost stumbled upon one of the clouds of floating smoke that betrayed the presence of a spirit.

The woman's demeanor cracked, and she jumped to one side with a shriek. Warned by this, Mariko saw the spirit in plenty of time. She could have avoided it easily.

But she didn't. She walked calmly into the space the spirit had occupied.

The mistress was upon her in an instant, fear of the supernatural overcome by the frantic realization that her precious cargo might have been damaged. Her hands traced the contours of Mariko's face while she repeated, over and over again, "Are you all right, are you all right?"

Mariko pretended confusion. "Yes, why?"

"There was a devil. You walked right into its arms. I saw it!"

"That's not possible. I would have seen it, would have felt something.

"But I saw it."

"It must have been a trick of the light." She took her mistress' hand and led her forward. "Come, it gets late."

Comforted by this, the mistress resumed her place in front of her. They arrived at the bridge without further incident, an unlikely pair: a young woman under a heavy waxed umbrella, a stately older woman, wide-eyed in the rain.

The bridge was a huge wooden affair of round logs and wooden boards. The guardhouse was thirty paces along its length, over the water, insuring that the earth-spirits could not molest the imperial troops stationed there.

A quick, curt goodbye at that guardhouse was all Mariko got on the moment in which she left everything she'd ever known behind. Her mistress turned back towards the comfortable confines of Lesser Boso, and the impulse to reach out to the receding woman was almost too strong to resist.

The guards removed the choice, however. They explained politely but firmly that she was expected on the far shore.

Mariko nodded numbly and walked out onto the boards, her umbrella rigidly upright in the slightly acidic rain that fell in this area, product of the island's fumaroles. Her footfalls echoed dully as she advanced towards a vast world that was, she was certain, empty of anything she wanted.

It was important to hold the umbrella upright. Only that way could the carefully sealed canopy do its work, keep everything on the correct side of its surface. Holding it this way meant she was getting wet, but that didn't really matter.

The bridge, a few hundred paces long, took her an eternity to cross. The walk gave her the opportunity to remember every detail of her childhood, even those vaguely remembered sensations that were her only true memory of her mother. Did she have the right to keep others from knowing their mothers, even if, with that, they would become complete with the earth in a way they'd never known before?

Wet grass met her feet as the bridge ended. A small honor guard huddled under an awning some distance from the edge of the bridge, barely visible in the moonlight. Mariko noted that the structure didn't have a guard house on that side.

She stepped off the boards onto the wet grass. The guard had just noticed her, and she would have some moments before they got themselves organized. She shook the umbrella and nothing happened. She gave it another shake, fearful that all had been in vain.

A small cloud of dust motes, felt more than seen, dropped from the umbrella and coalesced into a smoky specter.

I have never felt such agony, but the barrier held me down against the energy. It is done.

Mariko said nothing, watching the guards approach, wondering if, even in their worst nightmares, they knew what was coming.

You have done well. You were always worthy. We thank you.

She finally managed to pull herself together enough to formulate a question, just as the cloud of smoke sank into its new shore. "What's going to become of us? What's going to happen?" she whispered.

Something new.

POUPÉE'S PEOPLE

A tin teapot fell from the workbench and tinkled onto the floor. Poupée shot after it, climbing down the chair like one of the jungle lizards. She recovered it from between the rotting wooden boles that made up the floor of the hut and hugged it to her chest.

"You big oaf!" she yelled.

"Sorry." Even his voice was huge, a rumbling boom that seemed to shake the building to its core.

It wouldn't take much to bring the old hut down, she reflected. If Harold gave it another couple of bumps like the one that had dislodged the teapot, it would likely collapse around them and she would be crushed.

Harold probably wouldn't even notice—he'd been too big to live inside the house ever since he'd been born, hatched or whatever one called the process in which the late, lamented doctor had created the oversized lizard.

Poupée, on the other hand, needed the safety of the walls. The larger animals in the jungle around them tended to avoid the place because it still smelled of human—and animals in this little corner of the world had learned long ago that being too close to a human would mean a quick end. Even the larger predators stayed well clear.

Of course, nothing smarter than an insect would approach

when Harold was around. She had no idea what Dr. Philippe had been planning when he designed the creature. He'd once told her that the dragons had been hatched small, and should have taken thirty years or more to grow into their full size.

Whether that meant that Philippe's calculations were wrong or whether it meant that Harold would grow to become the size of one of the buildings she'd seen in the pictures in the books on the shelves, she didn't know or care.

But she did know that she needed to find a new and more solid shelter right away, or, one night, she wouldn't be there when Harold returned from his hunt.

"Come on, Harold, I need you to take me somewhere."

"Where?" he asked.

"I'm not sure yet. We need to look around. And we need to take my people."

The huge head turned to look at her. Harold knew what this meant.

"Are we leaving? For good, I mean?"

The question had weight. Harold had been living in the swamp, among the mangroves and wildlife, but Poupée was different. She'd stayed in or around the safety of the hut since Philippe had brought her from Paris. To a creature of her dimensions, the swamp was a dark, dangerous place.

"Yes," she said. "We'll need to bring my people."

She picked up a small dark-brown bear, the one possession Philippe had thought to bring for her when they'd escaped down the servant's stairs of his old apartment. He'd brought nothing for himself. "You'll need to carry Roger."

Roger was a huge stuffed rabbit, half-again as big as she was. Harold would only be able to carry him in his mouth… and he'd be soaked and torn by the time they arrived wherever they were going, but she wouldn't leave him behind. The enormous reptile obediently popped his head into the hut and emerged with the rabbit held gingerly in his teeth.

"It might be better if we tied him to your neck," she said.

This operation complete, she mounted behind the bunny and told Harold to set off into the swamp.

Poupée wanted to look forward, not glance back at the small shack where she'd lived and where she'd decided to murder her creator.

She failed.

***

Inland.

The jungle went quiet when they passed. Poupée could hear the sounds of birds, insects and even the occasional tree-dwelling monkeys off in the distance, but none of the sounds originated nearby. The dwellers of this forest were well aware of Harold, it seemed. And it was no wonder: his tail trailed behind them, several times the length of a human and much larger than anything in the swamp. It was a tail that corresponded perfectly with Harold's teeth.

Within an hour, the swamp gave way to a muddy river, just deep enough for them to navigate, but with a definite current. Harold's tail went from being a useless, dragged-along appendage, to a navigational aid as he moved it from side to side to propel himself forward.

"Wait," Poupée said. "Stop here."

"Why? What happened?" the dragon rumbled.

"Look there. A snare. That means that there are people nearby."

They sat silently, listening as only two creatures brought up in a jungle could. Birds and insects chirped happily in the distance, but not nearby. It was clear that something had disturbed the natural rhythm of the jungle—but Poupée couldn't quite figure out what had done so.

There! A ripple, small and subtle but completely out of place, drifted in from a slight inlet where the shallows were obscured by mangrove growth.

Harold, following his instincts, turned toward the movement. All thoughts of stealth were forgotten as he advanced toward the origin of the rogue wave.

A small form scurried between the mangroves, emerged from another inlet and ran across the shallows, in the direction from which they'd come. Poupée realized it was a small girl, perhaps eight or nine years old, dressed in the typical hodgepodge attire of the Gabonese villagers—in her case a pair of faced pink shorts and a t-shirt that may have once been white.

"Quick, after her! We can't let her get back to the village!"

Harold didn't wait for further instructions and leapt into motion.

That was one of the nice things about the dragon. Poupée knew that he trusted her implicitly, and would jump at any command she gave. It was the kind of loyalty that was rewarded by safety. Harold seemed to understand, without being told, that the tiny monkey-like creature would always protect him from dangers the dragon didn't even know existed.

Harold's trust was well placed. Poupée knew that, if the girl made it back to her village with tales of dragons and goblins—or whatever other derogatory moniker Poupée herself would merit—it would bring the townsfolk out in force. And even a creature the size of Harold wouldn't last long against armed humans.

The small form weaved between the tangled mass of undergrowth along the riverbank, making it impossible for Harold to catch her—and Poupée wouldn't stand a chance, even against a human as small as the girl they were pursuing.

"There, go through that gap in the trees and get onto the shore. We'll force her back into the river."

Harold obeyed, crashing through the opening and into a small trail behind the first line of trees. Poupée thought the trail looked ominously human-made, but she kept quiet. If they did run into someone, it would only make a bad situation worse.

As expected, the little girl shrieked and dove into the water. "Now! Back in the river!"

But it wasn't quite so easy. The next gap in the trees was thirty meters ahead, and Poupée could only grind her tiny, mismatched teeth in frustration as the girl swam towards the far bank.

When they were finally able to reach the river, she realized that their prey had reached a small grassy islet in the center of the current, and climbed into the branches of its only tree, high enough that Harold couldn't reach her.

They swam lazily to the bank and Hubert placed his head on the shore so Poupée could walk onto dry land without getting her feet wet—ironic considering that, after the splash-filled chase, she was drenched from head to toe.

Poupée looked up at the girl, who was attempting to use the foliage to conceal herself, with pathetically ineffective results. "I can see you, you know," she said.

Large eyes stared down at her. "Are you a spirit? Are you going to bewitch me so your dragon can eat me?"

Poupée paused. That had hit a little too close to home—being eaten by the dragon was definitely in the girl's future, if they managed to get her down. "No. I only want to talk to you."

"You sure look like a spirit to me."

The girl spoke the local patois, but since it was rooted in French, Poupée had little difficulty understanding her, but still wondered whether she wasn't misinterpreting the word for "spirit". She'd read every book that Dr. Philippe had in his library back at the hut, and she had looked at herself in the mirror dozens of times every day. She knew that most of the people in those books would have called her a monster, and been disgusted by her. That was how humans acted to those that were ugly and deformed.

This girl should have been one of the first to call her a monster. After all, she would have no way of knowing that

Poupée actually represented a triumph of science over nature—the creation of an intelligent being from printed DNA. She shouldn't be able to see past the ugliness to ask herself how Poupée had come to be.

"Harold won't hurt you. Come down."

"I don't believe you."

"Harold, please move away from us. Go onto the other side of he river."

The dragon did as she asked. They both knew that, without trees in the way, Harold could cross the few meters separating them in the blink of en eye—quickly enough to protect Popupée if that became necessary. He could also very easily catch and devour the girl before she had a chance to climb back up. But the girl wouldn't know that.

"Will you come down now?" Poupée asked.

The girl stared at the dragon, and for some moments it seemed like she wouldn't move. But then, deciding that she'd be safe, she clambered down with the same agility she'd shown going up.

She stood, her back to the trunk of the tree, staring at Popuée with wonder and more than a little fear visible in her face.

"Are you a spirit of the jungle, or of the river?"

"Neither. I am…" words failed Poupée. How could she explain to a child that she was the product of advanced genetic engineering carried out by a rogue scientist who'd ended up in Gabon after fleeing the French authorities? "My name is Poupée."

The girl giggled at that. The word "poupée" meant "doll" in Dr. Philippe's native French, and the name had seemed fitting to his twisted sense of humor. It seemed that that was one of the words that had made it into the local patois. "Yes, the man who created me thought it would be funny to name me after a doll. I am small and ugly after all."

"You're not ugly," the girl said. "But you're funny."

Poupée studied the girl and cursed her limited experience with human expressions. Though she'd studied every nuance of Philippe's facial movements, she'd only caught glimpses of others, usually from concealment that made it as difficult for her to see the people as it did for the people to see her. But even with these limitations, she convinced herself that there was no trace of disgust evident. There was laughter and wonder—and the fear was still present despite the humor—but no disgust.

"What's your name?"

"Shanel," the girl replied, uncertainty taking over again.

"Do you live nearby?"

"I live three villages down the river."

Poupée thought about that. It would take the girl a couple of hours to reach her village and tell the people there what she'd seen, and that might be enough to keep them safe. On the other hand, she could stop at one of the nearer villages and raise the alarm. Harold was big, but not big enough to fend off an armed mob.

It seemed that there was no choice. The girl had to be silenced. It was for the best, and besides, Harold hadn't eaten since they'd set out. Poupée gestured and suddenly, before the girl even had time to scream, the dragon had materialized, knocked her to the floor and immobilized her on the ground with one gigantic foot.

"Let me go! Help! I was right, you're monsters!"

"No one can hear you," Popuée said. "You took us quite far from the villages. And we're not monsters." Poupée felt that she had to explain herself, despite everything the world had done to her—actions that had sealed this girl's fate. "We just can't risk you telling anyone about us."

"I won't tell anyone, I promise!"

"We can't take that risk."

"I wouldn't lie to a spirit."

"I'm sorry." Poupée began to turn away, not wanting to watch, even if it was necessary. Dr. Philippe, after all, had been directly to blame for her condition. This girl was only guilty of being human.

"No, please! Who could I tell? I'm running away."

"Wait Harold!"

"What?" Harold asked, claws already extended to deliver the killing blow, already savoring the morsel in his mind. "Why?"

The girl had fainted when Harold spoke.

"Just stop. I want to ask her something."

"But she's already dead. Look. She isn't moving. Let me eat her now before she gets cold."

"She's not dead. Just wait." Poupée walked to the river and tried to capture some water in her misshapen hands. She threw it over the girls face like they always did in the books.

The girl moaned and opened an eye. Seeing them, she tried to sit up suddenly, but Harold still had her firmly pinned to the grass.

"What are you running away from?"

The girl just looked at them, eyes wide, nearly panicked.

"Answer me, or I will have to let Harold eat you after all."

"I'm running from my village. From my mother…" she stopped, a sob breaking through. "From Louis."

"Who is Louis? Is he your father?"

"No!" the girl replied vehemently. She spat. "Louis is my mother's… I'm not sure what he is. He gets drunk and comes to our house sometimes, late at night when I'm asleep. My mother opens the door for him. I think she's afraid to not have a man. She hasn't been the same since my father died. Sometimes she begs him to leave, other times she laughs and says she's been waiting for him. But she always opens the door when he comes. At first I pretended to be asleep, but one day I couldn't take it and I screamed at him to leave. But he didn't leave, he just laughed and…" The girl broke down again but tried to go on, tried to keep the flood of words flowing. "And ever since that time, they wake me up and…"

This time she truly couldn't continue she cried and cried, seemingly forgetting that she was about to die.

Poupée looked around. This was taking much too long. This wasn't a particularly populous branch of the river, but it couldn't be long before someone came along. If they had to kill too many humans, discovery pursuit would not be far behind.

She was torn. They had to kill this girl. There was no option. Everyone would respond to them the same way she had: they were monsters to the people of this forest. But she couldn't give Harold the order for some reason.

And then she knew why. She remembered clearly the girl's wonder and fear at seeing them, but most of all, she remembered the lack of disgust.

"You will have to come with us," Poupée told her. "And you can't talk to any humans."

"And you won't kill me?"

"Harold will kill you if you try to run away from us. He will kill you if you scream. He will kill you if you try to talk to anyone. And he'll kill you right now if you don't come with us."

"All right. I'll go with you." She got up as Harold removed his foot. "But where are we going?"

"We're going as deep into the forest as this stream will take us." She tried to look at the girl kindly, but her face really wasn't much good at expressions. "You see, we're running away, too."

The girl brightened as if they'd suddenly become best friends. "Then it's good that I'm coming! Who are you running from?"

"Everyone." For a fleeting second, Poupée wondered if she was making the biggest mistake of her short life… and then wondered if everything wouldn't end up all right after all. "Come on, we have to move. And come here—if you're going to be coming with us, I need to introduce you to my people. They aren't much to look at now, but should clean up OK once they dry out."

"Dry out?"

Harold snorted impatiently, but refrained from eating the girl while Poupée introduced the stuffed animals. He even let the girl climb on his back with only a token amount of grumbling.

As they set off down the river, Poupée reflected that such an odd assortment was just the kind of group one would expect to be put together by a half-baked genetic experiment.

It could, she reflected, have been worse.

A POSITION OF POWER

In the introduction to "Eyes in the Vastness of Forever", I mentioned that I'd suffered some trepidation in setting stories in my home country of Argentina. By the time I wrote "A Position of Power", I was confident I could pull it off, not only well enough for international audiences, but also for my own countrymen.

Of course, I cheated a little, and while the Argentine temperament is well represented here, the rest of the world has traveled a very different path.

This one was originally published in *The Worlds of Science Fiction, Fantasy and Horror, Volume 3*.

"Bon jour, inspector."

"Bon soir." The Frenchman shrugged apologetically. "I'm sorry that my Spanish is not nearly as good as I might wish."

"And you just used up all of my French," the commissioner responded. "Fortunately, Alberto here is very good at his job. His mother was French, you know." The two men turned to look at the translator, who squirmed a little in their direct gaze. He was obviously a man who preferred to do his job from the background, balding and dressed in trousers and a shirt made of the coarse cloth that all the laborers in Buenos Aires wore. "We should be able to avoid any unfortunate misunderstandings that might lead to unpleasantness."

The inspector pulled a pair of spectacles from his nose and wiped them slowly. "I am not necessarily here to avoid unpleasantness. I am here to make sure that my Emperor receives all the information he needs… and that the responsible parties are not protected by elements inside the city walls."

"You shall have our full assistance. We've all seen your balloons up there in the sky, waiting to rain death on our unprotected people. I assure you that there will be no protection of any sort. Ask for anything you need, and my men will get it for you."

"Thank you," the inspector said, and left, with Alberto on his heels.

As soon as the door closed, Commissioner Fernández looked to the heavens and swore at every member of the Napoleonic line, up to and including the current blot on society, Napoleon V. Then he stopped to wonder why in the world, at the dawn of the new century, this glorious twentieth century in the Lord's light, American powers still had to make way for the decadent French imperialists.

He also wondered what would happen if he allowed the steam cannons to fire on the airships, but only in passing. Other cities had been foolish enough to do so, and the conclusion was that airships were harder to hit than cities.

He sighed and ordered his secretary to bring over the rest of the day's work.

***

The inspector moved through the throng of the station-house, avoiding rushing clerks and excited young constables with the dexterity of long practice, seeming perfectly at ease in the chaos of that warren of corridors and offices. The familiarity in his motion was completely at odds with the imperial blue cape and luxurious moustache, elements that clearly indicated that this was a man who did not belong there, among the drab policemen of Buenos Aires.

Finally, a draught of fresh air hit them through the doorway and the Frenchman inhaled deeply. "It is so strange to find a city whose air smells sweet," he said. "You are blessed to have done away with horses altogether."

"It is hard on those who cannot afford to travel, especially when they have to leave the city, Monsieur l'Inspecteur," the translator responded.

The inspector gave him an appraising look. "We shall be

together for a few days. Surely we do not need to be so formal? I know your name is Alberto, I would prefer it if you could call me Philippe."

"I would be honored," Alberto replied, and they shook hands.

"Good. The commissioner tells me that you will be a good guide to the city, especially to the area where my unfortunate countryman was killed. He says you have helped the police before on little errands, and that all his officers know you well."

The translator nodded.

"Excellent. We have little time to waste. Let us make haste to the place where the body was found. Did I understand correctly, that the officer who made the discovery will be there to walk us through the scene?"

"Yes, Monsieur Philippe. Also, the scene has not been touched since the murder. You will be able to see it as it was when the body was discovered." Philippe was interested to see the pride of this translator in the work of the police. But all of a sudden, doubt crept into his features. "Except for the body, of course. They moved the body the first day. Is that all right?"

"Of course. Perfectly all right."

It seemed to be a relief for the other man. They walked along in silence, and the inspector observed the translator. He was young enough, not much over thirty, and looked strong—not muscled like a dock worker but lithe and wiry. The inspector wondered why he had chosen to help the police force at arm's length instead of joining. Also, he wondered about the man's French. It immediately reminded him of the docks of Marseilles—and that was enough to put any French policeman on edge.

"Ah, here we are," Alberto said.

They had reached a stone wall two stories high with a polished brass door in it. The door was clearly designed to withstand attack, as it was thick and reinforced. The translator rapped it four times with his knuckles and it opened inward, revealing itself to be six inches thick. A man in a round cap and grey coveralls peered through the opening and asked a question.

Alberto spoke with him at length, and showed him an orange card. "Could you please pass me your credentials," the translator said. Philippe fanned out all the official papers that had been issued to him upon entering Buenos Aires. The translator chose a bright green card similar to the orange one and showed it to the man.

The man's face was transformed immediately. He babbled at the Frenchman, falling all over himself in an effort to get out of the way and to let them in. He showed them each nook of the passageway beyond the door, and Alberto kept up a running translation.

"This is where they keep the boilers. Actually, they are under ground, because the pressure is so huge, and if they were above ground, an explosion would kill thousands… behind that other door, there is an access tunnel for pipe maintenance. Over there we have the safety valves… and here, here is the cannon room."

The corridor had opened into an impressive stone-lined courtyard in which stood the largest cannon Philippe had ever seen. Painted dull black and at least five stories tall, it stood on a platform of steel.

"Most of it is also underground, but this is the part that is maneuverable. See the joints, there, and there?"

Philippe had heard of this marvel—who, indeed, had not?—but the idea of crossing the city this way seemed absurd. And yet, it was reputed to be utterly safe.

The man in the cap deferentially assisted them in entering a small cylinder through another thick door in its side. Within the cylinder, there were eight seats, and they were ushered onto seats opposite each other, which the man explained was a way of keeping the capsule balanced. He added, with a touch of pride, that their tests had shown that the balance made no difference anyway.

As the man worked a series of buckles and harnesses, Philippe nearly panicked, nearly screamed to be let out, but when he saw how calmly Alberto accepted his fate, he was shamed into adopting a façade of stoic tranquility. "You'll enjoy this," the translator confided. "It's one of the few things Paris doesn't have."

There was a reason Paris lacked a steam cannon transport system and that was the fact that the middle class would never have accepted a type of transport reserved exclusively for officialdom and the elite. Here in Buenos Aires, however, the complete subjugation of the masses made that a non-issue, allowing them to enjoy their wonder in peace.

The door slammed with finality, leaving them in sudden darkness. Philippe's heart beat like a whole regiment of drums, and he could feel it almost in his throat. Sweat accumulated under his arms as a series of clunks and bumps could be felt through the hull. Blessed stillness and silence allowed him to relax, but only until he remembered what it meant. Then he nearly cried out that he wanted to leave.

It wasn't bravery that stopped him from begging off. It was the fact that the capsule suddenly moved as though it had been kicked by a giant. All the air was removed from his lungs, and screaming for mercy was rendered impossible. Then there was silence—or rather, not silence, but a soft rushing of air and a strange feeling of weightlessness—and Philippe knew that they were suspended in midair, that their lives depended now on the mathematics of the ballistics team and the integrity of the nets on the far end. He held his breath until forced to inhale, then did so only under strict control. Panic was a deep breath away.

Suddenly, with a jolt as sickening as that which initiated their trip, it came to a shuddering halt. Philippe thought his neck must have been torn from its roots, and that his eyes certainly must have ruptured in their sockets. He would have bruises all over his body tomorrow.

But that was a small price to pay for the fact that they were at rest. At rest and alive. He allowed himself to breathe again, as the jots and thumps of the crane lowered them into an upright position.

Much to his chagrin, Alberto was smiling in a knowing way. "It's actually much nicer now that they've installed the damper systems in the capsules. They used to flood the capsules with water to keep the initial acceleration from the cannon from breaking your bones. If you didn't seal your oversuit correctly, you'd get where you wanted but you wouldn't be dry. A lot of people actually preferred to walk in the winter."

They left the cabin and, barely glancing back at the huge metallic catch-nets of the station, emerged into a sea of people, all heading south. The architecture, the people and even the air itself bore witness to the fact that they had left the genteel surroundings of the administrative center, and had entered a working-class area. Actually not a working class area, but a working area, Philippe reminded himself. The working classes, after all, were not permitted to live within Buenos Aires' brass walls.

"These people, where are they going?" Philippe asked. He knew the answer, knew the barbaric customs, but wanted his guide to tell him what he knew. After all, one could never predict where the knowledge to break open a murder case might come from.

"They are going towards the south gate, the one by the Riachuelo. They have a little less than forty-five minutes to reach the exit, but we are near enough that they should make it easily."

"And if they don't?"

Alberto shrugged. "Well, it depends on who catches them. If it's an official, they will simply have their red cards revoked and won't be able to enter the city to work any more. A Sweeper might accept a bribe… but a Sweeper might kill them, too, just to stay in practice."

As the crowd passed, Philippe smelled the air. The unmistakable odor of damp—damp walls, damp floor, damp cobbles—told him what he needed to know even though the wind was blowing in the wrong direction: they were near the rivers, the place where the Riachuelo drained into the Rio de La Plata. The place the government called La Boca, and the locals called Tangolandia. The neighborhood where the man from Marseilles had been killed.

"This way," the translator said.

Philippe followed him through the crowd, moving against the flow, and getting resentful glances from anyone near enough to notice. It seemed that the poor weren't particularly happy with the way things were. They soon turned off the avenue, into a street that ran between gaily painted wooden houses, and finally down a broad staircase that led to an arched cellar. Three uniformed policemen were standing beside a large boiler at one end of the room. The area around them was illuminated by the flame of a single lantern.

"This is where he was found," Alberto said.

"I thought this was where he was killed."

"Yes, that is what I meant. He was killed three nights ago. They found him the following morning. You have arrived very quickly." There was awe in that voice, and Philippe did nothing to lay it to rest. The rumor that the Empire could respond immediately to any insults would aid them in the long run—and therefore it was unnecessary to clear up any misconceptions about the speed of French Airhsips.

"Who found him?"

"A young boy, maybe seven years old, there was no way he could have struck him with enough force to… to kill him that way."

"Where did the young boy come from?"

The translator hesitated but went off to speak to the policemen. They conversed for a few moments, and then one of them accompanied Alberto to where Philippe waited. "The boy is one of the couriers for the steam station further up these lines," the policeman said nervously. "The offices often employ them because they never seem to get tired, running from one place to another."

"But the body was found at four in the morning. Surely the gates are not open at that hour? Would an office boy be in possession of a citizen's pass?" Without one, the detective knew, it was illegal to be inside the city walls at night.

The policeman and the translator exchanged glances. Philippe wondered whether what they were hiding was important information or just petty corruption. It was always the same; even within the Empire, the further one got from Paris, the less laws meant to the people. In places where Napoleonic law failed to assert itself it was even worse.

"No, Monsieur," the translator said. "The boy clearly should not have been there."

"And did no one ask him why he was there?"

The policeman responded: "No. Since he was clearly not the murderer, and had done his duty in reporting the body, the officer on patrol chose instead to preserve the evidence. The boy ran off, and hasn't been heard from since."

Interesting, Philippe thought, but just nodded, as if dismissing the boy's existence as immaterial. "Do you mind if I look around?"

The policeman looked a bit confused. "I thought that was why you came," he stammered.

"Yes, it is," Philippe replied, and walked towards the corner where the officers had been standing earlier. He pointed to a small area where a dark patch of rust could be seen on the ground even in the uncertain light of the lamp. "Is this where he was found?"

"Yes, sir."

The policemen cooperated fully, and Philippe immediately

understood why. The man from Marseilles might have been found there. He might even have been killed there, but any evidence that might have been left in the dust by a careless criminal had been obliterated by the passage of what seemed to be hundreds of people. In places, the dust was almost all gone—probably on the soles of countless police shoes.

He wondered whether it had been deliberate; after all, any flat-footed gendarme who demolished a crime scene this thoroughly in Paris would have been sent back to the farm immediately. However, he dismissed the idea: the Argentine police had nothing to gain from covering up that he could discern—and quite a lot to lose. Until he could find a motive to suspect them, he would have to assume their incompetence.

But he didn't have to accept it gracefully. "I wonder," he said to the nearest policeman, the only one who'd spoken to him thus far. "Did you destroy the crime scene on purpose, or do you employ elephants for constables?"

The translator stumbled over the second part in his surprise.

Instead of being moved to anger, though, the policeman just shrugged. "Actually, we generally don't pay much attention to these dock killings. This man had no ticket—he shouldn't have been here at all, not after dark, anyway. The first officer at the scene probably thought he'd run afoul of one of the Sweepers, and that we'd get a bounty call later. It was mid-morning before anyone realized that this guy might be important."

Of course, no one had bothered to tell Philippe that a visit to the crime scene would be a waste of his time. They probably loved packing foreigners into that cannon of theirs and shooting them all over the city, just to see which would vomit.

"And how did you manage to figure that out?"

"Well, he got a crowd. Bodies in the morning don't draw crowds anymore, but this guy…"

"Yes?"

"Well, this guy was a bit of a celebrity. Everyone knows

El Francés. Or they knew him," the constable finished with a grin.

"El Francés means the Frenchman, right?"

"Yes," Alberto replied.

"So this was the end of Jean-Claude Dornier; killed anonymously by some bruiser in a cellar at the end of the world." He turned to the cop who'd been silent so far. "And did you know that he was working for the Emperor?"

The officer sputtered, and Philippe waited patiently for the translation. "We knew we had to stay away from him, but we didn't really know why."

"And the people he met?"

"Yes, them as well. We knew they were important, but most of us didn't know why. Sometimes policemen would be requested to escort valuables, or stand guard outside a meeting room, but most of us never knew what was going on. Mostly, they took place on French ships, or in the warehouses."

"So, just guards, then?" Philippe waited as Alberto relayed the question to the policeman, and also as the man took his time to respond. The translator turned to the Frenchman.

"Sometimes they were also requested as messengers. They took packages to various addresses, sometimes nearby, at others as far away as Belgrano." The man seemed to remember himself. "Belgrano is a neighborhood in the northern half of the city, where some of the wealthier merchants have their homes."

Philippe nodded. He'd studied the map of the city for two hours the night before—he'd suspected that the case would soon move away from the docks and into the upper crust. After all, he knew the dead man by reputation if not in person—a distant cousin of the Emperor's who'd been offered a post as a special envoy on the other side of the world in order to keep certain peccadillos out of the public eye—and he believed that he wouldn't be the kind to be satisfied with a civil servant's salary. And with contacts in France, there would be merchants who wanted to do business.

"I'd like to speak to González Guereño."

"What?" The translator's eyes grew wide. It was clear that he'd been caught by surprise by Philippe's knowledge of the name, and only managed to bite back follow-up questions with an effort. "We would have to check if he's available."

"Is it possible that he might not be available for an Emissary of the French Empire?" Philippe enjoyed watching them squirm. It was clear that they didn't want to bother any of the commercial barons in their Belgrano mansions, but were not brave enough to defy their orders. They were probably also wondering where the detective had gotten the name—and were probably afraid of which other names the detective might have.

"Oh, I'm certain they would never dream of that. But we'll need to get hold of him, and he might not be in town."

"I have a better idea. Let's go knock on the door."

They paled, but nodded. Quick learners. But only Alberto came with him—the other cops were probably headed towards the merchant's house, to warn him of the official scrutiny coming his way.

"Would you like to take the tram?" Alberto asked him.

Philippe wondered what the merchant needed to be warned about, wondered why they were going out of their way to get to the man first. He smiled benevolently. "I think we should take the cannon. It isn't to my taste, but something tells me that time is of the essence." He winked at the translator.

The trip back was just as nauseating as the first one, and Philippe was only just able to keep his food down, but at least this time they landed in a pleasant park-like area from which the river was visible in the distance. Plus, there was no way that the cops at the dock could have beat them there. They might have been able to signal—although Philippe hadn't seen any signs of telegraphy—but the most likely scenario was that the merchant would be unaware of their coming.

The servant certainly was, at any rate. The liveried black man who opened the door of the mansion clearly wasn't expecting to find an official delegation on his master's doorstep that late in the afternoon. His attempts to stall them hadn't been coached, and despite Alberto's difficulty in putting forth the arguments, the evident fact that Philippe was not going anywhere eventually got them invited inside.

Guillermo González Guereño was a man in his mid forties whose blond hair had all but abandoned his head, with just a few wisps remaining along the edges. He didn't look particularly happy to see them there but also didn't seem particularly concerned. His handshake was firm, but brief.

Having weighed the man, Philippe looked around. The room they were in—some sort of drawing room, perhaps specifically designed for meetings such as that one, was a dark-paneled room in the English style (Philippe dismissed the possibility of an attempt by the servant to insult them by bringing them into that room). There was a small automaton of the sort that had been in vogue in Paris a few years before—a thing of clattering brass and rubber tubing, powered by the house's internal steam pressure—crawling about in a glass cabinet on the central table. Chairs upholstered in dark leather completed the room, which seemed almost excessively masculine.

"I am here to discuss the murder of Jean-Claude Dornier," Philippe said without preamble.

Guereño received the demand with a neutral expression, the only movement a slight glance in the translator's direction, as if to verify that he's heard correctly. "I heard he'd been killed, but I can assure you that I can't be of much help with any of the details. Surely the police have all the information you could need."

"Well," Philippe paused, "they do and they don't. They were extremely helpful in showing me where he was killed, and in explaining their theories of how he was killed, but neither of those could ever lead me to the killer—I think the key lies in why he was killed. Once we understand that, we won't need to go far to find our killer. I believe you might be able to help me with that."

"Me? I have no idea why he was killed." Guereño finally showed some emotion, a little bit of anger around the edges. Good, Philippe thought, the man was playing his part as expected.

"So you're saying that there was no reason for him to have been killed? No one would have wanted to kill him?"

Guereño started to say something, but paused. Alberto didn't even bother to translate the truncated phrase. "Of course there are people with reasons to kill him. It kind of came with his business."

"And what would you know of his business?"

"A man in my position has to deal with many people. Dornier was very good at getting stuck wheels to move again."

"Meaning he would take care of your bribes when something was detained at the port in France?"

"I don't know how he did it. All I know is that he would take his fee, and the paperwork would appear as if by magic. As you know, everything I do must be legal, or I stand to lose quite a bit. I can't take any risks with my position. So I need those papers."

Philippe thought it strange that a man in the import-export business would be so risk-averse. That wasn't how one built an empire, bought a mansion in one of the great metropoli. All importers were smugglers, and most were pirates, and everyone knew it, which meant that either Guereño had become a little too enamored of his wealth and status or he was lying.

And, strangely, Philippe didn't think he was lying.

"So, to get merchandise into France, you had to go through him." Paris was the world's largest market for... everything.

"Getting merchandise in wasn't my problem. Getting it out was more of an issue—the real profit comes on selling in Buenos

Aires at the outrageous prices we can charge here, at the nether-end of the world."

"And what happened if things didn't go through him? Were there problems at this end, too?"

"I wouldn't know about that. El Francés was always involved from the start."

Philippe said nothing.

"Perhaps he controlled the dock gangs here, but I wouldn't really know if that were so, or why. After all, all he had was connections of some sort in Marseille. Not much of a power base if you ask me."

The arrogance of the rich, and the cluelessness that came with it was always a surprise. Here was a man able to create and control a commercial empire with tentacles in various continents who seemed unable to grasp the way the real world worked.

"So you think it might be possible that he was murdered by someone who wanted to take over the gangs on this end?"

"That seems logical, although it wouldn't be worth much unless he was connected in Marseilles as well. After all, it's the most important port—and the airship freight to Paris all goes through there."

"And you don't know any of his contacts on the French side?"

"Of course not. Without wanting to give offense," Guereño began, the lie visible in his eyes, "all Frenchmen are either too proud or too arrogant to learn any other language—and I don't speak a word of French."

"Perhaps you are too proud or too arrogant as well."

Guereño smiled. "Perhaps. Do you have any more questions?"

"Only one: who do you think murdered Dornier?"

"Someone with the connections and the knowledge to take his place." He smiled. "I suppose he will pop up sooner or later, offering to help solve troublesome import issues. I might even know before you do."

"Oh, I doubt that very much," Philippe replied.

The doorman let them out.

***

On the street again, Philippe turned to Alberto. "He's right, you know."

"About what, Monsieur?" the translator inquired politely.

"That the man who killed Dornier would be his logical successor. It's really a pity that Dornier turned out to be important, that was the only piece the murderer was missing. Who would have expected the murder of a mere dockside criminal to create an international incident? It would have, it should have been a single morning's entertainment for the poor in La Boca, and forgotten within a week." Philippe shook his head. "Instead, here we are with inspectors from France making a mess of things. One almost pities the criminal mastermind."

"One almost does."

"After all, whoever tries to fill the Dornier-shaped void will immediately come under suspicion, unless the murderer is caught first. And the government of France is not stupid enough that it will accept some stand-in, caught in order to take the fall for this. Even a man as dull as Guereño knew that only a very specific type of person could have profited from this particular crime."

"Obviously," Alberto replied.

"So my question is: what are you going to do now? Are you going to run, or are you going to try to brazen it out?"

Alberto began to respond. Philippe held up a hand.

"Yes. You do know what I'm talking about. And no, I'm not insane. So unless you really, really want to go through with that charade, let's dispense with it. I imagine you are impatient to get moving."

The translator was white as a sheet. "How…"

"You should have paid more attention when I spoke to your police chief. I never said that I didn't speak Spanish: I only said that it wasn't as good as I might wish. I understand Spanish perfectly. Well enough, in fact, to note what you omitted when you translated stories, well enough to note that the dockside cops spoke to you with more reverence than they did to me, and well enough to notice when you asked them to tell me things that they knew you already knew."

Alberto's hand went towards his coat pocket.

"Are you suicidal?" Philippe asked. "I don't yet know how high this goes, but I can assure you that if anything at all happens to me on your watch, you will be turned over to the French, and you will be turned over to the French in a coffin. If you run now, perhaps some of the official protection you still enjoy will be enough to keep you alive." Philippe looked him straight in the eyes, unafraid. "Run along now."

Alberto hesitated only for a moment. Then he turned and fled unceremoniously around the nearest corner.

Philippe smiled. The man would be easy enough to find; his mind worked in predictable patterns. The only real problem would be those damnable cannons. Why couldn't Buenos Aires have a subway system like a normal city?

He walked in the general direction of the police station, composing his report in his head. After all, he couldn't just say that he allowed the criminal to escape so that he could spend a little time there, could he?

THE BARBER OF MANAUS

Another tale set in Brazil, this one explores a city I find fascinating: Manaus, set on the banks of the Amazon in the middle of the jungle. Like Brasilia, it seems to me to be the epitome of a country in nation-building mode, forcing it's people to live in the most illogical of places.

It's a quieter piece, and was originally published by *Little Blue Marble*.

Felipe Santos da Silva swallowed. His palms were slick with sweat and he wasn't certain whether it was due to the tropical heat or his nerves.

He looked at the city that, twenty years earlier, had been a boomtown, the jewel of the Amazon rain forest. But then the population decline that had started in the early 2030s had begun to take its toll. Today, there was no one on the street. The encroaching vegetation was reclaiming the asphalt.

He pushed open the door.

The large wooden panel squeaked as it moved. Wind disturbed dust and paper in the foyer. There was a time when someone's head would have rolled for such things. He sighed.

The staff was gathered in the auditorium, thirty people lost among the hundreds of seats inside the Amazon Theater. Built in the 19th century to host the high society of the time—and to bring Caruso to the Amazon—the majestic, gilt-and-plush room seemed too grand to hold these men and women in worn grey work clothes.

"What's the news, Felipão?" Simona asked. Big and boisterous, she was the self-appointed spokesperson for the staff.

Felipe shook his head, unable to speak.

Alarm broke out on the faces in front of him.

"Are they going to shut us down?" Joao asked.

Felipe found his voice. "No. But they're not going to pay us any more. We're allowed to stay on as volunteers, but there's no more funding for the opera house."

Shock rippled through his audience. "But this is a national treasure. They can't close it."

"Tell that to Brasilia," Felipe said, no longer able to hide the bitterness.

"What did you tell them?" the person speaking was Andrés, a mulatto who'd come in from Sao Paulo five years before.

"They didn't let me tell them anything. They sent me a letter."

"Call someone. Tell them about us."

"There's no one to call."

"There has to be someone."

"I don't know who."

"Some director you turned out to be." He man stormed out, followed immediately by a couple of others. Others trickled away, giving him regretful looks as they did so, but leaving all the same.

They knew how Brazil worked. On one hand, one heard stories of the state paying people for jobs that no longer existed until the day they died. But once it acted, that same bureaucracy ensured that decisions were irrevocable. It took so long to get anything done that it was often better just to walk away. His former employees knew that.

When the exodus ended, fewer than ten people remained. Every single one of the faces looking back at him had been employed in the theater before he arrived. Most of them had been born in Manaus and had families there.

"What will we do?" Simona said.

"I don't know. Maybe you should go to Rio like everyone else."

"This is my home. I'll stay here and live on a boat if I have to. I won't leave."

The rest nodded their agreement. They knew about life in

the big cities. Better to be poor where one could maintain one's dignity than packed into a teeming shantytown.

Another woman spoke up, one of the few stagehands still on staff. Her peers had resigned in disgust when it was announced that there would be no more national productions, that the theater would only be open to local plays. "Why are they doing this to us?"

How to explain to her that the migration to the megacities that had emptied the streets had also opened the door to the ecologists who wanted to return the Amazon basin to its native state? How could someone born and raised in a city, and who'd lived their entire life there, understand that they were actually the expression of an ancient colonial aggression, and therefore not worthy of the government's money?

"The world is changing," was all he said in reply.

"Can't you do anything?"

Felipe nearly said no and turned away, leaving his former employees to dwell on his failure.

But the thought about what he would do next stopped him. What prospects did a fifty-five year-old director of a failed opera house in a vanishing city have in a place like Rio? He would disappear into the slums, never to be heard from again.

"I think I have an idea," Felipe said.

Heads turned his way, the faintest glimmer of hope visible under the despair.

"What?"

"How would you," he took a quick count, "just the nine of you, plus myself, feel about becoming the owners of the theater?"

"That's stupid. What would we do with it?"

"To start with, we could live here and maintain it. Then we could see about staging plays."

He could see the gears in their heads turning over. Each of them seemed to be thinking about their own homes —most of them were in bad areas which flooded and often consisted of two or three small rooms—and comparing them with the grandeur and luxury of even the smallest of the theatre's chambers… and there was more than one room available for everyone, with rooms to spare.

"But the government…"

"They only said they would stop paying me, but I'm still the director. The deed to the land is in the vault in my office. They left it here when they closed the last bank. If I can find a notary public, I can transfer the property to anyone I like. It's within the authority of the position although, admittedly, it's a bit unconventional." No previous director would have dreamed of it.

"They'll throw you in jail."

"Perhaps." Felipe didn't think so. If any bureaucrat even noticed the transfer of what was now officially jungle land to a small group of locals, they'd likely approve. If not, he would face the consequences. "But by then it will be too late. Should I go get the deed?"

Simona smiled. "Yes, please."

GUALICHO DAYS

I once wrote a story called "Tehuelche" which was probably my most successful story ever, readership wise. It was picked up by Pearson for one of their test cycles and hundreds of thousands of Texas high schoolers were forced to answer questions about it. It doesn't appear here because it is neither science fiction nor fantasy, but it is related to the story that comes next. "Gualicho Days" is one of my takes about what happened after "Tehuelche" ends.

I didn't think Pearson would want this one for their test cycles, so I offered it to Third Flatiron for their *Not Superstitious* antho. Luckily for me, they liked it and published it!

In a hospital in Patagonia, an old woman lay dying. She knows the end is near. She can tell from the expressions on her doctor's face, and even by the young woman. She isn't completely certain who the young woman might be, but she can see a certain resemblance to her people despite the much lighter skin and modern clothing. Something in the shape of the lips, or perhaps in the arch of the eyebrows. Or maybe something else—perhaps the spirit of the people shines through even wrong-colored eyes.

It occurs to her that the young woman is a member of her family. She can't quite recall. There are so many things she can't remember these days, and she just can't afford to waste the energy on them. The only important thing is the plea. Without the plea, life would not be worth living. She was proud to never have missed a day of the plea, not once, not since she was a little girl.

The old lady can't tell if the young woman is of her family, or if she is even of her people, but she will have to do. She takes hold of the girl's hand. "Listen well. I must tell you of Kóoch, and how he orders the world, and I must tell you of why he gave the Tehuelche people the responsibility of reminding him to do his work against the ravages of Gualicho. Listen now, my time is short…"

***

Dr. Alejandro Benetti hated this part of the job. "I'm sorry Jimena, but your grandmother passed away early this morning."

Jimena nodded, a slight tightening of her lips the only sign that she was affected by the news. They'd been expecting this for a couple of days at least. "I'm not sure what I have to do now."

"Don't worry. Selena handles all the administrative side. She'll have the paperwork ready in a couple of hours, and we can also arrange the burial, if you want to bury her locally."

"I think that would be best. As far as anyone knows, she never moved more than walking distance from the house where she was born. Esquel is all she ever knew. My mother said that the always insisted that she would stay with her people. They've been gone for years, but she stayed anyway."

"Yes, you told me. The Tehuelche." Benetti paused. What he wanted to say next might not be what a recently bereaved family member wanted to hear, but he decided to risk it anyway. "It was actually an honor to be here, in a sad kind of way. It reminds you that there are bigger things than what we think about every day. I can't imagine a whole civilization just dying out."

She shrugged. "I guess. But they're not really dead. They had children, and those children are just regular Argentines. They're not actually gone."

"But the language. What she was speaking yesterday was Tehuelche, wasn't it?"

"I guess. She was the last known speaker, so only she would really be able to tell us. It did sound like what she used to speak with the other women, back before she quarreled with my mother, so it must have been."

"Do you know what she said?"

"Not at all. I never learned the language."

Alejandro felt the blood run to his head, felt his cheeks grow warm. "I recorded some of it. It just seemed important to get it on audio. It might be the last time in history that those words will be heard. I hope you don't mind."

"I don't mind." And now she hesitated. "Do you think I could see her?"

"Oh, yes. I'm sorry. But are you sure? We'd have to see her in the morgue… wouldn't you prefer to wait until the funeral?"

"Just let me see her."

With that, Dr. Benetti was all business again. He led her through the small hospital to the morgue, and stood beside her as she said her final farewells. Then a group of tourists out rock climbing had stumbled down an incline, and he had contusions and a broken femur to deal with, and the day picked up speed. It would be quite a while before he thought about lost languages again.

***

A few days after the old lady was buried, the deaths began. No one noticed, and most people just shrugged them off. It was understandable.

Ten block's worth of street signs suddenly indicated that the one way street they signaled had changed directions. People who'd been going down that street for years ignored the signs—most of them didn't even notice them. A stranger driving an SUV, however, took it literally, and—just as he was turning in—encountered a number 5 bus full of children on their way to school. The driver and three of the children died in the accident.

A few minutes later, an elevator on the twentieth floor of an office block in Buenos Aires opened, revealing an empty shaft, and sending a pair of hurried market analysts the their deaths.

Gas leaks abounded. Electric wires fell into convenient puddles. People died, and no one, macroscopically speaking, really cared. It was just life.

But someone was eventually bound to notice. This role—perhaps understandably—fell to a young woman in Buenos Aires called Vanesa Federini. She was a journalist's assistant at a newspaper called Crónica, a sensationalist rag whose associated TV channel had become fleetingly famous worldwide for a headline that that said "Multiple dead in accident: two people and a Bolivian".

She was desperately looking for better employment but, in the meantime, she did her job, and did it well. And her job was to investigate the death of a man in a suburb who'd died when a car driven by the owner of a local dry-cleaner had accelerated in a multi-story parking facility and burst through the retaining wall, dropping on his head. The woman driving the car had been pulled out of the wreckage, unconscious, and wasn't expected to recover. It was a bizarre enough occurrence that it merited a trip to the local police station—but not important enough to send a fully accredited journalist.

The police station in Merlo was about what one would expect. Surrounded by run down light-industrial buildings in one of Buenos Aires' less-fashionable areas, it was manned by a single overweight woman with sergeant's stripes on her shoulder. She sat under a 100 watt bulb in a small office and chewed gum as she gave Vanessa a quick once over.

"How can I help you?" she asked—bored, but evidently not bored enough to bother concealing her contempt at the other woman's fashionable clothing, completely out of place anywhere near where they were.

Vanessa outlined the situation, expecting to be tossed out on her ear. To the journalist's surprise, the woman's demeanor changed completely.

"Oh, yes. It's the strangest thing. Did you know they knew each other?"

***

"...so it turns out that she actually had some of his clothes at the dry cleaner. He was actually walking over there to get it when the accident happened."

A single editorial eyebrow raised. "So?"

"It doesn't end there. It seems that the dry-cleaning lady was on the way to her son's kindergarten, where another little boy had been hit by a bus. The driver claims that he was distracted thinking about an accident he'd heard of that morning…"

"Where are you going with this?"

Vanesa paused. "I'm not really sure. The police woman was convinced that there was a chain of strange little connections to each of the deaths we've seen over the last few days. And that each was slightly related to the last. Looks like all the cops are comparing notes, building a chain."

The editor sighed. "And I suppose she told you all of this before you told her you worked for Crónica?"

"If you'd looked into her eyes, you'd believe me."

"And if I had a coin for every time some journo used that overused phrase, I'd be a rich, rich man."

"Look, they mean it. And the police are actually doing it. Won't you let me look into it? They're adamant that there's a connection, just that it's never an obvious one. Never the husband or the brother." She smiled. "Heck, you're the editor of the girl who went to Merlo to look into it. You could be next."

"If I let you look into it, will you go away?"

***

"It's actually a huge opportunity for me. Having actual journalism work on my resume means that I might be able to get a job at a real news outlet."

Ernesto laughed. "Yeah, as long as you don't tell them what you actually did."

"Can't you be supportive, just once? I don't spend all my time throwing mud all over your dreams."

"All right, I'm sorry. Tell me."

"Anyway, the cop lady is looking at me like she's telling me the secrets of the universe, and she whispers that anyone could be next. She says that none of the officers want to work on the case because they're afraid that it might just be enough to set the curse on them."

"The curse… Sorry, go ahead."

"That's what she said. Even when the story runs out of steam, we can run an article on the lack of professionalism in the police force. They believe in malicious spirits who kill people. Not really the kind of people I'd want guarding my security in this city."

"What kind of sprits?"

"The say it's something called a Gualicho."

"I thought that was some kind of spell. Anyway, no one would believe that the cops are really that stupid."

The conversation was interrupted by a loud buzzing. "I'll get it," Ernesto said. He walked to the door, looked through the peephole, then shrugged and opened it.

A huge bang sounded and Ernesto fell to the floor. From the hallway, Vanesa heard voices. "That wasn't Luciano, man, you shot the wrong guy." This was followed by silence, then a single word. "Shit." And then footsteps running down the hall and into the stairwell.

Vanesa ran to her fallen boyfriend, and looked at the bloody mass of entrails that came from the gaping wound in his abdomen. She'd been a journalist's assistant long enough that she could recognize a shotgun wound, and she also knew that pressing her hands to his stomach would do no good.

She did it anyway, crying as she did, watching bubbling blood ooze from between her fingers and out of Ernesto's open mouth. His eyes stared emotionlessly at the wall beside which he'd fallen.

***

Alejandro hugged her, not letting go, allowing Vanesa to cry herself out. It took quite a while, but eventually his brother's young widow managed to get herself under control. Even through her tears, she was an amazingly pretty woman, and he'd always been amazed that Ernesto, the quiet, unassuming one, had managed to convince her to marry him.

"I can't believe he's gone…"

And she broke down again, unable to hold it in.

It was midnight on the night of the funeral when she finally ran out of tears. Alejandro just kept her company, holding her when she needed it, and bringing her occasional cups of coffee. Even when Ernesto and Alejandro's mother begged off to get some sleep, he stood by the widow.

"It's my fault, you know."

"Don't be silly. It was random. An accident. You know it as well as I do."

"No. I know it was the gualicho. I just know it."

"Vanesa, you really need to relax. Maybe you should get some rest." The funeral home was a good one, and had plenty of room for family to lie down.

And yet… and yet the word gualicho nagged at him, left him with the strange feeling that he'd heard it before somewhere, and the fact that it didn't come immediately to mind irritated him. Where had it been? He set it aside, drawing her closer, intending to lead her to one of the couches.

She pushed him away. "I know you don't believe me. I laughed at the police woman as well, but now look at me. There's something going on, and if you don't believe me, you'll be crying over someone you love one of these days as well."

That was unfair, Alejandro thought, and yet he said nothing. He would have time to tell her about the endless summer afternoons he'd spent playing football with Ernesto on deserted sidewalks, or riding bicycles across the park… or just playing video games inside and fighting about whose turn it was to be "Player 1". The memories he had of his brother were no less important than the ones she had of her husband, and neither was the gaping hole torn in his life.

He held his tongue, trying to think of something helpful to say, but his mind had other ideas, and kept circling around and around that single alien word.

Gualicho.

Gualicho.

Gualicho.

Unexpectedly, it clicked, and Alejandro found himself remembering a dying old lady in a Patagonian hospital speaking what the doctor knew were her final words—and the final words that would ever be spoken in a language about to disappear from the face of the Earth.

"I recorder her," he said.

Vanesa looked into his eyes, clearly not knowing where he was going with this, clearly expecting to have to reproach him for bringing up a subject both banal and unrelated to her suffering. But he explained anyway.

***

They were scheduled to meet the linguist five days after the funeral, and on the morning of the appointment, Vanesa showered, dressed, and sat down to breakfast. For the first time since the murder, she opened up the paper—not the one she worked for, but a serious national sheet—and proceeded to ignore the difficulties in Europe and the violence in the Middle East. Local news was not much better and she was about to push it away in disgust when one article caught her eye.

A cab driver in one of Buenos Aires' endless suburbs had, against all logic, managed to run over himself with his own cab, dying in the process. It was printed as more of a curiosity than as actual news, but strange nature of the accident chilled her to the bone. She left her half-finished cup of tea on the table and walked out of her apartment.

She waited an hour for Alejandro, but that was preferable to staying in her empty apartment, looking for Ernesto's ghost and waiting for the curse to catch up to her.

They drove to the University in silence, broken only by Alejandro's soft cursing the inevitable aggressive drivers cut in front of him. Vanesa wondered if that would be the way the gualicho did away with her: an anonymous car crash, far from notice. But no… That wouldn't be its way. It was playful, wanting not just to kill, but to kill in such a way as to satisfy a sadistic need.

The linguist turned out to be a middle-aged woman in a large wood-paneled office that looked like something left over from a more bureaucratic era. Stacks of paper in faded yellow and pastel-green folders littered every available surface. The sign on her door said Prof. Serena.

"So, tell me," Serena said. She didn't sound like she was in any hurry to get rid of them, but she didn't sound particularly interested, either.

"I'm a doctor, and I made a recording of a woman speaking in what they say is Tehuelche, and we were wondering if you could help us understand it. We think it might be important." He pressed play and let her listen to the old woman's rasps and gurgles, until they faded to silence.

Serena suddenly looked animated. "When did you record this?"

"Maybe two months ago, in Esquel."

"And who is that woman? She's speaking the lower-base Tehuelche tongue. We thought that was extinct years ago. We might be able to decipher a few things that have been bothering us for ages—or at the very least get the words on record for the archives. Tehuelche is a very endangered language, you know."

"Oh, you don't understand. The woman died right at the end of the recording. I thought that was clear. I'm sorry."

The light went out of the Professor's eyes. "Then why did you even bother recording it? Why bring it to me?"

"I recorded it because I thought it might be the last time that

Tehuelche was heard on the face of the Earth—and I thought it would be important to keep some record of it.

"As to why I brought it to you, I wanted you to tell us about the use of the word "gualicho", and what the woman was saying."

Serena shrugged. "Oh, that. Nothing important. The old woman was just telling someone that it was important to say the invocation to Kóoch. Standard stuff. The Tehuelche religion believes that if their main deity, Kóoch isn't reminded, at least once a night, to keep the world in balance, the spirit called Gualicho will take over, sending the world spinning into chaos and ending human life. All the indigenous people in South America have something like it in their lore."

"And do you know the invocation?" Vanesa blurted.

Another shrug. "There may be some versions, incomplete versions, at the sound library, but you'll have to wait until next week if you want to hear it. Gómez is on vacation, and he's the only one who knows where everything is. A lot of it's still on tape, you know. Old native languages aren't really a high priority for the government."

Alejandro and Vaneesa listened to her diatribe and then politely excused themselves.

***

That night, Vanesa was watching the news, waiting for a sign that she was right. Just when she thought nothing would come of it, at the very end of the program, a short piece about an accident in a styling salon aired. It seemed that a very well-known hairdresser had, most uncharacteristically, stabbed a client through the eye with a very sharp scissor, sending it all the way into the brain with fatal results.

Vanesa managed to stay calm when she heard that the incident had occurred aa mere twenty blocks from her apartment, but when the woman's name was mentioned…

"I tell you it's getting closer. The gualicho is coming for me."

"Calm down. Why do you think that?" Alejandro asked.

"Because she had the same last name as the driver from this morning. And because it was right here, just a few miles away. She must have been a cousin or something, and now the curse is in my neighborhood. How long do you think it will take to get here?"

"Listen…"

"No, you listen. I'm going to the archive on Monday, and I'm going to learn that prayer. I know you think it's stupid, but I know what I'm doing. I'll barricade myself in my room, I'll make sure the gas is off. It won't get me. I'll—"

"Look, I have to go. My family is waiting at the table, and I've been away too long. If you have something to calm your nerves in the house, take some—and that's a professional order, by the way. I'll call you, to see how you're doing after dinner." Alejandro hung up.

***

Through a huge effort of will, Vanesa managed to convince Alejandro not to send one of his friends from the psychiatric wing of the hospital to see her. She apologized for sounding insane, and she promised to seek professional help.

But that had been a front. She barricaded herself in her room with nothing but a few supplies and a computer, and spent the next four days on Facebook, as insulated from the real world as any human could be, just waiting for Monday to come around. She ignored all incoming calls, especially those that seemed to come from her colleagues.

Isolation did not breed tranquility. Vanesa jumped at every sound, squealed every time the wind blew against her shutters. The days dragged by at a snail's pace.

Eventually, Monday morning rolled around and Vanesa showered, making certain to step carefully into the tub, and to hold on to the handle—a nice fall in the shower might just be banal enough to satisfy the spirit. She survived the bath and had a quick breakfast, scanning the Facebook updates that had been her constant companions over the course of her withdrawal from society.

There were an unusual number of them, and most from her old high-school classmates. It seemed that a girl in her graduating class had slipped and rolled down a staircase, breaking her neck.

The consensus was that it was an awful thing to have happened to the family, at the funeral of her cousin, no less. Another comment said that, yes, having two young women in the family die in accidents so close together was truly unfortunate. A more curious classmate wondered what had happened to the cousin.

"Didn't you hear? She was the woman killed in the styling place last week."

Vanesa ran out the door, muttering under her breath. "You won't get me. You won't get me. You bastard. I'll beat you. I'll get Kóoch to send you back to wherever you came from."

A chill came over her as she reached the elevator hall.

Are you so sure about that?

Vanesa froze. She wondered if she might be going insane, wondered if the stress had finally gotten to her. There was no way that voice could have been real. Why would an ancient native spirit care about her? And even if it did, why would it be able to talk to her in a language she understood. It was ridiculous.

Still, she pressed the elevator button repeatedly. She would get to the archive and repeat whatever the prayer said. "You'll be gone this evening, you little piece of shit." She knew there was no one, and nothing, there, but she had to get the fear out of her system.

Now that isn't very nice, is it?

"Where are you? What are you? Leave me alone!"

I think you know who I am. As to where… Maybe above, maybe below. Maybe right next to you.

Frantically, Vanesa looked all around, but saw nothing. She pressed the elevator button again and again, until, finally, the door opened. Still looking around, trying to make sure that nothing could enter with her, she rushed in.

As she fell down the empty shaft, all she heard was a dry chuckle, but the echo of her screams soon drowned it out.

A GATHERING OF ASHES

Every once in a while, I go back to a story that I wrote and simply can't believe I wrote it. This one touches the heartstrings—at least mine—in a way that doesn't happen to me with my prose every time. It's a super short piece which is still one of my favorites ever.

It originally appeared in *Every Day Fiction*.

A lone firefighter walked through the deserted street.

He saw the playground where he'd run as a boy, and watched for a moment as the swings, faded but intact, swayed in the autumn wind. A yellowed piece of paper blew across the street and caught in overgrown brambles by what was left of the road.

When he first woke, he thought it had all been a dream: the frantic emergency call, the smoke in the distance, the horror when they learned that the destination, and the huge blaze was at the power plant, the helpless watching as other succumbed to the radiation as opposed to the flame, and then the blindness.

The firefighter had woken many times since, but never as a fireman, always as a patient. In and out of treatment, of comas. In his dream, he'd never walked and he'd never been free of pain. Waking and sleeping was the same to him; his blindness made night of everything. He'd heard great events unfold in his dream: revolution, democracy, independence, but they'd felt to him like the hallucinations of a fever dream that lasted years and decades.

And then, from the frantic sounds of panicked nurses rushing to an emergency chime which had faded to darkness, he'd unexpectedly woken to a glorious sight: an autumn sunset over Pripyat, the place he loved most in the world. He was standing, free of the bed and the grey hospital. The pain was gone.

He could see.

He could see Pripyat before him, and the black hulk of

Chernobyl behind, but neither was as he remembered them. The plant had been rebuilt, some huge structure replacing the old squat buildings. The city was deserted.

It wasn't the deserted like it was on Saturday mornings. Pripyat had the look of a place that had been empty forever. Grass, even trees grew in profusion from cracks in the pavement. The windows on the apartment buildings were either gone or broken.

An abandoned bicycle lay in the center of the road, rusted into a bent mound, tires bleached by the sun. There was no question of finding anyone here—humanity had gone completely.

But still the firefighter walked the overgrown streets until he came to the playground where he's spent so many happy days. It should have echoed with the happy cries of children, but instead, the only sound was the slight swaying of the rusted swing-chain in the wind.

He covered his face with his hand, and that was when he realized that he could see through the outline of his arm.

So the other had been the waking, the pain, the hospitals, and this was the dream.

The fireman fell to his knees and cried out to the heavens they'd taught him not to believe in. He poured his entire spirit into one keening sound that he knew no one beyond his dream could hear, a primal cry that emptied his existence and should have carried him up to the sky with it.

But when he finished, he was still there, kneeling in a deserted, weed-choked playground.

He cursed the fact that he was unable to cry, unable to completely bury his head in his hands.

Eventually, a feeling made him lift his eyes to an amazing sight.

There were people there watching him. Thousands of people, tens of thousand, stretching as far as he could see. They were mostly oriental, but a few towards the front were European, and seemed to be half-remembered figures from the past. The entire multitude was as translucent as his arm.

A thought reached him. "We heard your call."

"I didn't call you," he replied.

"You did. We heard the pain, the burning of the radiation, the years of suffering. We came to help you, to tell you that you are free now."

It seemed the entire group spoke as one.

"This was my home," he said.

"This is not a fit home now. You must break away from it."

"I cannot."

"Perhaps not now, but you will."

And, deep inside, the firefighter knew they were right. There were better places to be.

"Will you wait with me until I am ready?"

"Yes, we will. We understand."

And they did. And none of the living were ever aware of it, save for some in the cities of Hiroshima and Nagasaki, who felt a slight breeze as the massed ghosts of their towns rushed to the Ukraine to help a single lost soul.

BELIEF

"Belief" is interesting in that, though the framing is right out of *Arabian Nights*, the story within the story is utterly European. Some people love this, others prefer to take their medicine straight.

I'll let you decide where you fall on that spectrum. It was originally published in *The Worlds of Science Fiction, Fantasy and Horror Volume 2*.

"…the evil grand vizier lost his grip and fell from the wall, leaving the kingdom in the hands of the prince, who ruled much more wisely from that day forth, and lived unto his ninetieth year and was much mourned by his people when he passed." Scheherazade paused. Both of them knew what was coming. "That was the end of my story, my liege. If it please you, I can begin another."

Shahryar nodded. "Do so, but it must be finished by dawn. This cannot go on any longer."

"Of course, my lord. Your wish is my command." She smiled demurely and lowered her eyes, playing her part to perfection. "Up to now, I have told you of great deeds from the past, of colossal struggles for riches and kingdoms. But I know also of things that are to come, stories that have not yet come to pass."

"How can this be?"

"You are a great king, and it is the will of the spirits that you should hear of all that would please you. A man of your stature cannot be limited by that which has been."

Shahryar smiled, well pleased at the compliment. Long gone were the days in which he mistrusted everything she said. Long gone also were her nights of terror.

"It is the story of a woman, my liege. A woman from the infidel lands to the north and west, who took up arms for her infidel king."

"Against whom did she take up arms?"

"Against other infidels, my lord."

"And why should this interest me? There seems no chance of a triumph of truth and justice." And yet Scheherazade could see that he was intrigued. Perhaps because the heroine had taken up arms, perhaps because it was a story of something yet to be. Perhaps simply because he no longer wished to have her killed.

"You may decide whether the story pleases you as I tell it," Sheherazade replied, knowing that the king would enjoy anything that reached his ears from her mouth. "In a small village far to the north and west…"

…the greatest general in the history of a proud nation strode down the corridor acknowledging the bows and reverences of the people. Ministers, clergymen, powerful nobles, lesser messengers, all of them men accustomed to places of power, all of them looking the general's way with eyes that burned brightly. Hope lived there, and the love of a leader that had turned a desperate situation into a winnable war.

The general reached the door at the end of the corridor, closed it, leaned against the rough wood, and sighed. She wasn't sure how much longer her strength would hold. A polished piece of metal served as a mirror, inherited from the previous commander of the king's troops. He, like all the generals before him, had used it to shave. She used it to study the rings beneath her eyes and her short light-brown hair. Sometimes, only sometimes, she wished she could allow it to grow, allow herself to find a husband and forget about the complexities of war.

But her God had called, and she had answered. No one could recognize her except in man's attire until her land was freed from the foreign scourge and her king was secure upon his throne.

But as long as no one recognized her…

She opened the solid wooden chest, the only piece of

furniture she'd allowed in the small room other than the desk, chair and bed. The troops were convinced that the contents of the chest were the paraphernalia of leadership and communion with God. They imagined maps, hair shirts and crucifixes within. The fact that the punishment for tampering with the general's chest was death only lent strength to the rumors.

The truth would have shocked them. The first item that emerged was a wig of long, lustrous black hair that fit over her own short hair like a glove. She adjusted the angle until she was satisfied with the effect.

After putting the wig on, she discarded her male attire. As always, she cursed herself for putting the wig on before doing any of the rest, but knew it was something she couldn't avoid. For some reason, she couldn't truly think of herself as a woman until that long black hair framed her features.

The dress she selected was a dark brown affair, beautiful but practical since the color would hide the stain of travel, and especially mud from crossing the fields.

She refrained from putting on her delicate indoor shoes—they would be ruined long before she reached her destination—and instead kept the boots from her general's attire. No one would see them under the dress, and she would hide them when she arrived and donned the other pair.

Finally, she extracted the single item that, even had the rest not been shocking enough, would have resulted in her being removed from the head of the army, incarcerated, and quite probably burned as a witch. A small wooden casket which, when opened, revealed a powdery white substance: powdered lead paint. She applied a light coating to her face, and secreted another small quantity in a pouch under her dress, whispering a prayer to her God for forgiveness as she did. Her country needed her to act on its behalf, and if God could tolerate, indeed command, that she dress as a man, small womanly sins could also be forgiven.

As she looked into her mirror, she was satisfied to see that the instantly recognizable sight of Jeanne was gone. In her place stood the Countess Renée, an equally well-known figure often involved in political intrigue and court politics. Mistrusted by Jeanne's people and the treacherous Burgundies, she was grudgingly tolerated by both because she was considered useful.

Neither faction had looked into her credentials, for she came bearing documents with the general's mark, an irony that made Jeanne smile.

Getting out of the general's complex—a small noble house, more of a large farm, really—would be simple enough in her disguise, but she had to be certain that no one witnessed the exit from the room itself. Any further connection between the Countess and the general would incite comment. Some of the sharper-eyed among the staff might notice the physical similarities, and that would lead to unpleasantness.

So she waited by the door, looking through the keyhole until no one was visible in the corridor and let herself out. She turned the key in its socket once to insure that the general's absence wouldn't send the troops into shock and walked out of the door, imperious and unchallenged.

The trip across the fields between the small town and the enemy city was full of risk. No woman was safe in those days, but a noble woman would be twice as vulnerable. Brigands would value her for flesh and purse, a much more profitable proposition than ravaging some penniless farmer's daughter.

Jeanne managed to reach a small clump of trees just outside the town without incident, but just as she was bending over to remove her muddy boots, she felt the touch of cold metal against her back.

"Straighten up and turn around so I can see you," a rough, uncultured voice commanded.

She did so, slowly. By the dim light coming from the town itself and the bonfires lit by the defenders, she could make out his features. A round, dirty face with a gap-toothed grin and beady eyes gave him a drunken look, but he held the spear against her steadily, keeping it in contact with her dress as she turned.

***

"It is dawn, my liege."

"It cannot be!"

"See for yourself."

Shahryar sighed. It was always thus. "I suppose you want to continue this tale tomorrow."

"I think it would be best," Scheherazade replied.

He sighed again. "One day I shall lose patience with your games, woman."

"But until that day comes, I assume you wish for me to continue in attendance."

"Very well. I shall hear the rest of this story tonight."

"Until tonight, then."

***

As the spear jabbed painfully into her stomach, just about to break the skin, Jeanne considered the man before her. The uniform identified him as a soldier of the Auxerre city guard. It was a bit frayed and definitely unclean, but there was nothing to suggest that the man wouldn't do his duty, and do it zealously.

"Ah," Jeanne said, pulling herself up and swatting at the spear with a dismissive gesture, showing a calm face when she felt like screaming. "The city guard. Good. I need you to take me to the Mayor."

This caught the man completely off guard. "The mayor? Not likely. I shall take you to the dungeons, and let the captain decide what to do with you. A spy in our midst will probably be put to death without much of a trial."

She scoffed, hoping to bluff her way through. Though she knew very well that she would never be put to death, a trip to the dungeons would take time she didn't have—and losing her wig might bring more problems than that. "A spy, you say? Hah! Are you blind as well as dirty, man? Do you not recognize the Countess Renée when you see her? Mayor Luc will have someone put to death if you take me to the dungeons, but I can assure you that it will not be me."

The effect on the poor guard was what she expected. No peasant would take the risk of incurring the displeasure of a noblewoman—at least not when her screams would be heard by the men on duty upon the city walls. He honored the tradition of all low-ranking military men and turned her in to the commander of the night guard, who sent her up to the castellan. Less than half an hour after being discovered among the trees, she was face to face with Luc Alphand, the mayor of the town.

He stood to greet her, a smile touching the corners of his mouth. "Countess, I was beginning to think we would not be seeing you tonight." He was a stout man, with thinning blond hair and bags under his eyes. He did not look as though he'd been getting much sleep.

Jeanne laughed inwardly at the use of the royal plural. The man had driven every one of his retainers out of the dark, candlelit chamber in preparation for her arrival. He knew the Countess' reputation well, and wished to add to it. He would not succeed, but without witnesses, he could claim anything he wanted. "I very nearly didn't arrive. Your city guard detained me at the gate and caused me an unconscionable delay. You must have a word with them, explain what is proper and what is not."

"I'm sorry Countess, but these are difficult times. Rumor has Jeanne's army stationed not a stone's throw from here. They say it is millions of men strong. Some claim that demons march with her, others avenging angels. They say she will not be stopped until all the world is part of France." He grinned at her, to show the sophisticated countess what he thought of such peasants' babble. "So tell me, what is the true news from the front?"

"For once, the rumors have more truth in them than lies. The army of France has won victory after victory, and they advance upon this city as we speak. The English have been unable to stop them, and they are much more concerned about reducing their own losses than in aiding their Burgundy allies lying in Jeanne's path. Whoever told you that they are nearby spoke truly, as their general headquarters is less than an hour's walk from this very chamber. They have been in position for two days."

He paled, well aware that though the countess was not allied to either faction, her information was always reliable. "If they are that close, why haven't they attacked us yet? And why have my scouts been unable to spot an army of that size?"

Jeanne waved his concern aside. "The army is not as large as they have led you to believe—it is large enough to put this city under siege, and more than enough to reduce your pathetic city guard if they create a breach or crest the walls, but it is easily hidden." She looked straight into his eyes. "Do you have some wine?"

Two goblets appeared as if by magic and Jeanne sniffed one. She nodded her approval—Burgundy might have been following the devil's path against the true king of France, but there was little wrong with their wine. She took a sip, watched intently as he drank and relaxed when he swallowed.

"Even with a small force, I still don't understand why she hasn't attacked us yet. She must know that we cannot hold."

Jeanne wondered how much to tell the man, and decided that the truth would serve her better than any dissembling would. "Jeanne has not attacked because she believes in the goodness of all French people. She thinks that Auxerre will come to its senses, renounce the treaty with the English and open her gates to the true king of France."

"That is ridiculous. She knows that all of Burgundy supports Henry. Why would we renounce our honor by forswearing?"

"Because Henry is an Englishman," she said, more harshly

than would have been natural for Countess Renée. She took a few deep breaths to steady herself. Her plan had already been put into action. Offending her host would serve no purpose. The next words she spoke were much calmer. "She believes that you will see the light and surrender the town."

His eyes blazed. "Does she think me craven? I will fight her to the last man, if need be."

"She knows you are not craven. But she also believes, truly knows, that God is on her side. She has told her troops that Auxerre will either open her gates on your command, or that you will be struck dead before noon tomorrow and Auxerre will capitulate under the orders of your successor."

He laughed. "Do her troops believe this? Has anyone been struck dead by her prayers in this campaign?"

"Thousands of the enemy have died as a result of her prayers. She has received guidance that can only be described as divine. Even your own peasants whisper that the city will open its gates. She is convinced that God guides her actions, sends her plans in the night and keeps her from death no matter how badly she is wounded. Her troops would lay siege to hell itself if she told them that it stood against the interests of France and her rightful king."

"Yes, I'm aware of the loyalty she commands, and I know full well that the city cannot hold out more than a few days. But I'm prepared to delay her progress for as long as possible. Perhaps reinforcements will arrive in time, or perhaps we can use the time for other purposes. And besides, I'm not at all certain that Jeanne isn't a witch who has cast some kind of glamour over half of the nation. How can they accept a woman who refuses to act in a seemly way? Even the way she dresses must be an insult to God."

"Not if God has commanded her to do so."

"No, but that is difficult to believe. What other news do you have for me?"

Jeannne sighed inwardly and gave the man an accurate, although incomplete assessment of the loyalist forces in the field. Enough that the Countess Renée's reputation would remain intact, not enough that the information would cause suspicion.

She left the man with a heavy heart, but content that her decision had been the correct one. Luc was a proud man, who would never surrender his city. His death would be a tragedy, but he would not be able to live with the decision she needed him to take. God was merciful in these matters.

Her return to headquarters was much less eventful than the road out, and dawn found her sitting at the head of a table speaking to her field commanders.

"We need to strike immediately," one man said. He was just a young artillery captain, but older and wiser heads around the table nodded their agreement.

"No. The city will capitulate."

"Why do you insist? They show no signs of capitulating. Luc is a proud man, and loyal to his Duke."

"If Luc wishes to resist, he will not survive the morning. The city will be ours by noon, and no French blood will be spilt. God has told me so."

There was a shuffling around the table as the men shifted uncomfortably. No matter how often she was proved right, they still would not believe. Only her iron grip on the army kept them from openly resisting her commands. Still, it was better to show confidence in their abilities than to crush them under her heel.

"I know that it will not be necessary, but I will allow you to plan for an assault. If the city does not capitulate before midday, you may attempt to storm it two hours after noon."

Another shuffle, tinged with relief, spread across the table as the men left to prepare. The artillery captain stopped on his way out. "Pardon me, general, but will you want to review our plans?"

She smiled at him. He was loyal, if misguided. "There will be no need. I will wait here for the emissaries."

His eyes widened, but he just nodded and left.

Jeanne prayed as the morning advanced. She didn't pray for the surrender of Auxerre. That had been promised, and the promise would be kept. She prayed for the people of France and the expulsion of foreign armies from her beloved soil. She prayed for a swift end to the bloodshed. And she prayed for her own soul, which had been forced, for the good of the light, to do things that many found questionable.

When the emissaries from Auxerre arrived at midmorning, surrounded by her own bewildered officers, she just smiled wanly. "I hope Luc's death was a painless one."

"No, Your Grace, it wasn't. He died horribly, screaming to the last."

She ignored the incorrect form of address and nodded. "God works in mysterious ways, my friends. I take it you are ready to surrender."

"More than that. We want to join you." His eyes widened and he made the sign of the cross. "We believe now."

"Good. All Christians are welcome in my army. I accept your offer." She gestured to her officers to take the men away. They could deal with the details, and with pacifying any resistance that might still smolder in Auxerre. She had to pray a little more.

She thanked God for the guidance, and then prayed for the soul of Luc, former mayor of Auxerre, struck down in his prime by the hand of god and a goblet of wine with just a little face powder in it.

She resolved to throw away the last of that powder, though it would make disguising herself as the Countess much more difficult. But the evidence was there: it had to be a product of the devil. Why else would something calculated to make men and women sin contain both lead and arsenic? But it had done its job.

Jeanne, her prayers complete, got up to face the rest of the day. It would be a busy one…

***

"…because her army needed to replenish, and establish its new base within the walls of the city, to plan the rest of the war." Scheherazade said. "And she was successful. The war ended with her king, the man she believed was the rightful king, on the throne of that far land to the north and west."

Shahryar smiled, satisfied at the conclusion of the tale. But then his eyes saw what he'd never seen before. "Scheherazade," he said, "the sun is rising, and you have not begun your next story."

She cast her eyes towards the floor. "I have told you a thousand stories in a thousand and one nights," she said. "I have no more tales to tell. Over this time you have come to know me well, have given me three sons for your greater glory. I believe the time has come for you to decide what it is you wish to do with me."

Shahryar smiled. "Have you poisoned my wine?"

"No, my liege. But I hope to have planted seeds of doubt in your heart."

He looked into her eyes for a long time, and the hour grew much later than what was customary for them. Finally, Shahryar spoke. "I will tell you your fate this evening. Come to me at the usual hour." And then he smiled, something she'd rarely seen, even after the most thrilling of her tales. "There is no need for you to prepare a story."

DARKNESS ENDS

This is another tale inspired by my travels in Syria. I was in Palmyra before the current war, and will never forgive the barbarians who could destroy such a jewel of human history just to get a political point across. I hope the Romans get them.

It was originally published in *Atomjack*.

Tita Livia Siriana basked in the silence. Her audience, composed of the best and brightest, the great leaders of the great families of both inner and outer Empires, hung on her every word. She'd barely begun to speak, but the little that had leaked of her work, the little she'd allowed to leak, was enough to have them on the edge of their seats. By speaking softly, she guaranteed that only those seated nearest the stage would hear her words, but then again, those seated nearest were the truly important men and women. The rest could get a transcript.

"I am honored to be here, among the leaders of the Empire, honored that you have chosen to travel all the way to Palmyra to hear my presentation," she said. "I only hope that the fruits of my research will meet your expectations."

Once again, Tita cursed her father for his untimely death. He hadn't lived long enough to see the triumph of his family. While his precious sons threw away their advantages and became an administrator in the Australis Province and a merchant, respectively, his daughter, unheeded, unaided and ignored had not only become Governess of one of the Inner Provinces but was also the Empire's foremost physicist. Her father, of course, had died before her moment of triumph, broken by his sons' failure.

Taking a final, deep breath and looking one last time over the arched skyscrapers of Palmyra Nova off to the east, she launched into her speech. "As you are all aware, the greatness of Rome has spread to all corners of the globe. Our invincible armies sit in a state of boredom as they become less and less relevant. The great expansion that began more than two thousand years ago, when this amphitheater was new, seems to have ended."

The audience stirred. They hadn't come all this way to listen to a political speech. Tita held up a hand.

"I am here to tell you that, in a few more months, the great expansion will begin again. New worlds will open for our conquest. And this time, we won't have to fiddle with rockets and wormholes."

She smiled. Needling the space agency was always an enjoyable pastime. All those well-funded rocket scientists from the Han Provinces, with their promises of glory and their endless string of disasters would become obsolete overnight if she succeeded.

And she would. All they needed was a little help.

***

Bassam al Aama was in his element. Nothing in the world was quite as satisfying to him as squatting over a shallow trench with a brush in his hand and the secrets of an ancient civilization coming to light as he carefully pushed away layers of dirt. Perfection would have required a hot sun beating on his hat, but the powers that were had decided to erect a tent. He wasn't happy with the fact that they'd blithely hammered four poles into the ground around a dig, but the main thing bugging him about the tent was that he wasn't working in the open. Archaeology was supposed to be hot and sweaty.

But even this couldn't dampen his enthusiasm. Who could possibly have imagined that, after nearly two hundred years of study, there would be a new discovery here in Palmyra? The Syrian government had immediately repurposed its best team of archaeologists into the area.

Basaam had been delighted: his former task, rebuilding the

shattered city after the disaster created by ISIS in the previous decade's civil war was his duty… but he'd always yearned to do something more, to make a true mark on the field.

Better still, he'd been allowed to choose his own collaborators. So he'd invited teams from France and Italy, and had gotten to work. After all, once the rebuilding was complete, this would once again become Syria's most important tourist attraction.

"Alia, please come over here," he called.

His assistant, bent over another section of the grid a couple of meters away straightened, stretched to get the stiffness out of her back and walked over. "Have you found something?" Her eyes flashed with excitement.

"I think so. But I'd like your opinion." He moved aside to allow her to climb into the trench beside him and pointed towards a flat grey area, about ten centimeters square, shining in the reflected sunlight.

"Ceramic?" Alia said.

"It seems to be, but I've never seen Roman glazing that looked like that."

Alia nodded. "Much too shiny, almost translucent." She knew as well as he did that while glazing had been known to survive intact, the shine they were seeing was extremely unusual.

Alia knelt beside him, and they got back to work.

***

"Why do we need a linguist?" Aulus Fabius, her assistant, seemed puzzled as he viewed the hologram showing their meetings for that day.

Livia shrugged. "Do you truly believe that these savages speak Latin? We'll need someone who can communicate with them. From what we've seen, the ones in Palmyra don't even use the semi-civilized alphabet the rest of their world uses." She shuddered. "You don't even want to know the kind of writing that the Han equivalent use. It isn't even real writing with letters—they use pictograms to represent words. Incredibly inefficient."

"How far can we trust him? If he's the one doing the communicating, then he'll have to know exactly what we need the savages to do in order to open the gateway. Do they even have the technology to do what we need them to do?"

"A small electric current through the key? Of course they do. You're being silly, and underestimating them. Some of the tribes even have nuclear weapons. They might not have had the benefit of Roman leadership, but even the densest people would have developed electricity given more than a thousand years! Anyhow, we can't just tell them what we're doing. We need to have someone who understands their language find out more about their culture before we send our message." Taking months to observe the world they were trying to enter before being able to communicate was frustrating, but necessary. The only way the barbarians would be able to stop them is if they refused to activate the key.

He shook his head. "I know. It's just that I don't want to involve anyone else. What if word gets out that we need their help to open the gateway? Where will we be then? Dishonored and disinherited, that's where."

Livia knew that if it hadn't been for his family connections, A. Fabius would never have been allowed to work on this project. But the Caesar's nephews, even the illegitimate ones, were due a certain respect. Still, it was hard for her to believe that anyone, participating in one of the world's greatest scientific discoveries endeavors could be thinking such inane thoughts. It was almost insulting. "If we succeed, it doesn't matter. And if we fail, the linguist will share our disgrace. I don't think there's much risk of his mouth opening inconveniently." Besides, she thought, this man's loyalty is to my family, and where my fortunes run, so do his. But she kept silent on this point—it was never intelligent to let well-connected assistants have too much information.

A chime announced the linguist's arrival.

***

Bassam had refused to consider the idea. The single most unusual find ever made in the Palmyra dig would not be turned over to the western archaeologists unless it was done over his dead body. He didn't care about the tourist value, didn't mind the consequences. His team would be the first to study it.

The Minister of Tourism had been angry with the decision, but the Minister of Culture had supported him: a Syrian artifact found by a Syrian team in Syria was to be analyzed locally, if there was anything the foreign teams needed to know, they would be informed. And the defense minister, the one with the true power, had not disagreed—which was better than nothing. For now, the artifact would remain in the war-ravaged halls of the Palmyra museum, less than a mile from where it had been unearthed.

This meant that they had it to themselves. They'd x-rayed it, weighed it, measured it, scraped it (yet another reason not to let it fall into the hands of overly timid foreigners) and generally studied everything about it over the past few weeks before giving their report to the Minister of Culture.

"We've never seen anything like it," Bassam admitted. In his experience, it was better to get this kind of thing out of the way early, in order to focus on what he believed was important. In this case, the central mystery surrounding the artifact.

Excitement shone in the minister's gaze. "Do you mean it's a significant find? Something that might lead to new theories? Or a confirmation of old ones, or whatever it is that you do?" The minister, like most of his peers, was a military man who had very little actual knowledge of archaeology. The only importance a significant find held in his eyes was as a tool to increase his influence at the expense of other ministers.

"Not exactly. What I'm trying to tell you is that we don't recognize the material. It isn't anything we've encountered before in any ancient civilization. If it hadn't been buried in a strata that dates it at nearly two thousand years old, I'd say it was some kind of high-tech ceramic."

His superior frowned. "High-tech in what way? Like it was Greek instead of Roman?"

Bassam ignored the absolute ignorance involved in the question itself and answered what his boss was aiming at. "No. Like it was a ceramic from the heat shield of a space vehicle."

"Have you analyzed it?"

"I'm an archaeologist. I don't know anything about modern materials."

"All right. I'll send someone over to help. You'd better be right, because I'm going to have to call in a favor to get your expert." The minister dismissed Bassam with a wave.

***

"I find it enormously hard to believe that their world functions as well as it does." Gaius Severus remarked, shaking his head. "While it's obvious that their social structure is far from perfect, and their decentralized governments completely inefficient, I still admire the fact that they seem to be able to function as a planet with so many languages. Some of them aren't even based on Latin!"

"Their world doesn't work all that well. At a glance I'd say they're running three hundred years behind us technology-wise." Tita Livia was bored of this conversation. Since most of the team had had no real work to do while Gaius Severus worked on deciphering the language of the Syrians in the parallel reality, they'd taken to using the gateway as a giant looking-glass into the lives of people whose fate, except for a lucky break over fifteen hundred years ago, could have been their own. Imagine growing up in such a chaotic world, a world in which the rationalizing influence of the Empire simply wasn't present.

"But they should be a thousand years behind—at least! From what I've gathered of their history, they actually went backwards, both socially and technologically for a millennium after Rome was defeated."

The words 'Rome was defeated' seemed science fictional, even after months of looking through the portal. Such a thing had been inconceivable even when the Empire consisted of a few hills in central Italy, and had grown more and more impossible as time went on. Tita sighed. "How much longer until we can communicate through the gateway?"

"I've got the language nearly down pat. I need to check a couple of cultural references but, by next week, we should be able to transmit something that is not only intelligible to the other side, but also culturally relevant. I think we'll convince them."

"For all our sakes, I hope you're right."

***

Alia fumed. She couldn't believe that she'd been summarily expelled from the meeting just because she was a woman. No matter what strides Syrian women had made towards emancipation—and she didn't pretend not to be grateful, since most of the Arab world was much worse—there were still moments when the women were dismissed as fluff.

The most galling part of it was that, though she respected Bassam's experience, neither of them had any doubt as to which of the two would, eventually, become the archaeologist remembered by posterity. She'd already put forth a couple of theories more significant than any he'd ever thought of by himself, explaining the social interaction between lower-class Palmyrans and their Roman and local masters. Theories that, unlike the currently accepted thinking, matched all the evidence and fit with Roman practices in other parts of the Middle East.

Worse yet, the three government ministers locked in with him were probably illiterate. All they knew how to do was drive tanks. Judging by their record in the wars with Israel, they weren't very good at that, either.

Making it worse was the so-called 'materials expert'. He'd taken one look at the artifact and proclaimed it 'just pottery', but had hung around ever since. He presumably had nothing better to do.

The cleric was the final insult. Even the most moderate among their number felt that women's rights were an aberration. Her khaki field pants would have offended him greatly.

But there was nothing she could do about it. Despite their limitations, all four of the men outranked her. She stormed through the dusty halls back into her office and dropped hard onto her swivel chair. A single touch on her computer's mouse brought the screen back to life. An image appeared on the screen, the flowing Arabic lettering perfect, as if drawn by Allah himself.

She glared at it. It was this message, which had appeared unexpectedly on the surface of the artifact they'd found, that had led to the emergency meeting being convened, and to her offhand dismissal.

Syrian Brothers, chosen of the prophet Muhammad, we greet you from the world beyond, the Paradise of your forefathers.

It is with great alarm that we have observed the decline of Allah's faithful at the hand of the infidel. With great sadness we see that decadence is creeping, even as we speak, into even the greatest Muslim societies.

We cannot condone what you've done to yourselves since the days in which all eyes turned to the Muslim world for their science and their healing. For it must be said that you have brought it down upon yourselves.

And yet, we cannot bear to watch our descendants become nothing but an irritant, a minor problem, on the world stage. Our destiny is to bring the word of the Prophet to all, tirelessly converting the infidel to the love of Allah.

For this reason, we have been allowed to give you one gift. The block you have found in Palmyra is a gateway, a gateway to Paradise.

But there is a condition. You must prove your worthiness to possess such a gift. You must activate the gateway before the next full moon. If you do so, an army will come to you, an army the likes of which the world has never known. An army that brings back all the glory of the past.

From Palmyra, the entire world shall be conquered, and once more, you will be allowed to bask in the radiance of true godly light. Life, for you, shall be as it was always meant to be.

All you must do to signal your desire to accept our gift is to pass a small electric current of any type, through the message box. We shall understand.

Alia shook her head. The message made no sense.

She was a good Muslim, if not too devout, and if not particularly enamored of the way Arab society treated women, but she still didn't get it. The message was obviously some kind of joke. An elaborate one, to be certain, but a joke. Which made it no surprise that the men had taken it perfectly seriously.

And yet there was something vaguely sinister about it. Why would Allah, or the spirits of his followers in Paradise need for the Syrian people to pass an electric current through the artifact? It was ridiculous. If the message were even remotely genuine, wouldn't it be sufficient to declare their willingness in a loud voice? Wouldn't spirits in paradise be able to hear that as well?

She stormed back to the meeting room and burst through the door. "Don't do it," she shouted at the men, who jumped away from their coffee. The cleric spilled a large slosh down the front of his tunic.

Bassam recovered first. The look he gave her was icy. "Alia, what is the meaning of this?"

She refused to back down. "The artifact. There's something wrong with it. I think it's a trap. Maybe it's a bomb."

One of the men, the one who'd been introduced to her simply as the Defense Minister laughed. "It's not a bomb. I would have recognized it immediately if it were such." He turned to Bassam, and smiled, a condescending, paternal gesture. "Don't be too hard on her, Bassam. She's young." Then his eyes twinkled. "And perhaps frightened of having to abandon her western clothing. Don't worry dear, once the true faith is restored, you will find peace."

"It isn't that! I think something terrible will happen if you do what the message asks. Think a minute—"

"Alia, that's enough. Please leave us. We have important matters to discuss, and can't spend any more time with your fantasies." Bassam's expression brooked no argument, and Alia found herself moving towards the door in spite of herself. In spite of the fact that she knew she was right.

Outside once again, she took a deep breath. And what if she was wrong? What if they were right? What if the army came through the portal on command, and the world was allowed to fall into strict Islamic law? Could she survive in some sultan's harem?

She knew she wouldn't sleep that night.

***

On the day, Alia couldn't help noticing that the government, despite its support, was not running the show. They'd shrewdly let the church take center stage. No official communiqué had been made, no invitation to attend. It was obvious that they didn't want to look like idiots if things went wrong or, even worse, if nothing happened, and everyone just stood in the desert trying to avoid each other's embarrassed looks.

Nevertheless, there were plenty of people in attendance, bused in from the surrounding villages, and even from Damascus, a long hot journey away. The imam in charge was one of the old-school type, who glared at the tourists, especially the women in their shorts and t-shirts. He ignored Alia, though. Her relatively conservative jeans and the hat she habitually wore out in the sun seemed to make her the least objectionable female in the crowd who wasn't wearing traditional Muslim dress.

Flashes, visible even in the midday glare, popped continuously as the imam placed his holy implements on a specially prepared stone, the flattened yellow base of what had once been a Roman column. The greatest ceremony and prayer were reserved for the rectangular artifact, but Alia was amused to see that the battery—a twelve volt automobile unit held inside a jeweled green box—and even the cables received similar treatment.

The priest spewed a litany of extremely acid predictions about the ascendancy of Islam and the subjugation of the infidel in every corner of the world while the oblivious tourists smiled and took pictures of him.

Finally, the blessed message, the blessed battery and the blessed cables were ready for action. With agonizing slowness the imam placed each item in its assigned position and connected the cables to the battery, one to each pole.

Alia just wished he would get on with it so that whatever was going to happen would just happen and she could get back to her dig. She'd been perfectly ready to miss this particular bit of mumbo-jumbo, but Bassam had insisted that, after her outburst at the meeting, it would be much better for her if she went along with the official delegation.

With a final prayer, the cables touched the block.

Nothing much happened. A gust of wind stirred the sand a little further up the road, but that was it.

The imam raised his arms, already in damage-control mode. He wailed a prayer about the unworthiness that kept everyone from receiving Allah's gift. Alia snorted, and was about to turn away—she had better things to do with her life than watch the scene become a circus with each faction blaming the other—but something stopped her. Out of the corner of her eye, she thought she saw movement.

Suddenly, in the middle of the road that led from the west, a massive vehicle appeared. Alia was no expert on military hardware, but she could tell a tank when she saw one, even though it looked like no tank she'd ever seen before. It had no tracks, no wheels of any sort, and floated, in complete defiance of all natural laws, half a meter above the ground. But there was no mistaking the purpose of the pair of long tubes that protruded from the turret.

Two figures protruded from the top of the tank as it moved soundlessly towards them. Behind it, an identical vehicle appeared, and another. Soon there was a column moving towards the crowd, each vehicle seemingly appearing out of thin air.

The tourists backed nervously away, but the imam moved forward, welcoming the wondrous intervention of God's legions. He stood before the tank, arms upraised. The figures on the tank ignored him and kept moving forward. The imam held his ground until, with a sudden whooshing sound, he was sucked below the tank and simply disintegrated into red mist, leaving a gruesome splotch on the dry pavement when the vehicle passed.

Panic broke out. The tourists ran for their buses. Some of the soldiers opened fire with their ubiquitous AK-47s, but nothing happened. No retaliation, no effect, not even the pinging of bullets on metal. The people in the tank acted as if the shots weren't there. The soldiers, seeing this, threw down their weapons and ran.

In moments, the only people remaining were Alia and a group of government ministers.

"Do you think it's Allah's aid, as promised?" one of them said.

Another snorted. "Were you watching when it ran over the imam? That man had been selected because he was the holiest, most dedicated person in all of Syria. Would Allah have done that to him?"

"Perhaps, even now, he is in Paradise." But the rest of the group ignored him.

"Those markings on the tank. That isn't Arabic," Alia said.

She surprised herself by speaking in this company, but no one seemed to mind. They were too frightened.

"What is it?"

"Latin. It says 'Third Legion of Palmyra'." Even Bassam looked surprised at that, even though he could read Latin as well as she could.

The vehicles came to a stop ten meters in front of them. Someone began barking at them through some kind of speaker system. A woman's voice. Unintelligible gibberish in a high-speed delivery. The words flowed over the uncomprehending group.

And all of a sudden Allia could understand what they were saying. It didn't sound anything like the stiff, formal language she'd learned, and some of the words and grammar were unfamiliar, and she suspected that she was missing most of the technical terms, but it was Latin, and she could understand it.

"… We will give you until noon to answer," the woman finished.

A man's voice broke in. "Maybe they don't speak Latin."

"Then they'd better learn. They're going to need it."

"Should we repeat the message?"

A sigh. "All right. People of the former nation-state of Syria. I am Tita Livia Syriana, governess of Palmyra in the true universe and commandant of the Palmyran Legions. We declare that your former nation-state is now part of the glorious Roman Empire. Rejoice at your fortune. Soon, if you behave, you will qualify for citizenship. Even if you don't behave, the survivors will be treated humanely until you earn our trust. In order to make the transition as painless as possible, we will allow you to bring us a list of customs you wish to preserve. Otherwise, we will establish Roman law and customs. You have until noon to answer."

Alia turned towards the confused group of men, mouth already open to tell them what the woman had said. To explain that, if they wanted to save any part of their way of life, they had to make a list immediately. Noon was less than half an hour away.

And then she thought about the customs that would likely be saved, the veiled women, the right of each man to four wives. She thought about the way the woman on the tank spoke. Imperious, commanding.

She said nothing, and the sun inched its way towards the top of the sky.

SUPERIOR BEINGS

This tale is original to *Off the Beaten Path* and closes a chapter in the Poupée Cycle. As this is the most recent tale I've written about her, I don't actually know where she might be going next, but I have a feeling we haven't seen the last of her.

"It shines in the sun," Shanel said. "See?"

"Yes," the dragon rumbled. "Now stop shining it in my eyes. It hurts."

"And look. It's hard." She tapped the object against a flat rock at her feet to produce a sharp clacking sound.

Harold watched, mesmerized. His own clawed forelimbs were much too large to hold the object, of course, but it fit into Shanel's palm perfectly. When she held it up so he could take a better look, he cocked his head to focus on it with one plate-sized yellow eye. "But what is it?"

"I have no idea."

"It's trouble," Poupée said, dropping out of the trees. As always, the creature seemed to arrive whenever anything interesting happened in their little realm. Shanel felt a mixture of guilt and relief; guilt that she hadn't taken the thing straight to their leader in the first place, and relief that the matter was now out of her hands.

"Let me see that."

Shanel bent down and held it out. Poupée's features were irregular, obviously mismatched even under her long brown fur, and no two of her limbs were the same length… but that made little difference: she could move along the trees both swiftly and silently, and her tiny, fully-formed human hands were dexterous and skilled. "This is a broken cellphone," she declared. "Where did you find it?"

"On the path," Shanel said. She led them to the only lane that led in and out of their little world. It had once been a well-worn footpath through the mangrove jungle, leading to a small fishing village of five huts on a narrow spit of land. Some event had left the place abandoned, and they'd moved in. Now, the only feet that trod the path were Shanel's. Harold seldom came ashore—his bulk made him unwieldy and his wings were much better suited to moving under water. Poupée, of course, used the trees as her highway. There, she moved with all the grace she lacked on the ground.

Right at the very end of the path, where Shanel seldom dared to tread because it led to the mainland, sat a rough pyramid of fruit: guavas, bananas and mangoes. "It was sitting on that pile."

Poupée stared at the pile for a long moment. Then she did something uncharacteristic: she sat down on the path and sighed.

"What? What does this mean?" Harold said.

"It means they know we're here."

"Who?"

"The villagers. Probably the ones to the north. They're the ones with the banana tree."

"How can you tell?"

She nodded at the pile. "The fruit. It's an offering, the kind you make to the spirit of the forests. The kind they think will either keep them safe from us or entice us to grant a boon."

Shanel looked at it critically. "It's not much of an offering. We can get any of this for ourselves from the trees. And why the… what did you call it? Cell phone?"

"The cell phone is the actual sacrifice. It must have been the shiniest thing in their village, a valuable possession. It probably worked at some point, or one of them saw it working on a trip. People in big cities use them to talk to each other, but I haven't seen them working this deep in the forest."

"What are cities?" Shanel asked.

Poupée sighed again. "Not now. I think we may be in trouble."

***

Shanel looked around, tears brimming in her eyes.

The miniscule hut had been her home for the past seven years. She'd come in as a little girl, frightened of the jungle, frightened of the dark, almost frightened of her own shadow. She could only sleep if Poupée stayed with her, and she would wet her bed almost every night. Fortunately neither of her companions seemed to care about that.

But time passed and the forest became her home, the darkness became an ally… and her shadow became the closest thing she had to a companion that looked like her. She was well aware of how she looked—she'd been watching her reflection in the clear waters of the lagoon, watching it change with the years, watching her chubby child's face morph into the high-cheekboned features she had now—and knew that everyone else who looked like her, everyone human, was an enemy who meant them harm.

It was the best structure that remained in the abandoned village. Over the years, Shanel had made it better, decorating the walls with leaves and feathers, and replacing the rotting wooden floor with clean sand from the lagoon. Pretty rocks and, the centerpiece of her collection, an ancient glass bottle on which white lettering could still be seen, completed the decoration. Now, those possessions—the bottle carefully wrapped in old cloth—sat in a bag in the middle of the floor. The room seemed empty without them, but Poupée had been adamant: she was to pack immediately. It never occurred to Shanel or Harold to disobey.

Now that she was finished, however, Shanel decided to seek explanations. She spotted their leader in her favorite observation post, the top of a lone okoumé tree where she could watch the world beyond their borders without being spotted.

Shanel shimmied up the bole to where the branches sprouted,

five times higher than she was tall. Poupée heard her coming and motioned for her to stay where she was, so Shanel rested in the crotch of a branch until the small, furry creature made her way back down.

"What's happening?" Shanel asked.

"We might need to leave at any moment."

"Why?"

"Because they know we're here. Our survival depends on not being seen. We must have slipped up somehow."

"Maybe they spotted Harold. He's getting too big to hide."

Poupée reflected on that. "He was always too big to hide. But you're right. It's getting worse. Every time he leaves the water in daylight, he can be seen from a mile away."

Shanel didn't know what a mile was. Poupée often used words that she didn't know, words she found in the books she was always collecting from... Shanel had no idea where her friend got the books; she'd certainly never seen one in the jungle.

"Do we really have to leave?" The question almost died on her lips. It was difficult for Shanel to even contemplate it without crying. But she had to know.

"I... I don't know. I don't know what to do."

Somehow, that admission of helplessness hit Shanel harder than a cold, clinical confirmation would have. Poupée was their guide, their wisdom. She always knew what they had to do. Always.

"How can that be?"

Poupée sat silently for long moments before she responded. "I suppose you're old enough to talk to now," she said finally. "I remember when you were just a little girl, ready to believe anything I told you, ready to go anywhere I said."

"You saved me."

"Yes, I did. I don't even want to think about what your life would be like if you hadn't run into us. But even after everything that happened to you, you were a complete innocent. And look at you now."

"What about me?"

"You're a woman. Strong and tall… so tall." The little figure chuckled ruefully, as if lamenting the fact that she, herself, was condemned to be tiny her whole life. "But you still think we're spirits of the forest."

"I don't really think that."

"Then what are we?"

"Well, Harold is a dragon and you… maybe some kind of magical monkey?"

This time, Poupée's laugh was much heartier. "So you have been thinking about this."

"Of course. Why wouldn't I have? You've left all the books lying around, after all."

"Because you were supposed to be an innocent little girl forever. You weren't supposed to turn into a beautiful young woman with a brain." The tiny figure threw some leaves out into the forest. "Come with me."

They climbed down to ground level and entered the council chamber, a hut that contained all their most important possessions, and one which Shanel had only entered a handful of times. There was no lock on the door, no impediment to access apart from the fact that Poupée had asked her not to intrude. It was the little creature's sanctum sanctorum.

Arrayed in a semicircle around the center of the hut were Poupée's People, a tiny stuffed bear named Roger, a giant stuffed rabbit whose name Shanel never learned, and a carved wooden turtle who'd washed up against their shore one night and that Poupée had adopted. On the wall opposite the entrance, two makeshift shelves—planks stacked on large stones, held Poupée's precious books, the one thing that Poupée truly couldn't live without.

In the light coming from the door, the little figure nimbly climbed onto the upper shelf and pulled out a volume half her height. She carefully leafed through it until she came to a page with several images, and opened it.

"Look."

Shanel peered at the image. At first, she was completely puzzled by what she was seeing, then she remembered machines from her childhood in the village, and had a sense that the thing in the image was a machine of some kind, but the contrast between the gleaming and polished metal she saw and the rusted and battered memories of the village generator was too great to reconcile.

"What is it."

"That's my mother," Poupée said.

"I don't understand."

"What you see there is a BGI-Shenzen gene printer. It can create creatures… well, the stuff that creatures can be made out of, from pieces of other animals. I was made in there."

"You were… made?" Like every girl in the village, Shanel knew exactly where babies—human and animal—came from: they came from inside their mothers. And birds came from inside eggs, which came from inside their mothers. The generator couldn't make babies. "How can that be?"

"The world is a big place, and not all of it is peaceful, beautiful jungle. There are many, many people like you out there. They build all sorts of things. One of them built me."

"Who?"

"A man. A man named Phlip." She smiled at that, as if there was some kind of private joke in the simple mention of the man's name. "I think of him as my father. And that there is my mother."

"What happened to Phlip?"

"He… died. It was a long time ago, before we found you. But the important thing is that he made us—me and Harold—and… well, we are the only ones like us in the world. People won't be happy to learn that we exist, which is why I have doubts about what to do if they find us."

"I still don't understand."

"The question is whether to set out and try to hide somewhere else or to use this situation to our advantage."

That didn't clarify much.

"What I mean," Poupée went on, "is that if the nearest villagers think we're spirits, they won't come to try to kill us. But if we try to run and get discovered… well, anything could happen."

"Why would they try to kill us?"

"Not you, Shanel. Us."

"I'm one of us."

Though her face was furred, Shanel could easily see the look of infinite sadness that crossed Poupée's features. "Of course you are. Could you go, now? I need to think."

Shanel left, taking her own worries with her.

***

They came in the night, or at least one of them did.

He didn't get very far. The night belonged to Harold.

The commotion woke Shanel and she ran through the moonlit darkness, soundlessly as only a girl brought up in the jungle could, to where the shouting came from.

Harold's bulk loomed, and Poupée's soft tones reached her ears long before she saw the third person. She knew he was there, though—he was the one making most of the noise.

Poupée, on the other hand, spoke softly. "No one can hear you."

"Let me go. I'll banish you back where you came from. I've got a charm."

"Your charm…" Poupée hesitated. "It's not powerful enough to save you."

"We gave you fruit."

"And you think that gives you the right to come here and disturb us?"

Shanel finally located him. He was lying on the ground, held inexorably in place by one of Harold's colossal feet. He wouldn't be moving unless the dragon allowed it. He seemed a wretched thing.

As she watched, he began to thrash desperately.

"Ouch. Stop it. You're killing me!" the figure said. The voice sounded young, not like the rough shouts that carried across the water from unseen fishermen. Then, without warning, he began to cry, great sobs racking his dark frame.

This must have caught Harold by surprise. the dragon stepped back, easing the pressure for a single moment.

That sufficed. The young man under his claws twisted violently and disappeared into the underbrush.

"Get after him," Poupée piped.

They pursued, each in their own way. Poupée took to the trees and vanished. Harold rumbled off to try to cut him off at the narrowest point of the peninsula: where it made contact with the mainland. That was a smart move; Harold would have been slowed down by the thick tree growth if he'd tried to push through the woods.

That left Shanel. She darted through the spot where the invader had disappeared, thankful that he'd already pushed aside the worst of the thick vegetation.

Following his trail was easy, simply a question of finding the places of lowest resistance, where he'd already made a path. Even without the moonlight, Shanel would have been able to track him.

The moon was shining brightly though, and she quickly realized that if the man was planning to escape down the path to the mainland, he'd got hopelessly turned around. It was to be expected; if she'd found herself running from Harold, she would have been too scared to get her bearings as well. But it was still inexcusable in someone brought up in the forest.

Her quarry finally reached one of the paths. These were little more than the suggestion of space created by Shanel's repeated passage but compared to the thick trees and undergrowth they presented a natural highway through the forest.

The path allowed him to run faster, but he still crashed through the night. Shanel, with years of practice, began to close the gap, slowing only when she knew she was very close.

Was he trying to make his way to the water? she wondered. She hoped not. In water, like in the darkness, Harold held absolute sway. The invader would be dead and eaten before she got a chance to talk to him.

Shanel redoubled her pace, closing the gap. He pushed blithely ahead, thundering like an elephant, unaware of both her and of Poupée, gliding along the treetops. To Shanel, she was obvious, but the invader seemed to have no clue she was there.

There. A final lunge. She grabbed his legs and they tumbled onto the ground. Taking advantage of his surprise, she tried to pin him to the ground like Harold had but found herself struggling with someone much bigger and stronger than she was. He might not be a man full-grown, but he had iron muscles.

Soon, he had immobilized one of her arms and was attempting to pin her down when he desisted. "You're a girl."

She never got the chance to respond. A shadow flitted from a branch and ghosted past his face. He shouted and brought his hands up to defend his eyes.

It was the opening she needed. As Poupée swung out of reach, Shanel tackled him again and he went down hard, crashing between two mangrove trunks. He tried to regain his footing, but now the only thing beneath them were mangrove roots, some twisted, others near vertical. He stumbled again and fell into a stream with Shanel on top of him.

And then Harold was there, looming above them, silhouetted in the moonlight. All the fight went out of her opponent. He let go of Shanel and just sat there, looking up at the dragon.

"You aren't spirits, are you?" he said.

In the silence that ensued, Shanel studied him. He didn't seem fearful. Either his blubbering from earlier had been an act, or the chase had drained all the emotion from him, leaving only resignation. He was a young man or a large boy—she thought he might be about her own age.

Poupée dropped out of the trees and perched on one of Harold's shoulders. "That makes no difference. Right now, you should be more worried about what's going to happen to you."

"I suppose you're going to kill me, and that monster will eat me."

No one said anything for some moments, and Shanel watched—as well as she could in the moonlight—the realization that yes, he was most likely going to die, sink in. The boy's bravado melted away and tears welled up in his eyes again.

It amazed her how easily she could read his emotions after spending her life in exile. If Poupée's claim of being built by a man with a machine was true, the man must have mixed in something human because she now realized that the little creature's expressions were the guide she was using to read the young man in front of her. With a pang of sadness, she realized that Poupée's face showed human emotion in the same way that the wooden turtle in the council chamber resembled a turtle. The outlines were there, but it was a rough-hewn effort, a crude approximation that struggled to depict reality, and ultimately failed.

By comparison, Shanel could read every feeling the boy displayed as if he'd been telling her what was happening within.

Harold, of course, looked on impassively. If he'd been built by the same machine, no one had bothered to add emotion. But then? Harold didn't need to convey feelings; all he had to do was to loom large, solid and menacing.

"Yes."

With that single word, forced out between clenched teeth, Poupée condemned the boy to die. It was obvious she didn't want that, but also clear that she meant it.

"No!"

Shanel only realized she had been the one to speak because all the others turned in surprise. Even Harold's impassive features seemed bemused. She continued, desperate for an excuse. "Wait. He can tell us things. Like why the villagers left us the pile. And why he tried to come here alone."

Poupée studied the boy. "All right. Talk."

"Let him rest. Can't you see he's scared out of his wits? Let him rest. He can talk tomorrow."

Poupée didn't look entirely convinced, and for a second, Shanel thought her objections would be ignored. But in the end they put the frightened young man in Shanel's cabin, which was the only one strong enough to keep him contained. Then Harold lay down in front of the door.

Shanel decided to sleep on a blanket in the circular patch of ground between the houses. The open space was now softly padded with tangled grass. She was much more comfortable there than in her room.

Normally, the buzzing insects and calling birds lulled her to sleep after a few moments, but the excitement of the night and the stars shining down on her after the moon set kept her awake.

She thought about the young man locked in the darkness of her hut. She wondered whether he even knew what he'd done to deserve his death sentence. The crime of trespassing onto the spit of land and seeing its inhabitants should never have merited the snuffing out of a life

Shanel knew that staying unseen was the key to their survival, but the memory of how he'd felt when she threw him to the ground shone vividly. How his muscles had rippled as he struggled, the warmth of his body against hers, the mingling of their sweat. For some reason the boy's presence had woken a sense that something was missing in her life, shone light into a hole she hadn't imagined was there.

She toyed with the idea of trying to talk Poupée into letting the boy stay with them, but soon discarded it. Everything the little creature had done had been aimed at keeping them hidden. There was no way she would make their group bigger—especially when the addition would have no reason to keep faith with them. They couldn't watch him all the time.

Shanel tossed and turned and finally sat and looked into the night. In the dim starlight, Harold's form lay in front of the hut. He was snoring, and she knew from long experience that he would be sluggish when he woke. The dragon almost never slept at night, but when he did, this was the time for it, a couple of hours before dawn.

The boy couldn't take advantage of that, even if he'd known; Harold's body blocked the door, and no mere human could budge him.

But there was another way.

Moving quietly, Shanel crawled around the back of the hut and pulled aside three loose planks that were hidden behind the bedding, impossible to find if you didn't know what you were looking for. A hole opened, just big enough to let a person through, as long as that person was willing to drag themselves through the dirt to get inside. She hadn't used that exit in years; she'd dug it as a child, when she was still scared that her mother and her lover would find her.

She stuck her head through.

"Psst," she said.

"Who's there?" the boy's voice asked, tremulous.

"It's just me, Shanel."

"Are you one of the monsters?"

"I'm just a girl."

"The one that attacked me?"

"Yes. I was only trying to stop you."

"Why?"

She thought about it. "To stop you from talking about us."

Shuffling footsteps rushed toward her, but the boy didn't

know the room and, in the darkness, would never be able to find the opening fast enough to reach her. "Don't do that. Even if you manage to find me, all I have to do is scream for the dragon."

"Who cares? You're going to kill me anyway."

"I don't want them to kill you. I came to talk to you. What's your name?"

"Igotsu."

"Igotsu," she repeated, savoring the feel of the name on her tongue. There had been an Igotsu in her village before she'd had to run away, but that had been an old man with graying skin and few teeth. This name felt very different: rounder, fuller. "You can leave, Igotsu."

"How?"

"Through this hole."

"Never. You're some kind of witch woman."

"Witch woman? Why would you say that?"

"You live with spirits, or monsters, or whatever they are."

"They're my friends. They aren't monsters." As she said it, she remembered Poupée's words and the picture of the machine. Was the little creature right about him being there to destroy them?

"They look like monsters. The people in my village think they're spirits of the forest, but they haven't seen them from up close. I know the truth."

"You don't know anything about them. Us, I mean."

"I know you don't want to be seen, and I've seen more than enough since I came here."

"Why did you come, anyway? Did your village send you?"

"Of course not. They're terrified of you. I came because I wanted to prove that I'm a man. It was time." The voice was angry now. Evidently, talking about his village was enough to make him forget his plight.

She had no idea what he meant by that. Wasn't he a man because of other things? What difference could it possibly make to do something completely stupid? "And have you?"

"I don't think so. Everyone will think I ran away because I can't stand my life in the village. No one will believe that I was eaten by a dragon."

In the darkness, he sounded too loud, so she whispered her next words. "You won't be."

"What?"

"I said you won't be. I'm going to show you how to get out of here. Take my hand."

"How? I can't see you."

She wriggled a bit further inside and extended her own hand to where his voice was coming from. Her fingers found his chest and she felt him flinch, but held on and soon had her hand in his. "Follow me."

She led him to the hole in the wall and, with a struggle—he was almost too big for the hole—they stood outside. Even then, she kept hold of his hand, his warm, dry skin rough against her own, until they reached one of the paths.

"Do you think you can find your way back from here?"

He stood looking into the darkness for a few moments before shaking his head, the movement barely visible in the night.

Shanel sighed. "I'll take you, then. Hurry."

They set out through the jungle, following the quickest route to the exit, secure in the knowledge that Harold slept soundly beside the hut.

Without warning, something made contact with her throat, light as a feather. She thought it was a bug and tensed to brush it away. "Don't move," a familiar voice whispered in her ear. Poupée's voice. "That's a razor. If you move, you will die."

The voice of her friend, her mentor, her protector sounded colder than Shanel had ever heard it. She believed in the very depths of her being that Poupée would do exactly what she threatened.

"What's wrong? Why did we stop?" Igotsu demanded.

"There's been a change of plans," Popuée replied. "Now stay where you are or you'll die, too."

"Who..?"

"Be quiet. I'll deal with you later." Poupée turned back to Shanel, her tiny body barely visible in the thin light. "Are you really that ungrateful? Would you really trade our lives for his?"

"I'm not trading anything. I want us to let him go. He hasn't done anything wrong."

"What do you think will happen if he gets back to his village and talks about what he saw here?"

"We'll just have to move."

"Impossible. It's too dangerous."

"Dangerous for who? You can hide in the trees, and Harold can wait in the lagoon until they leave."

"What about you?" Poupée asked quietly. "if they find you, they won't stop looking for us." The blade pressed into the soft skin of her neck. Poupée might have been tiny, but she was strong—more than strong enough to cut through her, and more than fast enough to do it before Shanel could move. "So, unless he dies, we will have to run, and running is too risky. But if we kill him, maybe the rest of his village will be too frightened to come this way."

"Or maybe they'll be so angry that they'll come and get us."

"It's a risk, but we didn't ask for this. We need to kill him now."

"No."

"Don't make me do this, Shanel."

"Would you?"

"You're human. I've already killed my own father for being human and doing the things that humans do."

"The things that humans do?"

The edge dug deeper. Shanel was certain the skin must have split. "Yes. You know. Always wanting to be with other humans. Not caring about anyone who doesn't meet their standards of beauty. Being afraid of everything different. Do you know humans have killed off most of the other animals on the planet?"

Shanel was about to say that that was ridiculous, that the jungle around them was full of other creatures, but the cold metal against her throat made her think twice.

"I thought you were different," Poupée continued. "I thought you loved us. I thought you understood… and then, the first chance you have, you betray us."

A tear ran down Shanel's cheek. It must have rolled onto the blade because she didn't feel it on her shoulder. "How can you say that? I love you like my mother. No, that's not true. I hated my mother. I ran away from my mother. I love you like the mother I wish I'd had."

"And yet you freed him."

"I had to. Killing him is wrong."

This time the silence stretched long enough that some of the more courageous insects began chirruping again. "You still think we should let him go? Even though you know what it means?"

"Yes. He didn't do anything wrong."

"Then we'll have to run again." Poupée sounded old, tired.

"Then we'll run."

"No. We'll run. Harold and I. Like you said, we can hide in the lagoons. You can't."

"What?"

"Letting the man go means we have to split up. We'll go our way and you'll go yours."

"No!"

"It has to be this way. We can't survive with you along."

"We did it once already!"

"We were lucky to find this place. There aren't many abandoned villages where we can hide and you can live the life you're used to."

"I'll sleep on the ground. Please!"

"No." There was sadness in the voice, more than Shanel had

ever heard her friend express in all their days together. "It's better this way. You can have somewhere you belong, a place where you'll be accepted. You should treasure that."

"No. Please."

But the razor was gone, as was the barely-felt presence of her best friend and mentor. Moments later, the sound of something large slipping gently into the water echoed between the trees. She ran even though she knew Harold could swim faster than anything in the lagoons. Sure enough, by the time she reached the shore he was gone too.

She cried until a hand on her shoulder made her look up. Igotsu stood beside her, the pink of approaching dawn illuminating him. He smiled sadly. "She was right. Your place is with us."

"Us?"

"I'll take you back with me."

She swallowed down the sorrow. What else was there for her?

"I need to see something first."

She walked the twenty paces to the door of the council chamber, but the stuffed animals were gone. So was the book with the pictures and many of the others. The shelves stared back at her, gap-toothed. That, more than any words, made her understand that Poupée wasn't coming back.

Shanel bent to pick up the carved turtle. She suspected her friend had left that behind on purpose somehow knowing how Shanel felt about it.

"Let's go," she said.

"Aren't you going to take anything else?

She hefted the turtle in her hands. It was heavy with the weight of memory. "No. I've got what I need."

They walked into the night.

Together.

Scratching Through Rock

This story is brand new, original to this collection. In it, I dive deep into Argentine society without hiding it with distance or an alternative universe as I do in other tales in this book. This one goes straight to the heart of the single biggest thing to happen to Argentines in most people's lives, and the one thing in the past that, even after 35 years of peace and democracy, our society still has trouble getting over: the military dictatorship of the 1970s.

Well, that and our recent form in the Football World Cup... but I decided to focus on the dictatorship for this one.

Something pulled.

I didn't know what it was, all I knew was I couldn't resist the tug, so I picked some jeans and a shirt out of the pile beside my bed, grabbed my *alpargatas*, the cloth shoes that were all I could afford, and forced my sixty year old legs to function.

The stairs of my tenement creaked as I descended, a sound strange to me. During the day, the building was too full of noise to hear it: women calling to each other as they took out their laundry, children screaming up and down the steps, doors opening and closing and drunken men returning from yet another fruitless search for work.

Outside, the night was as silent as the tenement, the bright yellows and reds of the houses lost in the darkness. The tourists were long gone, and *La Boca* had seemed to revert to its true glory days, when it was a working port, never imagining that it would become a curiosity that, though everyone agreed it was dangerous as hell, always overflowed with tourists.

A fog had fallen. Not unheard of—we were close to the river, after all—but unusual. But the pull intensified, became a hint of music, and within a few blocks, the suggestion coalesced into a series of chords. I nearly went home. I didn't want to follow the chords. Not those. But my feet took me where I was called without awaiting my permission.

The cops were huddled beside a patrol car whose blue lights were barely up to the task of illuminating the area around it. But no one was watching the mouth of the alley, so I walked in.

I'd barely entered the alley when a hand took hold of my shoulder. "Where do you think you're going?" It was a woman's voice. She held a flashlight up to my face, blinding me.

"I'm going to see what's up there."

"You don't want to."

"No, but I think I have to."

"Why?" Now she'd pulled the light away I saw red hair and a face almost as old as mine. She was giving me that look cops must practice in the mirror, that said that you were the main suspect of every crime they could come up with?

So I shrugged and told her the truth. "I was asleep and I felt… I'm not sure how to describe it… a call, from here."

"A call?" The look changed from one of suspicion to one of understanding. She'd collared a crazy old loon.

"Yes. And I'm not crazy. It was a call, and it had music, guitar music. I can hear a riff, just a few notes, over and over again."

"I can't hear anything," she said.

"Of course not. It's calling me, and only me. I was the only one Guillermo ever played it for. We composed it one night in the back room of a bar in 1979, and Guillermo disappeared that day." The way I said the word "disappeared" left no question about where he'd gone. The military dictatorship had taken him to one of its clandestine detention centers and not many people made it back from those. "He's been dead for forty years."

She shuddered, then gave me a sharp look. "Did you say guitar music?"

"Yeah."

"I think you'd better come with me."

She didn't say it in the kind of tone you argued with.

***

El Comisario, the officer in charge of the precinct, was a tall man with an ample belly and a black moustache. He looked about fifty, but he might have been ten years younger. That was probably because people insisted on being murdered in the middle of the night, and other people insisted on waking him to look at bodies. He was sitting in the car, and when the young woman told him my story he gave me the same look she had. "So you're a musician?"

"A rock star," I replied indignantly. "You should be old enough to recognize me."

He shrugged. "I'm more into reggaetón myself. What group were you in?"

"Baltrauta."

"Never heard of it."

"We only lasted a few years. Our guitarist… well, he fell afoul of the military junta."

The man chuckled darkly. "Yeah, that can put an end to an artistic career. So you were revolutionaries."

"Not really. Only Guillermo was politically active."

"What's your name?"

"I'm Víctor Canales." I said it with pride. People who knew the golden age of Argentine rock knew the name.

This guy, on the other hand, just looked blank. He groaned and pulled himself off the car seat. "Come on."

We walked back into the alley, all the way to the end this time. There was a young man slumped against a wall, a guitar case beside him. Blood stained the front of his shirt and, when I looked closer, I saw it came from his throat.

"His throat was cut?" I asked, thankful that my dinner, like all my dinners for the past twenty years, had been meagre.

The big cop shook his head. "Garotted. Look." He bent down and, using a handkerchief picked something off the dead boy's shirt, a piece of cord that led to the boy's neck. "Any idea what this might be?"

I knew, and he knew I knew. Once again, I had to fall back on the truth; sometimes there wasn't any other choice. "A guitar string."

He nodded grimly.

And the music in my head suddenly stopped.

***

The grimy cell smelled like vomit, but it had a window. I smiled. The last time I'd been in a cell, it had been buried deep in the bowels of a colossal building. It had been tiled and spotless though, smelling of disinfectant. The military dictatorship hadn't allowed its cells to stay soiled.

Now, I leaned back on the metal chair bolted to the wall and smiled. This was just a holding cell in the neighborhood precinct station. They used it to detain drunks, and pickpockets who hadn't paid their bribes. It wasn't the first step on a walk to oblivion.

The hall in front of my cell must have been a convenient shortcut because a bunch of officers carrying photocopies and envelopes went back and forth along it without ever looking my way. I would have spoken to them if I hadn't been enjoying myself so much. Besides, they'd tell me everything in their own sweet time: cops loved to gossip. It might have been different once. I don't remember chatting with cops too much during the Junta years, but since then, they'd really relaxed, and you could usually find out anything you wanted if you were willing to stop and chat on a lonely night. They were human, underpaid and misunderstood by most, so they appreciated basic kindness just like anyone else.

A little before noon—I wasn't wearing a watch and my phone had been confiscated—a small guy opened the door to my cell and said: "You can go now."

"Thanks. But why did you lock me up in the first place?"

"The *comisario* ordered it. Guy is killed with a guitar string and a musician was first person on scene… if he hadn't taken you in, he thinks they would have taken away his badge."

"Come on, he was robbed. Do I look like a mugger?"

"He wasn't robbed. He still had money… and do you think they would have left the guitar behind? No. We think this is a contract killing."

"So, who was he? Drug dealer?"

"That's the funny part. He's just some college kid who plays the guitar at bars a few nights a week. We have no clue why anyone would want to kill him. He's never been on anyone's radar. Not even a speeding ticket to his name."

"So how come they're letting me go?"

"Another body turned up. Witnesses said the screaming started at five-thirty in the morning… you were in that cell by four."

I nodded and was about to leave when a thought hit me. "Bodies show up all the time in this city. Why do you think they're related?"

"The other victim was a young woman. She was getting home from playing a concert and she was garroted with a guitar string. I think we can assume it's the same guy."

And, just like that, the music in my head started again. The same riff, but with a triumphant feel to it.

***

I thought it would go away, but it didn't, and at around four in the afternoon, the need to see where it would take me became too urgent to ignore.

A bus, a subway, plus another bus saw me at the very northern end of town, diametrically across from where I started out. Parque Saavedra was crowded, which was to be expected on a Saturday afternoon… but it felt too crowded by about half.

I walked up to a girl in a short dress, like something out of my seventies college years, or one of Argentina's poor excuses for hippie communes, picture perfect down to the bright yellow flower in her hair. When she returned my smile I asked her what was going on.

"Rock concert," she replied. "Music with heart, none of the new crap. Acoustic guitars, the way it was always meant to be."

I chuckled to myself. She clearly had no clue who I was, and Guillermo, one of the rock gods of the generation she pretended to belong to, would have sold his soul to any demon that offered him an electric guitar. The only reason old rock was played on acoustic guitars was because secondhand acoustics handed down from our grandparents were all we could afford before the record companies took note.

She headed off towards a stage in the middle of the park and I bent and picked up a crumpled blue flyer. *Woodstock Saavedra*, it announced.

I chuckled. At least the call had brought me to something I might enjoy. I sat down in the grass about thirty meters from the stage. I was early. Only a few isolated spectators dotted the grass, smoking joints and talking amongst themselves. But soon more people began to drift in. Everyone seemed to have dressed for the occasion; flared pants and checked shirts competed with batik. Everyone wore flowers.

The ensembles made me wonder where everyone had gotten their fashion tips. I'd lived through most of the movement in Argentina in jeans and a t-shirt which, in those days, painted me a shiftless Marxist menace. I'd never even owned a tie-dyed shirt.

The show began an hour before dusk. Some things hadn't changed: the first groups were obviously just warmup, new kids searching for their sound or trying to copy sounds that had died away before they were born.

Of the rest, there was some talent—a bassist keeping time to his drummer despite the fact that the guy behind the pots was either drunk or stoned, a guitarist whose fingers danced like Joaquín Cortés—but you had to pick them out, and it took a good ear or, in my case, fifty years of music... even if the last thirty of them hadn't been particularly active.

Meanwhile, the riff inside my head had subsided into a strumming rhythm, no longer tugging hard, as though it was satisfied I was where I needed to be.

Finally, the crowd stirred and a new group walked onto the stage to actual applause. This must be one of this generation's preferred acts. I sat up straighter and turned to the guy sitting next to me.

"What's this group called?"

"*Los Que Quedaron*," he replied. The ones that remained. I wondered what that might refer to. They consisted of a pretty girl with straw-colored hair on the ubiquitous acoustic guitar, a bearded guy on a Yamaha organ, a female bassist—electric bass, I noted with amusement—and another beard on the drums. The two women were front and center with mikes on stands.

The first song started. I found myself relaxing back into my previous slouch and wondering what all the fuss was about. These guys weren't notably different from the groups that had come before, maybe a little more polished, but that was it.

The lead singer was the guitarist, with the bass player as supporting vocalist. The singer's voice was a bit thin and reedy—not unpleasant, but certainly not memorable. The song's lyrics spoke of holes in people's lives, about people who were missing.

I sat back to let the set wash over me, no longer truly listening, and squirmed with the discomfort of sitting on the grass for so long. Each group so far had gotten four songs, and the first three ended quickly enough. The crowd seemed to enjoy them.

"Now we're going to do something new," the lead singer announced. "It's the first time we've ever played it in public." She put down the acoustic guitar and picked up a red electric number.

I yawned as the bassist started what she probably felt was a powerful thumping rhythm, but which just wasn't doing it for me.

Suddenly, the riff in my head began again. It was louder, somehow crisper and more real; whatever was pulling my strings like a puppet must really want me to do something urgently. I stood almost automatically, ready to follow the tug.

But there was no tug at all, no sense of urgency.

The riff faltered.

I looked at the stage: the sound was coming from the group. The lead guitarist looked both confused and frightened. The bassist and the drummer were looking at her as if she'd really screwed up. I couldn't see the keyboard player.

Then the blonde girl shook her head and an expression of… well, it's hard to describe, but it looked to me like an expression of understanding… came over her. She said something to the bassist, nodded to the drummer and launched into the riff again.

This time it wasn't hesitant. This time the bass wasn't tenuous. And either the drummer was really good—which hadn't been evident before—or something magical must have happened, he joined the song as if he'd been one of *Baltrauta*. Because the song was a Baltrauta song, the very one we'd been composing that night amid cigarettes and girls whose names we wouldn't remember a week later. It was the riff, it was the bass, it was the drums. The only thing missing was my piano.

Then the girl began to sing and the lyrics, the first wine-addled draft of which I'd abandoned on a soggy paper napkin when the cops had stormed in, emerged in their full glory.

This wasn't the rough, incomplete version I'd half-set down that night. These were the words the way I imagined them in my head, perfectly shaped the way songs never were… as though I'd had time to polish them over and over.

Perhaps I had… or someone had… or something. They'd taken forty years to be sung in public, after all.

This was something special, and the crowd knew it. The

song raged, but it raged without excess, it moved, but without resorting to cheap shots. It had true substance. For three eternal minutes, *Baltrauta* lived again and everyone came to their feet.

Then it was over. She belted the last line in a deep contralto that was completely unlike anything she'd hinted before then stopped, placed the mike in its stand and walked off the stage, dazed, still carrying the guitar, which was still plugged into its amp. When she noticed, she removed the plug on the guitar end and just kept walking.

The remaining members of the group exchanged bewildered glances and began to put away their instruments. The next group was already onstage, setting things up.

I bolted through the crowd to the stage exit, which consisted of four black planks that served as steps. There were no barriers between the musicians and the crowd, so the girl with the guitar walked along the grass, absent-mindedly acknowledging the congratulations thrown her way.

I stood in front of her, forcing her to stop and look up. Vague recognition crossed her features, but she tried to step around me.

"I'm Víctor Canales."

She stopped dead in her tracks and looked at me again. This time she actually *looked*. Wonder bloomed. "Yes. You are. I knew I'd seen you somewhere, but I couldn't place it. It's from the cover of your album."

"You've seen our album?"

"I've worn out my copy of *Baltrauta Sings the Turtle*. Thank God for YouTube…. You were amazing, the greatest group of the seventies. It's a tragedy what happened to Guillermo." Then her face clouded over. "Just another thing the military junta has to answer for."

That was a long time ago, I thought but didn't say. She was what, twenty? Though she hadn't lived through those days, I knew her type: they burned with the fire of hatred for the police state and all the people involved with it, and nothing you could say would ever change their mind.

The silence stretched. She broke it. "I'm sorry. I imagine you miss him more than I ever will." She smiled with the mixture of confidence and insecurity that only a singer who's had a little success, but is in the presence of someone they consider more important, can pull off. "I'm Camila, by the way. Did you really want to talk to me?"

"Yeah… I wanted to ask about that last song."

The dazed expression returned. "Yeah. I'd like to know a little bit about it, too."

"What do you mean? You sang it."

"I… I guess I did. But I'd never heard it before."

"That's impossible. You performed it perfectly."

"It just came to me. I fought it…. Did we stop playing the first time?"

"Yes."

"I thought so. It's all a bit blurry, and I haven't had a drink all day."

"But after you stopped, you played it beautifully."

"Yes."

"And you don't know where it came from?"

"No. My fingers just knew what to play. My mouth knew what to sing. I've never felt anything like that before."

"I wrote it. The song, I mean. Forty years ago."

She looked aghast. "I'm sorry. I mean, I didn't know. We weren't trying to steal it…"

"I know."

"Oh." Flustered, she shut up.

I decided to make it easier on her. "It was the last song Guillermo and I ever composed. We were working on it the night he was taken in."

"I swear I'd never heard it."

"I know you didn't. No one heard it. As far as I know, the only person who heard the riff was me… and no one has ever seen a complete version of the lyrics."

"How…"

"Look, why don't you let me buy you a cup of coffee?"

***

It ended in bed, of course. It nearly always did.

Smoking a cigarette afterwards, I did what I always did on these occasions: tried to avoid thinking of why she'd climbed into the sack with a guy nearly three times her age who'd never been that good looking to begin with.

I knew exactly why, but I preferred not to admit it.

She wasn't sleeping with me in any but a physical sense. She was actually sleeping with my music and, through me, with Guillermo. She was celebrating the golden age of Argentine rock, before the reintroduction of democracy and the freedom to sing about whatever we wanted without fear of repercussions took the edge off. It was her way to connect to the seventies, her chance to tell all her friends about what she'd done.

I wasn't about to question her motives. All I cared about was that she was young and pretty and enthusiastic. She didn't even criticize my tiny room in the tenement, just assumed it came with the territory of bohemian rocker. Had she known what my royalty checks looked like forty years on, she would have realized the tiny space was all I could afford.

But it had a railed balcony, just big enough to hold a table for two—overlooking the touristy—if poor—section of *Caminito* in *La Boca*, and it was another glorious sunny morning.

"So, I'm curious," I said. "What does the name of your group mean?"

"You're going to think I'm making it up," she said. "It has way too much to do with what we were discussing last night. About the dictatorship and the Disappeared."

"Try me."

"Well, the group's called *Los Que Quedaron* because we're

literally the ones who were left. Everyone in the group has a family member who disappeared during the dictatorship. A great uncle, a father's cousin. In my case, it was my grandfather… and since I'm a direct descendant, I get to be the singer."

"I heard you sing. You would have been the singer anywhere."

"Not really. I don't have much of a voice."

"I disagree. Remember that I was there for your latest concert. I know about this stuff. The way you sang that last number…"

She looked uncomfortable. "What you heard… I'm not really sure where that come from. It wasn't my voice."

"It was coming from you."

"Still. It's like the words, I don't know where they came from."

I was about to argue, but what right did a guy who'd followed a guitar riff played by an invisible Pied Piper have to criticize a girl who pulled lyrics and a voice out of nowhere?

Instead, I grunted. "Yeah, strange things have been happening all over."

The strumming, too soft to be a riff, chose that exact moment to start up again, as if to warn me the strange happenings weren't done.

We finished breakfast and I offered to walk her to the bus stop, eager to get out into the sunshine. I tried to spend the smallest amount of time possible cooped in my little room.

The *Comisario* was leaning against a lamppost when we emerged.

"Hello, Victor," he said with a smile I wasn't sure I liked. "We need to talk."

"Can it wait until I walk the young lady to the bus?"

"Sure. I'll come with you."

The bus stop was a couple of blocks away, on the avenue, so it was just a matter of minutes before she boarded. Our goodbye was about as awkward as they always were. In daylight, the romance of sleeping with the seventies was eclipsed by the reality of the older man who'd been the vehicle. At the last moment, she tried to turn away from the kiss, and I got a little mouth but mostly cheek.

The cop surprised me. Instead of razzing me, he looked sympathetic. "The young are always fickle. They don't know how to appreciate the good things in life."

"So you're a poet as well as a cop?"

"Times have changed. It's allowed now." He smiled thinly.

"Fair enough, I guess. To what do I owe this pleasure? I don't imagine I charmed you so much that you just had to see me."

"Why not? Seemed to work pretty well on the girl last night."

So they'd been watching me. And the *Comisario* wanted me to know it. At least they'd had the decency to wait before picking me up.

"And yet, I sense that isn't why you're here."

"No. It isn't. I'm here because we had a bit of a breakthrough regarding the dead guy."

"So quickly?"

"We work fast in the police force."

He waited to see if I had any smart Alec comments, but I did my best to disappoint. I kept my peace and let him continue.

"Anyway, someone working the other case, the girl, realized both victims were descended from prominent members of the military in the seventies, officers involved with torture and execution of dissidents." He gave me a long, hard look to see how I would react. I tried to keep up my poker face. "And that got me thinking. Which guy that had just happened to appear at my crime scene last night had a serious beef with the dictatorship?"

"I didn't do it."

"I'm not saying you did. The only way you could have killed the girl is for the night watch at the *comisaría* to have let you out and then let you back in once the deed was done… all without telling me. I'm willing to believe they're all corrupt, but they're not all stupid. So no. You didn't do it."

"Then what…"

"But I think you know who did."

I said nothing. How could I tell him I thought a ghost was involved? He'd either think I was crazy or he'd be pissed at me for lying to him. "I really don't."

He sighed. "It's no use trying to protect him. We'll grab him in the end, and it will go hard with anyone who protected him."

"If I do think of anything, I promise to let you know."

"Make sure of it." He ambled away, unhurried. I wondered if that was the way he spent his days: issuing vague threats to potential witnesses, but it seemed too romantic, too literary to be real. He'd probably just looked me up because it was better than having to do paperwork all day.

***

I spent the Sunday sitting in a traditional café in the city center. I wasn't in the mood to remain in my neighborhood and watch the tourists or, worse, get harassed by the cops.

So I sat and listened to a couple of guys in their eighties discussing Perón. One was drinking coffee, the other gin, and both were wearing brown suits, probably bought back when I was still dreaming of playing in public. They'd likely commanded a bigger table once. But friends had been lost along the way, to death, to nursing homes, and these two were all that remained to fulfill the ritual.

That made me sad and I thought about my relationship with Guillermo. Not about his music—I thought about that all the time—but about our friendship. How we used to while away our evenings in dark places… anywhere you could get alcohol and where the cigarette smoke rose in billowed folds was good enough for us. That's where we'd sit and talk to girls, or when the girls realized there were more interesting things to do than talk to us, to write a song. Guillermo never went anywhere without his guitar.

Where had it gone? The cops who'd taken us that night hadn't been the understanding kind. They weren't the friendly neighborhood beat cop. They were hard men, killers without remorse, and they had told him the guitar wasn't coming.

When they put us in different cars, I didn't imagine one of the vehicles led to life and the other to death.

I asked the waiter for a napkin and pulled an old ballpoint from the pocket of my jacket. I started writing a poem. Well, it started out as one; it wouldn't be a poem when it was done, but the lyrics to a song. It was all about a girl with straw-colored hair and a song I hadn't heard in ages. It was about how friends had gotten off at different stations and were no longer along for the ride. It was about growing old and about leaving something behind. As I wrote, I cried.

I'd forgotten about the tears that came when I wrote lyrics. That hadn't happened to me since the last time I'd written a song. Decades ago.

Had it really been that long?

Yes, it had. Something inside had died with Guillermo, and it had taken a girl too young to understand anything, even her own motivations, to revive it.

I stayed in the bar until night was falling, and then the riff started again, a melody I'd never heard before, but it was undoubtedly Guillermo; I could recognize his style anywhere. It was an angry tune, almost all rhythm, but with enough melody in there that it would have been an instant classic if we'd ever played it in public. But we never had… In fact, I would have sworn that it hadn't been written when he died.

There was no resisting it. I walked out, and it led me from the city center into a residential neighborhood. I walked streets I knew, then many I'd never seen before, driven by an enraged guitar.

Then the pull relaxed and I found myself walking behind a young man with long hair who turned into a dark side street.

Suddenly the guitar screamed, a chord never intended for an

acoustic… it was a full on heavy-metal screech.

"I didn't know you had it in you, Guille," I said to no one.

My only answer was the wind picking up and swirling some leaves. Of course, that might have just been my imagination, but still, I peered closely into the dark corners. In the movies, ghosts made their presence felt this way, but I should have known better. Guillermo was never that subtle.

Twenty meters in, the young man I'd been following without knowing it—dragged along by the pull—suddenly stopped and straightened with a muffled cry. No… he began to arc backward as if he was being pulled from behind, and his hands reached out, trying to grab something behind him.

I rushed towards him. Was he having some kind of seizure? What were you supposed to do in these situations? Put something in his mouth to keep him from swallowing his tongue? One thing was certain: any action was better than just standing there watching.

By the time I reached him, he'd slumped over on his side, so I rolled him onto his back.

He was far beyond any help.

A sharp dark line was traced across his throat, already beginning to bleed. Looking carefully, I could spot where the guitar string emerged from the gore.

I turned away, thankful I'd had nothing to eat. Throwing up would have given the cops a clue. Could they use vomit to find me? I didn't know. From what I'd seen on TV, they could probably find out that I'd been here just from analysis of my footsteps on the concrete sidewalk but a pile of vomit would have been a dead giveaway.

The music in my head was already pulling me away. I didn't need to be told the obvious: I'd been taken there to witness the killing. Now, it was time to get the hell out of there.

An hour and a train ride later, I was sitting in a well-lit restaurant with a book and several dozen witnesses, nursing the single coffee my funds stretched to.

The book was for show. I'd found it in a box on the street and picked it up on a whim. I couldn't concentrate for the broken fragments of guitar music flying around in my head.

***

He came to me in my room. There was no mistaking it this time, no need to be sensitive or even intelligent. My scant wardrobe, scattered on random surfaces, fluttered in his rage. The leaves of my book turned themselves, even though my window opened onto a dead-still night.

But the real giveaway was the unmistakable smell: smoke and his terrible cologne. Did we really use that stuff back in the seventies? I suppose we did.

"You've got to stop killing people," I told the empty space where I imagined him to be.

That didn't go down well. Things flew, paper and used socks actually flew in the dark confines of the room.

"I don't care what they did to you. It was their parents or grandparents. You're murdering kids."

The rage this time seemed more subdued... petulant.

"Yeah. They're probably more like us than like their ancestors. Just want to share their music with people to make them happy."

Everything went still, and I realized I could actually, somehow, feel his moods. Now it was ice-cold fury, and I knew exactly why.

"No. It isn't fair they cut your life short. It isn't fair you couldn't share your joy at being alive. I think we lost even more than we imagined when you died. But you can't make that better by taking revenge... besides, no one will even know you had anything to do with it. The families will be hurting, but they'll never know why."

That stopped him. I felt the air around me calm down... if that makes any sense.

After that, we sat, the way we'd done so often, each lost in his own thoughts, when we were stuck on a song, or simply sick of listening to each other.

And then, as always did, one of us had an idea. This time, it was my turn.

"All of that music you showed me earlier. Did you compose it?"

His reply was a blast of riffs, rhythms, melodies and even something that sounded like a piano concerto—all different but still somehow unmistakably his.

"So let me write them down. We can get that group you showed me to play them, and send out whatever message you want, without killing innocent kids. I've even got some new lyrics." I pulled out the napkin from that afternoon. "Maybe a sad tune for that one."

Read them to me, the empty room echoed without sound.

So I did, and we worked, and guitar music was in my head again, and I wrote it down.

And forty years had never passed.

RACIAL MEMORY

Another of my favorite stories, and one which combines my fascination with early humanity and the Olduvai Gorge with the beautiful possibilities just beyond the veil of reality. I hope you enjoy reading this as much as I loved writing it.

It's another of my stories published by in Third Flatiron's anthology series, this time in *Keystone Chronicles*.

"Grandpa, can you tell me about the fairies?"

"Again? You really like the fairies, don't you? Do you want me to read you a bit of this book of fairy stories?"

"No, not those. Those are stupid. I want to know about the real fairies. You said you knew the story. You said you'd tell me where they went."

"Not where they went, but where they were last seen."

"Isn't it the same thing?"

"No, this happened a long time ago, far away from here."

"Far, like McMurray Street?"

"Much further."

"Wow. Where? Have I been there?"

"Hmm. I don't know, have you ever been to the Olduvai Gorge?"

"What? There's no such place, you're making things up…"

***

At the bottom of a deep, steep hole in Africa, a girl looked up at the night sky. She didn't know she was a girl, she didn't even know what a girl was. All she really knew was that the night sky had pretty lights in it and that there were things that were good to eat, and things that made you sick. There were also things that liked to eat things like her, but there weren't all that many of them that would dare to attack a big girl with a spear. Those things and the trees and the walls of the valley made up the category she mentally called 'the world'. The world was half of what she thought about.

Most of the rest of what she thought about was the group. The girl didn't know what a family was, she didn't know what a clan was. She just knew that there were other things like her living in the hole—which was actually a valley, but one with walls so steep that no one had ever climbed them—and that they shared their food with her and that she had to share her food with them. In her mind, they were 'people', and there were man-people and woman-people in the group.

The reason this girl had to think these things out by herself was that she lived very far back in time, in what is called prehistoric times. In fact, she lived so far back that the only people living in the world all lived in Africa. And of those people, only the most intelligent and adventurous had made it as far as the Olduvai Gorge, which does, in fact, exist, but it doesn't look like it did back then. Water and wind have softened the sides, and made it much easier to climb in and out of now than it was back then.

The girl's grandparents' grandparents had seen a lush forest which looked like it had food in it and climbed down the side, but, by the time she'd been born, there was no one left alive who knew how to get back out again. And even if there were, the group had broken into other, smaller groups, which had grown, and it was dangerous to pass their territory. They would keep any girls they saw tied up until they were old enough for children. The girl didn't want children because they cried and smelled and you had to give them food from your own body.

But right at that moment, she wasn't thinking about her people, and she wasn't thinking about the world. She was watching one of the tiny glowing creatures, about the size of her hand, that shared the valley with them. It was trapped, one wing caught between a rock and the floor, and its efforts to escape were achieving little, apart from putting a huge strain on the wing. It would tear off soon, leaving the creature—shaped like one of her people, but lighter-skinned and much, much smaller—to the mercy of the scurrying things that roamed through the underbrush.

The girl got into a more comfortable position, and sat still. She was afraid to touch the glowing creature—everyone knew that some members of her group had been touched by the glowing ones, and they had been driven mad by impossible visions and nightmares—but was perfectly willing to let something else come along to try to victimize it. Maybe whatever came along would be edible. Maybe it would just be fun to watch.

The fairy—and that was what it was, even though the girl didn't know it—saw her and looked straight into her eyes. It stopped struggling. Were it not for that useless, pale-colored skin that would have looked better on a fish than on a person who had to walk in the sun, it would have looked exactly like an adult woman-person. It stayed still, which kept it from breaking the wing, but wouldn't help much if a something hungry came along. The girl recognized that look. It was the look that trapped animals gave her just before she hit them with her spear.

But she didn't hit the fairy with her spear. She did something that surprised even herself.

The girl lifted the rock.

And the fairy… Well, the fairy flew away as fast as its injured wing allowed it to.

***

"It flew away?"

"Of course it did. What did you expect?"

"I don't know, fairy stuff. Gold. Treasure. Wishes!"

"But what would a girl like that do with gold?"

"You're right, she's like a caveman, isn't she?"

"Well, not exactly. They didn't live in caves there. And she was a girl, so she couldn't be a caveman at all."

"But like a caveman, or a cavegirl, or whatever."

"Yes, like one. But not exactly one."

"All right. But what about the fairies?"

"I'll tell you more about them tomorrow."

***

The girl walked through the densest forest.

Some parts of the great valley were open, grassy and ideal for hunting because you could see a long way, but the girl tended to avoid those places. What helped you hunt food also allowed things that ate people to hunt you—and it also allowed other tribes to hunt girls like her. She preferred the safety of the dark shadows and recessed nooks.

And besides, in the shadows, she could see the soft light of the flying people. Their loops and stunts made her smile—and some of the more amazing swoops actually caused her to laugh out loud.

But the main reason she went there wasn't for safety or for entertainment. It was so that she wouldn't have to share her food with the others. She knew how to get food from the forest and, if she were careful to wash off the blood afterward, no one would know that she'd eaten, and they'd give her a share of what the other hunters brought back with them.

Her method was simple. All she would do was to rub leaves and dirt on her body, and sit inside a bush next to one of the paths that the animals used to get to the flowing water that ran through the middle of the valley. If she stayed very still, one of the bolder animals would walk past. It was usually something a little too big to attack with her spear, but, egged on by its success, smaller forms would soon appear.

A small, furry creature walked bonto sight, moving slowly and raising its head to sniff the air suspiciously every two or three steps. The girl held her breath, hoping that this one wouldn't sense her and be spooked. Two or three of the glowing people flew above her head, but they were common enough that perhaps the small creature wouldn't realize that they marked her position.

It was close enough, now, to strike. But the girl waited. One more step.

All of a sudden, the creature seemed to realize its danger, looked straight at the place where the girl was hidden, and turned.

At the same moment, she threw the spear with all her strength, knowing immediately that she'd missed slightly to one side. The creature saw it coming and spooked, swerving at high speed away from the missile, and away from her. It brushed the branch of a low thorn-bush and then, with a crash, cartwheeled into the tangle of thorns. It lay there, twitching one limb or other experimentally.

The girl could see that it wouldn't go anywhere. Every time it moved, all it did was to bury the spikes impaling it a little deeper into its flesh. She watched it struggle, seeing no need to hurry and the flying people-things gathered around her.

But this wasn't a strange and possibly dangerous glowing person. This was food, and the girl picked up her spear and, without pausing, buried it in the creature's torso. It squealed once, and then struggled, freeing itself from the thorns.

The spear, however, was too much for it, passing all the way through its body. The food was dead within moments.

She danced with the joy of capture, of feeding and of life. She pulled the creature out of the bush, still impaled on the spear, and set it down before her. She knew that if she took it to her group, most would be taken from her. Maybe the group would use its captive ember to make a fire and cook some of the meat, and that would be delicious.

But it was worth sacrificing taste to have more for herself. She used the sharpened point of the spear to puncture the hide until she could tear the creature open to get at the meat under the hair.

The flying people-things came closer. She ignored them as she let some of the blood fall onto the ground, drying the meat inside enough that she could see what she was doing. She ignored them until one, the one she had saved earlier, still flying unsteadily on its bent wing, appeared right in front of her face, between the girl and her food. It looked straight into the girl's eyes and reached out an arm. Its tiny finger touched the girl on the nose and the world exploded.

***

"That's it?"

"Go to bed now."

"But that's a terrible ending. How could the world explode? And besides, you said this was a long time ago. The world couldn't have exploded. It's still here."

"It's a metaphor, I think."

"A what?"

"It's a word that means something else. I think the story will go on tomorrow."

"Tell me the rest now!"

"I… I can't. I haven't heard the rest yet."

"You mean you haven't made it up yet."

"If you prefer. Now, lights off and go to bed."

***

The girl sat down hard on the grass. The trees around her came into focus slowly, and, for the first time in her life, they had names. They weren't the names that you or I know, but they had ceased to be classified simply by whether they had thorns or not, or edible fruit, or the ones that made you sick if you ate the nuts. Each was individual, similar to some, different from the rest.

Likewise, the bloody animal she'd hunted—some sort of rodent—had a name. It wasn't just a walking piece of meat, too small to defend itself. It was a type of animal. The names, and many other words, more words than her group had ever formed, more words than could possibly exist, poured into the girl's head.

"Can you hear me?"

The girl looked around. Who was there? Only her people spoke, and her own group never came into the woods. She picked up her spear, pointing it in the direction she thought the sound had come from, but otherwise stayed very, very still.

"You won't need that."

The girl reeled. Her mind wasn't having trouble with the voice, and it wasn't having trouble with what the voice was saying. It was having trouble with the fact that such a difficult concept—the negation of something that hadn't yet happened—could be conveyed with words. Words were small things. One meant "food", another meant "danger". One meant "man" and another "woman". "Come" and "go". They were for basic things. Words were so few, so precious, that there was even a word for "word". But such a complicated structure was an impossibility.

Especially since it had been expressed in words she'd never heard before. She straightened, spear at the ready.

"Really, we mean no harm."

Again, her mind retreated in the face of impossibility, but enough of her consciousness remained to attempt to find its source. The words seemed to be coming from the forest itself, a small, piping note out of the thickest branches of the trees in front of her. "We?" she asked. Why she should know any words in that language was beyond her, but it was obvious that she did. "Who are you? Show yourselves."

Branches rustled just above her eye level and she adjusted her stance to face them directly. A single glowing form floated out of the tree. "It is I who speaks to you." It was a woman-shaped fairy, the same one she'd saved earlier.

The same one, she suddenly remembered, that had touched her face before.

The girl fell in a heap. "What have you done to me?"

The images of the mad folk, failing to keep their eyes focused, so useless that everyone had to share food with them while they gave none in return, speaking in gibberish and unable to understand what was said in turn. They were sad, forlorn figures.

And now she was one of them.

The girl cried, and wondered whether it would be safe to vent her anger on the shining creature floating beside her. After all, what could harm her more than madness? There was nothing left for her to give. But even without words, the rumors existed, and everyone in the group—new words like "tribe" and "family" floated through her mind, but she fought against them fiercely, knowing that they were but steps on the path of madness—was aware of the dark fate that awaited one who hurt a glowing creature. The word "fey" she also ignored. She wasn't sure what it meant, anyway, other than something much like "people".

But her new mind, actually her old mind with all the new words in it, wouldn't let her dwell on the misery that awaited her. It ate through the despair and threw it aside. One single question remained, burning like fire—not the tame fire of her village, but the hungry flame that lived in lightning. "Why have you done this to me?"

The woman-thing didn't hesitate. "Because you are different."

"I am different because you made me different. Now I will be useless to the tribe… to people. My food will all be shared food."

The woman-thing hovered right in front of her and met her gaze directly. "You were already different before."

***

"But why was she different? I want to know now!"

"You will go to sleep. Perhaps you'll find out more tomorrow."

"Don't you know?"

"It all depends on what I hear in the night."

"Is she a fairy?"

"Who, the girl?"

"No, the glowing woman."

"I think so. Yes, I'd say she probably is. Go to sleep now."

***

"Why did you make me crazy?" the girl asked the fairy. "I was happy." Happiness was another concept that was completely new to her, but one that immediately brought up an image of sitting on the ground near her tribe and watching the stars in the night sky.

"I didn't make you crazy. You are still the same as you were, but I just gave you the words to understand the world."

"I understood my world before you touched me."

"You might have understood your world, but you didn't understand the world. Now you do—or you will once you stop questioning what can't be undone and start thinking about things."

"Everyone else you've touched went mad."

The fairies—for the original woman-thing had been joined by two of the men-things—hovered silently for a moment. "Yes, they all have. Opening them up to the world was too much for them, their minds broke. We swore to leave you in peace, to let you be like the animals you eat, and like the ones that eat you." She paused to look at the girl again. "But I saw that you could tell the difference between beast and thinking creature."

"You mean because I saved you?"

"Yes."

"Maybe I did it because you were pretty." The girl was amazed at the way words—nothing but words—allowed her to express thoughts she wouldn't have had otherwise.

"Did you?"

"No." The girl thought. "What was it that broke their minds?"

"It isn't always the same thing."

"Is it two things?" Counting was easier than many of the

other things she'd learned, but she was still trying to get a feel for how the numbers related to anything but her fingers.

The fairy tinkled, a sound that the girl had come to know as laughter, but not to understand, no matter how many times the fairies tried to explain it. "It is many things, but it is mainly just two…"

"Tell me."

"I don't want your mind to break."

"I'll come to it myself sooner or later."

Eyes downcast, the fey replied: "Yes, you probably will."

"Tell me."

"The first thing is names. Your kind seems to have trouble understanding that people are different from other people, and that each can be called something different, not just man or woman. My name is Lenii, and that is Guoo and that is Drioo."

"You are all fey." The word was right for them.

"Yes, but we are different fey."

The girl tried to wrap her mind around this concept, she thought she could actually feel it breaking under the strain as things gave way. If they were different things, they could act as they wanted. They could go different places and hunt different food. They… And suddenly the world changed again. "Can I have a name?"

The fairy smiled.

***

"How could she not have a name? People always have names."

"I think this was before people knew they were people."

"Why do you keep saying that you think this and you think that? It's your story, grandpa."

"It is? Well, no matter. Lights out."

***

"The other question," Tiam said.

"What do you mean?"

"The other question that breaks our minds."

"That one is more serious."

"You thought giving me a name might do it," Tiam reminded her fey friend.

"None of your kind has survived this."

"I think I will," the young woman who, before the gift of the fairies, had thought of herself as just another one of the people, told her friend. She was lying. In fact, her mind was already beginning to fail. Over the past few moons, her understanding of everything had grown incredibly—but at the same time, her fairy teachers had grown more and more indistinct. There were moments in which she could see straight through Lenii—and the two males had long since disappeared. One thing that all of her tribe knew was that the fey were there, had always been there, and would always be there. So not being able to see them anymore could not possibly be a good sign.

Lenii hesitated, but spoke. "It is about the walls of the valley."

"What about them? They mark the edge of the world."

"No, they don't. There is another world beyond them."

"It can't be a very big world, or we would hear it."

"It is a world much bigger than the world within these walls. It is so large it would take you many, many years to cross it all."

Tiam stood, trying to see over the cliffs. "That cannot be."

"It is."

She thought and thought. The more she thought, the more her mind rebelled against the idea. Everything her family needed was inside the walls: water, food, stones and wood for spears. What need could the world have of anything else? She said as much to the fairy.

"I can show you the path to the top."

"Why has no one found it?"

"Because they don't believe it exists."

So they climbed among the shrubbery, and by the time they reached the final ledge, night had fallen. Even Tiam's strong young limbs were sore by that time. But the silver light of the moon showed nothing but a long, flat expanse. "See? It's empty. Let's go back."

"If you trust me, wait for day."

So Tiam wedged herself in the crook of a tree—the only way to be safe in the night—and slept as well as she could. Her family would probably have given her up for dead by then, but they would be happy to see her when they returned. Unlike the other mad members of the tribe, she'd tried to teach them a few things at a time. They thought she was simply some kind of very young elder—and elders were to be respected and revered.

The pink beginning of day woke her. She looked toward the rising sun, but her eyes never reached the horizon. In front of her, and to every side, a great expanse of land full of trees, bushes and animals of every description extended. It went on forever, until the land ended at the horizon. It was something that, after the close walls of the valley, seemed to be a fantasy. But it was there, in front of her eyes, and her eyes would never lie to her.

"Lenii, It's beautiful!" Tears came to her, and she was overwhelmed. "It's beautiful, Lenii," she said again, after the tears had subsided.

But no answer came. Lenii was not there with her. Lenii was nowhere near her.

She climbed back down, half-sliding, but her friend was nowhere to be found. In fact, not one single fey, not one single glowing tiny creature was to be seen in the whole valley—even though it had once been impossible for Tiam to move more than a few steps without seeing one.

Her tears came in earnest now. Not the crying of one moved by beauty but that of one sobbing for a huge loss. She knew that she would never know them again, and had been left with no company but that of her fellow people, who could barely understand the glimmer of what she'd been shown.

It would take a lifetime to teach them everything. A lifetime to make them understand even a fraction of the knowledge.

But she knew she would have to try. If she didn't, she would simply descend into madness like the others.

In another immediate decision, she knew that she would lead them out of the valley. She tried to tell herself that it was because the large land outside would give them more food, and that it was because they would follow her if she told them about more food.

But the truth was that she could hear that vast emptiness calling to her, telling her that it needed people to be complete.

It called her with a force too strong to ignore.

***

"Is that how people came here?"

"It might be."

"It's not a good story if you don't know how it ends!"

"All I know is what I hear at night. There are voices that tell me the stories."

"Have you always heard these voices, grandpa?"

"No, only since I began to get sick. I heard them for the first time on the day the doctors said my mind was giving out."

"Do they tell you stories every night?"

"No, they only tell one story, this one. They also say they miss us."

"Who are they?"

"I don't know. I've never seen one."

"Is it the fairies?"

"Maybe."

"All you ever say is maybe."

"That's true. And maybe you'll understand that when you get older."

"Maybe?"

"I really hope you will. Now it's time for bed."

"Good night, grandpa."

"Goodbye, dear one."

ABOUT THE AUTHOR

Gustavo Bondoni is an Argentine writer with over two hundred stories published in fourteen countries, in seven languages. He is a winner in the National Space Society's "Return to Luna" Contest, the Marooned Award for Flash Fiction, 2016 SFReader Short Story Award, and 2018 N3F Fiction Award. His sort fiction has been published in *Swords and Sorcery*, *Albedo One*, *M-Brane*, and many anthologies.

He has written several novels in multiple genres, including science fiction *Outside* (from Guardbridge Books), *Siege* and *Incursion*; comic fantasy *The Malakiad*; and modern thriller *Timeless*. Surely, more are to come.

He now lives in Buenos Aires with his wife and children. Follow him online at http://gustavobondoni.com.